Everything Is So Dark

Vicente Raga

(Valencia, Spain, 1966, currently living in Ireland)
An excerpt from an interview for *Tribuna Libre*

QUESTION: You studied Law, a Master's degree, you learned languages... Everything to end up being a politician and a writer.
ANSWER: Hahahaha, if you say it like that, it seems like I've been doing worse, right? Having been a councilman in my hometown for more than six years, apart from being an honor, is vocational, just as being a writer.
Q: How did you get here?
A: Because I believe there's a different story to tell. People are tired of always having the same. Curiously, we can apply these statements both in politics and in literature.
Q: Is this your third novel in The Twelve Doors Series?
A: It is its continuation, so it is necessary to read first The Twelve Doors and Nothing Is What It Seems. I have created a story that takes place over several centuries in different novels. It's the first time I have written something so long, although I'm not a newcomer. I wrote my first story at fourteen years old, and it won a modest literary contest in England. Since then, I haven't stopped. Now, I write opinion pieces in different media, and I keep my social networks active.

Everything Is So Dark
(The Twelve Doors part III)
Addvanza, 2022

Q: ¿Why this title?
A: It is a literal quote from the Valencian, Spanish, and European humanist Luis Vives, after a reflection about the Spanish Inquisition; in fact, he's one of the protagonists of the next novels. The literal quote was "**Everything is so dark and the night covers me.**"

Q: Now, is it about the Spanish Inquisition?
A: Yes. In my first two novels, the historical background was the life of the Jews in the aljama of Valencia at the end of the 14th century. In the next installments, we jump to the first quarter of the 16th century, with the action of the court of the Holy Office of Valencia, which was one of the busiest in Spain. Centuries went by, but the situation for the Jewish people didn't improve. In fact, which was already difficult, it gets even worse.

Q: The current plot, the one referring to the XXI century, is it still the same?
A: The main characters remain the same, with some stellar additions, but the surprises don't end and they are very important.

Q: Is it another historical novel?
A: I wouldn't dare to classify it as a historical novel. It's something else. It's a contemporary mystery and intrigue novel based on real historical events.

Q: Who is it for?
A: For all the readers, from fourteen years old that want to be entertained.

Everything Is So Dark

The Twelve Doors Part III

Vicente Raga

Translation supervised by Leyre Raga

addvanza books

Important warning

This novel is the third part of The Twelve Doors

In order to enjoy a better experience, **it is necessary to respect the reading order of the novels:**

1 – The Twelve Doors

2 – Nothing Is What It Seems

3 – Everything Is So Dark → Current book

4 – All You Believe Is a Lie

5 – The Uncertain Smile

6 – Rebecca Must Die

7 – Expect the Unexpected

8 – The Final Mystery

Each of the novels reveals facts, plots, and characters that affect the subsequent ones. If you don't respect this order, despite the fact that there is a brief summary of the previous events, you may not understand certain aspects of the plot.

First edition, March 2022

© 2022 Vicente Raga
www.vicenteraga.com

© 2022 Addvanza Ltd.
www.addvanzabooks.com

Phototypesetting and page layout: Addvanza Ltd.
Illustration: Leyre Raga and Cristina Mosteiro
Translation into English supervised by Leyre Raga

ISBN: 978-1-915336-12-5
COPYRIGHT PUBLISHER

To my family, friends, and schoolmates.
Knowingly or unknowingly, you have all contributed
to create the universe of *The Twelve Doors*

Index

Author's previous note

In the historical part of the novel, which corresponds to the XVI century, all characters are real and existed in their exact historical context. Nevertheless, the events narrated are fiction and didn't necessarily occur as it is described. In the contemporary part of the novel, all characters and events are fiction. The historical events described in both parts correspond with reality.

In the whole novel, dates are used according to the Gregorian calendar. For clarity and consistency, the Hebrew calendar is not used.

I MARCH 20th, 1500

"We are in great danger," Blanquina March said, the Number One of the Great Council.

"In danger?" several voices said, with a certain nervousness.

"We must take drastic measures immediately," Blanquina continued.

All the members looked at her with expressions of deep concern. Blanquina had called an extraordinary meeting of the Great Council. She looked really scared. They had gathered at the home of the late Salvador Vives and his widow, Castellana Guioret, Luis Vives' uncles. In one of the rooms of the house, a clandestine synagogue was hidden.

The Jews of the late 14th century in the Iberian Peninsula had accumulated an enormous amount of knowledge in a multitude of subjects, but they had it scattered in different places. Faced with the change in their relationship with Christians that was happening at that time, and with the fear of losing that great treasure, they decided to protect it, gathering it and hiding it in a single location. They chose the Jewish quarter of Valencia. It wasn't as important as those of Seville, Cordova, or Toledo, for example, but precisely for that reason, they chose it. It was medium in size, not too confrontational, and well connected. Ultimately, it was discreet compared to bigger ones. They created a kind of fellowship made up of ten people whose mission was to preserve that treasure through the centuries, and they called it the Great Council.

It was undoubtedly a very timely idea, since just over a year after completing the task, in 1391, the assault and destruction of more than sixty Jewish quarters throughout the territories of the kingdom of Castile and the Crown of Aragon occurred, which resulted in the death of tens of thousands of Jews. Most of the aljamas never recovered and disappeared forever. Fortunately, the members of the Great Council had an escape plan prepared, which they had called *The Twelve Doors*, which made reference to the twelve gates that were opened in the medieval wall of Valencia at the end of the 14th century. Their objective was to get to safety and preserve their cultural treasure. Once this plan was executed, they began to call themselves as doors.

As if all those misfortunes hadn't been enough, one hundred years after that disaster, specifically on March 31st, 1492, Isabella I of Castile and Ferdinand II of Aragon, later known as the Catholic Monarchs, ordered the expulsion of the Jews from all the kingdoms they dominated, exile that was completed in the month of August of that fateful year.

"How serious is the situation?" Number Six asked.

"It's very serious," Blanquina answered.

"What's happening?"

"It occurs that we are being watched," Blanquina answered. Her face was very serious.

Those who were gathered today in the synagogue were descendants of the first members of that original Great Council, which began to form in 1356 and was completed in 1390. They were still in charge of protecting that cultural treasure, which they called 'The Tree.' Its existence had been a great secret for over a hundred years.

"Watched? By whom? Who is interested in our activities?" Number Five asked, surprised.

There goes the first bombshell of the meeting, Blanquina thought.

"The Holy Office of the Inquisition."

The bombshell had the expected effect. The initial concern of the members of the Great Council turned into deep fear. The mere mention of the Holy Office terrified them. Everyone knew that the Court of the Inquisition of Valencia was one of the most active in Spain and also the one that condemned more Jews to the stake.

"How do you know they're watching us?" A scared Number Six said.

"I think you know we have a very important person in the City Court who protects us and keeps us informed. Just this morning, he sent me a warning note. Here it is," Blanquina said, placing a handwritten paper on the table.

There was maximum attention. They all read it. Indeed, the note reported that the Holy Office had detected 'certain clandestine meetings' of a group of ten people. Although it seems that they had known of its existence for six months, the Court's prosecutor had ordered special surveillance in the last week. The author of the note said that there was nothing more he could do to protect them since the Grand Inquisitor, Fray Diego de Deza, had taken a personal interest in the matter. The orders came from the highest authorities, so he couldn't further hamper the investigation.

"This is why we are meeting urgently," Blanquina said. "Isn't that serious enough?"

"Yes, of course, but apparently, they don't know about the Great Council. The note only says that they have discovered certain clandestine meetings, without further ado." Number Five said.

"We don't really know that, but they certainly suspect something. That's why they're watching us closely," Blanquina answered. "What worries me the most is the special vigilance this past week."

"Can't the person who wrote that letter be wrong?" Number Five insisted.

Blanquina stared at him with a certain indulgence.

"Do you know who the author of that note is?" She asked him.

"No."

"Don Juan de Monasterio himself."

Everyone was surprised to hear that name, as they perfectly knew who he was. He was one of the two inquisitors of the Tribunal of the Holy Office of Valencia. They had no idea that he was protecting them; it was something unexpected and unusual. The initial surprise turned into fear when they realized that, given who was warning them, the threat must be completely serious.

"And what drastic measures are you talking about?" Number Six asked, scared.

"We have to protect ourselves. I suppose you were surprised when I summoned you in this synagogue and at the start of Shabbat."

Shabbat was going to be that Saturday, the Jewish holiday which was equivalent to Sunday for Christians. It spans from *kiddush* on Friday afternoon to *havdalah* on Saturday night. During that period, they were forbidden by the Talmud to carry out almost any activity, so they never met on Friday night or Saturday. On the other hand, the meetings of the Great Council were held regularly in the warehouse of Number Eight, whose trade was being a merchant of *draps i sedes* and had large and discreet facilities.

"Protect ourselves? What do you mean?" Number Seven asked.

"Since we're being watched, I've thought it was wise to change the meeting's day and location. You know that this synagogue has a secret room. Also, observe around you."

All the members looked closely at the synagogue.

"As you may have noticed upon entering, we have lit the ritual lamps. We are in full celebration of Shabbat. If we were discovered, we could always claim that we are Judaizing. You know that's how the Inquisition likes to call the practice of our religion. Understand that the most important thing is to hide the existence of the Great Council itself."

Number Nine intervened. It was a woman's voice.

"Good thinking, but this can't be considered a drastic measure. I suppose you weren't referring to meeting in a synagogue at the very beginning of Shabbat when you used that word, did you?"

"You're very insightful; indeed, that's not what I mean," Blanquina replied.

"So?"

"Our safety is important, but above us is the safeguard of the tree. Let us not forget that the very meaning of the existence of the Great Council is its custody so that it can endure through the centuries."

"We already know that. Why are you reminding us that?"

Here goes the second bombshell of the night, Blanquina thought.

"Because we have to change the location of the tree as soon as possible."

The surprise was major. There was a small uproar in the synagogue, everyone wanted to speak at the same time, and with the noise, they couldn't understand anything.

"Do you understand what you're saying?"

"That's very dangerous."

"Do you think the tree itself is in danger?"

Blanquina tried to put some order, answering in a firm voice.

"It could be if they discover the existence of the Great Council. That's why I have called this meeting so urgently. I have the feeling that things aren't going well."

"And if they are watching us, how do you expect us to move it? They could surprise us red-handed, in the middle of a change of location."

"I've already thought about it; that's why I suggest entrusting the job to Number Eleven. They don't suspect anything about him since he's an old Christian with no apparent relationship with us. In addition, he's a member of the Catholic Church."

"He belongs to the Church and is the Eleventh Door?" A voice asked incredulously.

"He's even a member of the order of preachers," Blanquina replied.

The Great Council was made up of ten people, but in reality, there was an eleventh member who didn't participate in the meetings, whose identity was kept secret, and who was only known by Number One. The Great Council was organized in the likeness of the sephirothic tree of the Kabbalists. Although apparently, this tree contained ten spheres or sephirot. In reality, there was an eleventh sefirah, which is the singular of the word sephirot. That eleventh sefirah, called *Daat*, remained invisible and represented consciousness. It was another form, in this case, non-material and hidden, of the *Keter*, of the root of the Great Council, which at this time was Blanquina March. Consequently, only Blanquina knew the true identity of the Eleventh Door.

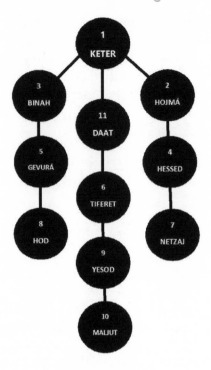

"A Dominican is the Eleventh Door?" another voice asked, surprised.

The Order of Preachers was also known as the Dominican Order because it was founded by Domingo de Guzmán in 1216. Its members were known as Dominicans.

"Yes, that's why he's the only one who can move the tree with guarantees of success. After all, he's one of their own, and they don't suspect a thing about him. They've never seen him in the company of any of us," she said, in the strongest tone she could bring to her words.

The meaning of the existence of the *Daat*, of the Number Eleven, hidden and secret, was the very preservation of the tree. Each of the ten visible members of the Great Council knew one-tenth of a message, which, once gathered, led to the site of their cultural treasure that they had collected and hidden. But these were dangerous times. Any member of the Great Council could die or disappear without transmitting part of their message to their heir. In this case, Number Eleven came into play. Along with Number One, both had two halves of a message of their own, which, once combined, also led to the tree. Thus, between the two of them, they could reconstruct the Great Council and the message, if necessary. It was a security measure to avoid any unforeseen misfortune that could mean losing the location of the Jewish millennial tree of knowledge, which had cost them so much effort and so many years to assemble and hide.

There was silence for a few seconds.

"What you propose is very risky," Number Four said at last. "Our ancestors in the Great Council conscientiously concealed it, safe from prying eyes."

Blanquina March insisted.

"Believe me. I wouldn't suggest such a drastic measure if I didn't consider it necessary and urgent. If we are discovered before the tree is moved, it could be lost forever. You will agree with me that the loss of the tree is a much greater risk than its own transfer. In no case can we accept it."

All the members were worried about what they were hearing. Until now, they weren't aware that the Inquisition could be following their footsteps. Fear paralyzed them and clouded their judgment. In addition, Number One urged them to accept the change of the location of the tree, which was a very delicate task.

"Then we agree?" Blanquina asked, looking at everyone present in the face.

In reality, they had no other choice. One by one, they all nodded their heads. It was an extraordinary measure for an extraordinary situation. No one dared to say a single word. You could cut the silence with a knife.

Suddenly, Castellana Guioret, the widow of Salvador Vives and the owner of the house, burst into the synagogue with a loud bang, almost knocking down the front door. They all stared at her, surprised by her gaze. Her face was completely contorted. It was the living reflection of terror.

Something dreadful must be happening.

2   NOWADAYS. THURSDAY, JUNE 21st

"So, they found an empty chest in the Patio de Los Naranjos of Valencia's Lonja? And what the hell was it doing there?"

"I have no idea. The only thing I know is what Rebecca said. She was with her aunt Tote, with the Jewish historian Abraham Lunel, with the actress Tania Rives and her husband, and with her friend Carlota Penella at La Lonja. It appears that the chest was discovered next to the star-shaped fountain, after detecting it with a ground-penetrating radar and digging it up."

"It's very strange."

"Of course."

"And what happened next?"

"Rebecca proved that the current Eleventh Door was Joanna Ramos, the University professor and her aunt's partner."

"What are you talking about? That isn't true."

"Well, Joanna herself confessed it in front of the whole group, with total sincerity."

"That can't be possible!"

"Of course, it can! I'm just telling you what happened at the meeting, nothing more."

"Are you sure you're not confused?"

"It offends me that you doubt me. You ordered me to inform you about my friend Rebecca, and I believe that I have always followed all your instructions. You can't have any complaints about me."

"Don't get angry. I didn't mean to doubt you. Of course, I have no complaints about you. You have always behaved with complete loyalty, but you understand that what you have just told me is surprising and, above all, completely unexpected."

"Do you think I don't know it? I can't understand it either."

"And you, that know the truth, how did you react to Joanna's confession?"

"The surprise was general for all of us who were sitting at the table and, as you will understand, even more for me. I hope no one noticed my reaction. I tried to hide it as much as I could, but you already know that both Rebecca and Carlota are extremely intelligent. It took me a lot to hide it. I hope I was able to do it." They were silent for a moment, thinking. "You know what? Sometimes, I have had the feeling that Rebecca might know, or at least suspect, my real identity."

"It's not possible; that's your imagination. Think that if she distrusted you, she wouldn't give you access to all the information, and I believe that she has never hidden anything from you. She has always made you a participant in her discoveries."

"That's true," they said, though they weren't quite convinced.

"You shouldn't worry; your identity is surely safe. What should really concern us is why Joanna said what she said."

"I know, it's unsettling. I assure you she was very upset. After her confession, she couldn't bear the pressure, she collapsed and went to her room. She left the rest of us staring at our faces, not knowing what to do or say. It was a very uncomfortable situation for everyone. Immediately afterward, Rebecca and her aunt ended the meeting. It was evident that they were also shocked by the revelation. It all seemed very real, I assure you. I didn't see any deceptive expressions."

They were silent for a moment.

"Why would Joanna confess something that isn't true? I swear she seemed completely sincere."

"I wasn't there, but if we think about it, there is only one logical explanation. Since you told me, I haven't stopped thinking about it."

"Oh! Yes? What is it?"

"That we were wrong from the beginning."

"Do you really believe that?"

"You know very well all the information we handle. We know even more than Rebecca herself. I'm afraid it's the only explanation that fits with all the facts."

"Then things will change."

"Of course, but we must act with the same caution. Keep reporting directly to me. None of this has happened, is it clear?"

"As clear as always. I don't know what will happen from now on. The Speaker's Club is not going to meet again until after the summer."

"Well, enjoy your break. It's well deserved."

They parted. They probably wouldn't see each other again for some time.

3 MARCH 20th, 1500

"They're here!" Castellana managed to say with panic on her face.

"Who?" Blanquina asked, almost rhetorically. Seeing the terrified faces of all the members of the Great Council, she realized that they had already guessed the answer.

"They have asked for the master of the house. They say they have a letter for him, but it's clearly false. I observed them through a window. There are five people. I'm guessing they are getting ready to enter the house at any moment," she replied as she dropped to the ground, completely upset, not knowing what to do.

Castellana Guioret, better known as Castellana Vives, was one of the people with the strongest character in the city's Jewish-convert community, which continued, clandestinely, to practice the rites of their true religion, the Hebrew. Therefore, all the members of the Great Council were shocked to see her in such a nervous state. It wasn't normal.

Noises could be heard at the entrance of the house. They seemed to be pounding on the door with remarkable insistence.

"They'll break down the gate soon," Castellana said, panicked. "Despite being resistant, I don't think it'll last much longer."

"Everyone to the closet! Now!" Blanquina cried.

The closet of the synagogue, where the Torah scrolls and the rest of the ritual books were kept, hid a secret door, which

27

gave access to a small room. Many of the clandestine synagogues had it so that they could hide in case of need. Those were very difficult times for the practitioners of the Hebrew religion, which was prohibited by Christians, and persecuted by the Holy Office of the Inquisition, so they had to take certain precautions.

Suddenly, they heard a loud crash. It seemed that the front door to the house had given in. Blanquina lunged for the closet, entered, and removed the false wooden plank that concealed the secret door. She opened it, stepped aside, and all the members of the Great Council rushed inside, seeking to hide.

The nerves were on the surface.

"Castellana, get up from the ground. You must enter the closet last. you know what your role is," Blanquina said, pretending to be as calm as she could, "and it's very important."

Castellana nodded, rising quickly.

"Don't worry, I know what to do," she said, her voice cracking. "We have rehearsed it several times; it's clear to me."

Blanquina went into the closet. In reality, although they might suspect it, they didn't know what was happening, but the terror was reflected on the faces of all the members of the Great Council. Perhaps it was what Blanquina feared. If confirmed, this was going to be a real disaster for everyone, of unknown proportions for the whole group, and even for the tree itself."

It wasn't for less.

4 NOWADAYS. SUNDAY, SEPTEMBER 2nd

Rebecca had finished her degree in History. In the end, the exams had gone better than expected. Not that she had gotten great grades, far from it, but considering that she combined her studies with a part-time job at the newspaper *La Crónica*, they weren't bad at all. Also, she couldn't complain because she didn't have anything in her favor. The past month of May had been a real madness with the matter of the Counts' drawings and all the events that happened later. She had barely had any time to study.

Rebecca lived with her aunt Tote since she was eight years old when her parents died in a car accident. Along with Joanna, her aunt's partner, and her professor at the Faculty of Geography and History, they formed a very happy family. The consequences of the events that happened in that fateful month of May ended up wrecking the family. Joanna had applied for a transfer to an American university and had left home in July, never to return. The farewell was heartbreaking. They still kept her vivid memory in their minds.

Once again, they were alone in life. It was a very hard blow, especially for Tote, since she lost her partner, her wife. Rebecca also had a hard time. Joanna was much more than her aunt's companion. She was also the Twelfth Door, an original figure that was created in 1391 when the plan of *The Twelve Doors* was outlined. Its sole purpose was to protect Number Eleven, who was alone and isolated from the other members of the Great Council.

Currently, the Eleventh Door was Rebecca. Due to a series of adverse circumstances, Joanna was forced to pretend that she was actually Number Eleven. She sacrificed herself to keep Rebecca's true identity hidden and also to keep the real location of the ancient Jewish tree of knowledge safe. We can't forget that it was being actively sought by Number Two and Number Three of the Great Council, Abraham Lunel and Tania Rives, respectively, after the death of the Countess of Dalmau, who had been the last Number One. No one knew who the remaining members of the Great Council were. In fact, it seems that they had ceased to exist for centuries. Now everyone was convinced that the tree had been lost forever, after Rebecca made them believe that the empty chest they found in the Patio de Los Naranjos in La Lonja de Valencia was, in reality, the tree that they were looking for with so much determination. That chest had been placed there by Rebecca herself in order to be found. After all the events that had happened that month, Tote had replaced Joanna as Number Twelve, and no one seemed to suspect that Rebecca was the real Eleventh Door, at least that's what she believed. Everything seemed calm.

Before all the dire events that occurred during the month of May, the three of them were close-knit family. Rebecca felt very depressed. She couldn't help but think that when she seemed to find some stability in life, the curse of Number Eleven pursued her with cruel fury, and the worst thing was that she dragged her aunt with her. She had it really bad. She had the feeling that no one could be happy with her. *Is it going to last forever?* She wondered, anguished.

Consequently, it was a depressing and painful July for both of them. Her aunt was crestfallen, and the last thing Rebecca wanted was to spend the month of August locked up at home. She persuaded Tote to take a three-week vacation and tricked her into a good trip under the pretext of celebrating the end of her college degree studies. Actually, what she wanted was to get her aunt out of the house and keep her distracted. They had to flee and leave the family home at all costs.

Rebecca had always wanted to see Norway, so they flew to Tromsø, the northernmost international airport in the country. They rented a car and drove through the entire coastline, enjoying the untamed beauty of the Lofoten Islands, passing through steep fjords, and ending the journey in its

30

cosmopolitan capital, Oslo. During those three weeks, they managed to disconnect from all the problems that haunted them. *They certainly haven't been able to catch up with us on this trip*, Rebecca thought, a little more encouraged.

But the holidays were over. Tote returned to work today. She was a police commissioner and was in charge of the Provincial Immigration Brigade. Rebecca was going to return tomorrow, Monday, to the newspaper. She had no desire to see Editor Fornell or his secretary, Alba. On the other hand, she wanted to greet her desk partner, Teresa, with whom she had a good friendship.

There was a subject that disturbed her. She couldn't forget that she had discovered that someone was spying on her in the newspaper. Furthermore, to her utter surprise, her aunt had identified the only complete fingerprint she took with her cellophane trick, and her identity didn't correspond to anyone on *La Crónica* staff. It was something unusual. She couldn't understand how someone outside the newspaper could access her desk so easily. There were always people in the editorial department, and a stranger would have attracted attention.

Her aunt had asked her to take some precautionary measures, although she didn't know exactly what to do. In any case, she had to admit that it was strange since she didn't keep anything interesting in the drawers of the editorial department. *Of course, the person spying on me doesn't know that. I suppose they'll hope to find something important*, Rebecca thought.

As for continuing her studies, she had enrolled in a postgraduate master's degree. In the end, she had opted for the Master's Degree in History and Identities of the Western Mediterranean, which spanned the 15th to the 19th centuries. She would study it at the same Faculty of Geography and History where she had studied her degree. She didn't have too many alternatives since, as Number Eleven, she couldn't leave the city to study at another university. It was part of her curse, although she had undertaken it since she was a child.

The meetings with the Speaker's Club would resume on Tuesday. Since the group of friends finished their studies at the Albert Tatay school four years ago, and before each of them left for a different Faculty to continue their education or start in the job market, Rebecca and her schoolmates conspired not to lose contact. They had been raised together for many years and didn't want to lose that healthy complicity. Thus, they decided to institutionalize a weekly meeting, every Tuesday, in a fixed place, in this case in the Kilkenny's Irish Pub in the Plaza de la Reina. Each one came when they could, but over time, even people from outside the school had joined the group, such as Carmen Valero or Jaume Andreu. It was the English bartender at the pub, Dan, who named them the Speaker's Club because, according to him, 'a lot of talking and a little drinking.' Even their usual table in the place was called, with affection, the Speaker's Corner, in honor of the corner where the speakers hung out in Hyde Park in the city of London.

In short, back to the delightful routine, but this time without the surprises of the recent past.

At least that's what she believed, deluded.

5 | MARCH 20th, 1500

"Now is the time!" Juan de Astorga said.

They had been monitoring the activities of this strange group of people for almost half a year. Now they were gathered at the doors of a house on Forn de l'Argenter street, in the parish of San Andrés. It seemed that, inside, a clandestine synagogue was hidden. From the outside, you couldn't see much since the windows were completely blinded, but a very significant amount of light came out through one of the cracks in a small porthole. It seemed that these were the usual ritual lamps used in the celebrations of the Mosaic religion.

Juan de Astorga, the prosecutor of the Inquisition of the Court of the Holy Office of Valencia, was accompanied by the notary Joan Pérez, the Fray Martín Ximénez, and two other supporters. They were all situated in front of the house, hiding.

"Check to see if the door is open," the prosecutor told Brother Martín.

In the end, this mysterious group seems like just another band of Jewish pigs, he thought with annoyance. During all the time he had been watching over them, he always had the feeling that they were more than just heretics. Inside, he felt a little disappointed. He thought that this time it would be more interesting. But no, again, more of the same. What surprised him was the meeting place. It was the first time they had done it at this location, and he was even more intrigued by the day of the week they had chosen: Friday night. *It's strange. If they are Jews, they are not supposed to meet at the beginning of*

Shabbat, the prosecutor told himself. Of course, this was really weird.

Martín Ximénez approached the door and pushed it.

"It's closed, sir."

Juan de Astorga would have liked more time to investigate the activities of this unique group, but he had received direct instructions from Fray Diego de Deza himself, Grand Inquisitor of Spain, who had been the successor of Fray Tomás de Torquemada since he died, just over a year ago. The Supreme Council of the Holy Inquisition also had suspicions of the existence of the clandestine synagogue in this house. The orders they had given him were clear and concise. He had to enter the house, arrest those present and close the synagogue. He had no choice but to comply with the instructions, although he wasn't entirely convinced that they were mere heretics. *They don't behave like such,* the prosecutor thought.

On the other hand, he also had other orders from the Inquisitor of the Tribunal of the Holy Office of Valencia, Don Juan de Monasterio. They had to be as discreet as possible and try to access the house without causing too much scandal in the neighborhood. The prosecutor didn't fully understand these instructions, but he was his immediate superior and had to comply with them.

Fifteen minutes had passed since the last person entered the house, and he thought it was time to go inside.

"Knock on the door and say you have a letter for the master of the house," he said to the friar. "We will try to do things with the utmost discretion, as requested by our superiors."

This is how Martín Ximénez did it. He knocked on the door. From within, a voice urged him to identify himself. The friar turned to his companions, shrugging.

"Knock the door down now!" The notary Joan Pérez, who didn't understand so many subtleties, ordered impatiently. "They already had their chance to open voluntarily. Let's capture these dirty heretics once and for all."

Juan de Astorga nodded his approval.

Martín pushed the door with all his might, but despite his heftiness, it was useless. The gate didn't give up. Noises were heard inside.

"They have realized we're trying to get in, sir," Brother Martin said.

"Try to bring down the door between the three of you," the notary ordered, addressing the other two companions.

They lunged at the door. Its construction and anchorage were solid, and it was reluctant to give way. On the fifth charge, it creaked and the hinges snapped. The gate fell to the ground with a great crash. They had an open passage.

They entered as quickly as they could. Brother Martín and the two assistants stayed at the door of the house to prevent anyone from fleeing, while Juan de Astorga and Joan Pérez went to the room where the light came from. They found the door closed.

"Open in the name of the Holy Office!" the prosecutor yelled.

They got no response. Joan lunged against the door, knocking it down easily. What they saw amazed them. It was a fairly spacious and highly decorated room, with three large lamps lit in the center. There was a table covered with a rich copper leaf, and in the four corners, there were some chandeliers placed with six burning candles in each one of them. On top of the table, there were three small lecterns holding a small Bible, the Talmud, and a box adorned with many jewels containing the Torah. There were also other books and papers. However, to his surprise, there was no one inside.

"There are more than thirty burning candles here. It's clear that they were going to practice some heretical rite," the prosecutor said.

"The decoration seems to be very valuable," the notary replied, who was fascinated by observing the opulent objects in the room. Not in vain, the king had promised him that he could keep them, in gratitude, for the services rendered to the crown and the Holy Office.

"Look at that corner. There is a lamp with the eternal flame. It certainly is a clandestine synagogue. Where are the dirty pigs?" the prosecutor asked.

Suddenly, they heard screams coming from the front door of the house. They left the synagogue and immediately rushed there. Brother Martín was found trying to prevent two people from leaving the house, who tried to separate the friar and his two companions without success.

"Stop in the name of the Holy Office!"

Both people froze upon hearing the voice of the prosecutor.

"Tell me, who are you that you insist on fleeing with such rudeness?"

"I'm Miguel Vives, lord of the house, and she's my wife, Castellana."

"Castellana? You can't be the widow of Salvador Vives. She was almost a damsel," Joan Pérez said, addressing the woman.

"No sir. I'm Castellana March, not Guioret."

"And where is the other woman named Castellana? And the others?"

"Others?" Miguel asked, with the most credible expression of innocence he was able to simulate.

"Don't waste our time! We have been guarding the house for more than an hour, and we have seen how ten people have entered through this same door." the prosecutor shouted angrily.

Miguel and Castellana remained silent.

"Martin, have you found anyone else in the house, apart from this couple of pigs?" Joan Pérez asked, addressing the friar.

"Yes, sir. In the kitchen, there are two servants."

"Then, bring them immediately into my presence."

Martin appeared with a maiden and a Muslim, who didn't appear to be more than fourteen or fifteen years old.

"I'm Joan Pérez, a notary of the Court of the Holy Office of Valencia," he said, addressing the young woman. "If you don't collaborate with us, we will arrest you and lock you in the darkest and more sinister dungeon in the Torre de la Sala, do you understand?"

As soon as she heard the mention of the Torre de la Sala, the prison of the Inquisition in the city, the girl began to tremble. She was completely terrified and the words wouldn't come out of her mouth. She just nodded.

"What's your name?"

"Caterina, my lord."

"Caterina?" Isn't that a Jewish name?"

"No, my lord. My parents were Christians, and I have been one since birth," the maid said, hurriedly crossing herself, trying to confirm her words.

"Caterina, where is Castellana Guioret? What about the rest of the people who have entered this house in the last hour?"

"In the synagogue," she managed to answer, frightened by the terrible threat from the prosecutor. Not for a moment did she consider lying to that wicked man.

"You mean the room full of chandeliers with burning candles?"

"Yes, that one."

The notary seemed angry and raised his voice.

"Do you dare to lie to the Holy Office? We just came out of that room and it was completely empty."

"The synagogue closet hides a camouflaged door. If you remove the rear panel, you can see it. You will enter a secret room. That is where all the people your lordship look for are hiding."

The prosecutor Astorga reacted immediately.

"Martin, stay here with these two heretics. Don't let them leave the house," he said, turning to Joan and Caterina. "You two, come with me."

The three disappeared in the direction of the room that housed the synagogue.

Miguel Vives and his wife Castellana March began to cry while they were held tightly by Brother Martín and his two assistants. They were aware of the tragedy they were experiencing. Their life was no longer worth anything, but they feared for the others.

6 NOWADAYS. MONDAY, SEPTEMBER 3rd

It was Monday, but it wasn't just any Monday. It was the first of September, also the first one after three weeks of vacation. According to psychologists, it was certain that today a multitude of syndromes came together, of those that they liked to define with pompous words such as post-vacation stress or adjustment disorder. Actually, all those terms could be summed up in one word: laziness. But very big.

Rebecca had a hard time getting out of bed. The alarm clock was trying to do its job, but she was trying conscientiously to disrupt its disgraceful work. It had already been playing non-stop for about ten minutes. At some point, she would have to get up. *At some point, but when?* She thought with immense laziness or with a strong post-vacation syndrome, whichever you prefer.

In the end, she succeeded. She didn't mean to be late on the first day of work after three weeks of vacation. She showered and went out to the kitchen. It was empty. Her aunt Tote had already gone to the police station. Devoted to her customs, she drank a good glass of fresh milk and left for *La Crónica* on her bicycle.

When she entered the newsroom, the first person she saw was Alba, the editor's secretary, sitting behind her desk. She wore her usual cheerfulness; she was drier than a mojama. She didn't even deign to raise her head. She headed to her place of work, greeting her colleagues along the way.

To her surprise, during the month of August, the configuration of all the tables in the great hall had changed. It even seemed different.

"Hi Rebecca, how was your vacation?" Tere told her while she gave her two kisses and a big hug. She was glad to see her friend and coworker again.

"Hi, Tere, what happened here?" She said, pointing to the tables with a shocked face.

"A small reorganization."

"Small?"

"Well, not so small."

"But they changed everything! Even the trash cans are different."

Tere was glowing; she hardly looked like herself.

"Yes, it's true, but that's not the most important thing."

"Oh! No? And what's the important thing?"

"We have a new guy in the office!"

"Good heavens! It seems that Editor Fornell was waiting for me to go on vacation to make all the changes: tables, staff, and trash cans included."

"You have to meet him!" Tere said with the enthusiasm of a schoolgirl.

"From your expression, I gather he must be interesting."

"Interesting? Please, Rebecca! Besides being smart, he's eye candy."

Rebecca couldn't help but laugh. Never, in the three years she had been working at the newspaper, had she seen Tere so excited about something or someone. She looked like a teenager. She looked for him with her eyes.

"And where is that candy right now? Why can't I see him anywhere?"

"Covering a press conference, I don't know at what time he'll be back."

Rebecca took a better look at the table settings. Before the big change, she and Tere sat facing each other, but now there were four people who shared the space.

"Who is the fourth person?" Rebecca asked, pointing to the empty chair.

"I don't know. Editor Fornell just told us they'll be joining us shortly, without further details. You already know how he is. Only what he considers essential counts; that is, almost nothing."

"Another new girl or boy?"

"So it seems," Tere replied, still excited.

"I certainly can't leave you alone. I went on vacation for a few weeks, and, when I come back, the whole newsroom is turned upside down."

"Hey, it's not my fault!"

"I just hope that the person who occupies that chair isn't another variety of candy because I see you working very little this year."

Tere laughed at ease.

"Don't be silly, Rebecca. I haven't had a partner for a year and I already feel like having one."

"A year without a partner, and you are worried? I have been almost twenty-two years alone, and I'm over the moon. Also, who needs candy when chocolate exists?"

Now they both laughed.

7 JANUARY 20th, 1500

"Hurry, we're running out of time," Blanquina urged the remaining members of the Great Council, who hurried through the camouflaged door inside the closet.

When everyone left the synagogue, Blanquina addressed Castellana Guioret.

"After I get in, it will be your turn. Make sure to close the double bottom of the closet and the door before hiding in the secret room. The access has to be completely camouflaged."

Castellana nodded. She went into the closet and left it as if no one had been there. As soon as they finished their work, they heard a loud pounding on the synagogue door. A voice was yelling, urging them to let them in.

"Open in the name of the Holy Office!"

Instantly, they heard the noise they caused when the door was smashed. They heard the voices of two people inside the synagogue and as they walked around it.

"There are more than thirty burning candles here. It's clear that they were going to practice some heretical rite," they heard a voice say.

"The decoration seems to be very valuable," they heard another person reply.

"Look at that corner. There is a lamp with the eternal flame. It certainly is a clandestine synagogue. Where are the dirty pigs?" the first voice asked.

Suddenly, from their hiding place, they heard the footsteps of the two people leaving the synagogue in haste, almost running.

"Thank God, they seem to be heading towards the door of the house," Blanquina thought, relieved. "I hope they don't discover us."

Meanwhile, Castellana Guioret was situated in her position. Her ear pressed to the wooden plank that concealed the access door, trying to hear what was happening. The tension was maximum. She couldn't hear anything. She didn't know what was happening around the rest of her house. *What would have happened to my son and daughter-in-law?* She wondered in alarm. She supposed that it wasn't anything good.

Within a few minutes, she clearly heard how people were entering the synagogue again. This time, from their footsteps, it seemed like they were three people. To her horror, she could clearly hear them approaching her position.

"Is this the closet?" She heard a voice say, the same one that had said just now that there were thirty candles.

"Yes, sir."

Castellana got stiff. It was undoubtedly the voice of her servant Caterina. *Has she betrayed us?* She thought in terror.

"I'm going to open the door," the notary said.

They came across several shelves, each containing various prayer books. There would be more than twenty.

"Let's put away all this heretic garbage," Joan said, slapping all the books violently, knocking them to the floor.

Castellana, from her position, could hear them perfectly. They were barely a meter from her, only separated by a plank.

"Where is the access door to that hidden room you told us about?" the prosecutor asked.

"You must remove the wooden plank from the back of the closet, and you will see it," Caterina replied.

"Joan, come in and do it," ordered the voice of the person who seemed to be in charge.

Caterina has betrayed us. They are going to discover the entrance to the secret room, Castellana thought with horror as she prepared to make it as difficult as possible for those strangers to enter the room.

The notary removed the wood from the bottom of the closet, and they could see how the maid had told them the truth. There was a hidden door there. He immediately lunged for it and tried to open it. It was closed and locked. He took a wooden shelf from the closet itself and began to beat it until it broke, and was able to open it. Joan Pérez stared inside the secret room. What he saw completely astonished him.

He already knew that there were ten people inside the house, but he didn't expect to see what he had in front of his nose in that small hidden room.

8 NOWADAYS. MONDAY, SEPTEMBER 3rd

"I still have more surprises to tell you," an excited Tere said.

"Don't tell me Fornell and Alba are getting married?" Rebecca replied, laughing.

Gossip circulated in the editorial department that the newspaper editor and his young secretary were a couple because no one knew exactly what Alba's functions were. At a time of economic difficulties for *La Crónica*, the reasons for her keeping her job weren't explained.

"No, idiot!" Tere replied, laughing too. "That wouldn't be a surprise to anyone."

"So?"

"During the summer, after the seven o'clock afternoon meeting, when we close the next day's edition, we joined the modern *afterworking* culture."

"To the culture of what?" Rebecca asked without understanding what she meant.

"Don't tell me that a girl as modern as you doesn't know what it is."

"The truth is I don't."

"Its name already gives you a clue. *Afterworking* consists of going out for a drink with your co-workers when the workday ends."

"Come on, that's what ordinary people call after-office drinks. What a stupid way to use unnecessary expressions! Of course, I can understand that a person as sophisticated as you uses that word," Rebecca said jokingly.

"Hey, don't make fun of me again!" Tere laughed.

"And I suppose you're so excited because that cultural *afterworking* also comes with the famous candy."

"No, Fabio hasn't actually gone to any of them yet."

"Fabio?" That's his name?"

"Yes."

"What a sophisticated name! Now I understand why you use the expression *afterworking.*"

"Not sophisticated, Italian."

They both laughed. Rebecca watched Tere carefully.

"You're telling me this whole story for some reason, right?"

"I see you know me well. Yes, I have a little favor to ask you."

"Come on, spit it out."

"We're going out for drinks this afternoon, as you call it, and Fabio is coming for the first time."

Rebecca immediately understood what her friend was up to.

"And you want me to accompany you because you are ashamed to go alone."

"How do you know it?" Tere asked with a surprised face.

"Because you have it written on your forehead with neon lights," Rebecca said, laughing.

"And would you do it for me?"

"Of course," she replied, feigning enthusiasm. "How am I going to leave you alone in front of that Latin lover?"

"You'll see how we are going to have a great time," Tere said, trying to cheer up her friend.

No way! Rebecca thought. What a boring afternoon awaits me, acting as a chaperone for the sophisticated Italian and the excited teenager.

She didn't know how wrong she was. Tere was a lot smarter than what the delusional Rebecca thought.

9 MARCH 20th, 1500

Joan Pérez and Juan de Astorga were confused and dumbfounded. The room was small, square in shape, and had neither doors nor windows. Clearly, this was a camouflaged hiding place. In the center of the room, there was a single chair, somewhat rickety, and on it sat a barefoot woman, a book on her lap, eating what appeared to be slices of unleavened bread. The image was completely unsettling.

"May I know who you are?" The prosecutor asked, astonished by what he saw in front of him. That was quite unusual.

"I'm Castellana Guioret, widow of Salvador Vives and owner of the house."

The prosecutor looked around. There was nothing and no one else in there."

"Where are the others?"

"Who are you talking about?"

"Don't make me waste my time! You know exactly who I mean."

"I'm sorry, sir, I don't know what you mean. As you can see, I'm alone in this room."

"And what are you doing alone and barefoot in a room whose access is hidden behind a closet?"

"I'm a regular reader, sir. You already know that the books of our Mosaic religion are prohibited by the Holy Office of the Inquisition, and that is why I use this small room to hide when I want to study them, away from prying eyes. I take off my shoes because I read more comfortably, and I also take the opportunity to eat something," she said, pointing to the bread on her lap.

Castellana was aware that she had just signed her death sentence and that she would possibly drag her son Miguel and her daughter-in-law to the stake with her, but she had to protect the Great Council above everything, even their own lives. So, she limited herself to follow the plan they had drawn up to the T.

"Prying eyes? Do you know who you're talking to, you fool? I'm Juan de Astorga, the prosecutor of the Court of the Holy Office of Valencia, and my partner is Joan Pérez, notary of secrecy. We come in the name of the Grand Inquisitor of Spain, Fray Diego de Deza.

Castellana didn't seem impressed. She had already assumed her destiny.

"I order you to tell me where the ten heretics I have seen enter this house are, damn wretch!" he said in a clearly threatening tone.

"Listen, both of you, Mr. Prosecutor and Mr. Notary. I've been sitting here for a long time reading this book and haven't heard anything at all. Besides, I'm barefoot. Do you see me looking like fleeing from a room that has no doors or windows?" She lied as best she could. "There is no one here but me. There isn't even room for those ten people you tell me."

Juan and Joan took a closer look at the room. There was no way in or out, apart from the door that concealed the closet. The small room was bare. There was no furniture or paintings that could hide another escape route. The floor was made of tile, no grating was visible, and the walls were solid. It was clear that no one could have escaped from there.

Was it possible that the dirty pig was telling the truth? The prosecutor put that idea out of his head.

He turned to the maid, who was at his side, looking genuinely surprised.

"You didn't claim that heretics were hiding in this room?"

"I'm sorry, Mr. Prosecutor, I guess I was wrong. Have pity on me. I swear I thought I was telling you the truth," a terrified Caterina replied.

"I'll take care of you later," he said in a deep voice.

Now he turned back to Castellana.

"Get up from that chair and get out from your hiding place immediately. You are coming with us to the Torre de la Sala. I have reserved for you the filthiest of dungeons," he said with all the contempt he could. "The worst of torments awaits you: I will take care of you especially."

Castellana rose slowly, with an enigmatic smile on her face. *Although we barely made it, thank goodness they had time to escape*, she thought to herself, not without some relief.

The prosecutor was very angry. He didn't understand how the group of people he had seen entering the house could have vanished from inside the house if there was no other way out than the main door, which, moreover, had been guarded at all times. The notary also looked puzzled. They didn't understand anything.

"I have to find out what happened here," the prosecutor said in amazement.

"Perhaps there's no need to discover anything, sir," Castellana dared to say.

Juan de Astorga stared at that strange woman.

"What do you mean?"

"You just discovered a clandestine synagogue and caught three pigs, as you like to call us the converts who continue to practice our old and true religion. What else do you want? You don't have to obsess over the unknown. Think that the last synagogue in the city has just closed. It's certainly a great triumph for you. Your mission has been completed with enormous success. Why brood over the matter?"

Juan de Astorga was thoughtful. He had to report the results of his inquiries directly to the Grand Inquisitor of Spain, Fray Diego de Deza, and also to Don Juan de Monasterio. He didn't want to leave any loose ends or give them a reason to reproach him. Perhaps that strange woman, after all, was partly right, and it was convenient to omit certain details for which he had no answer to offer. He didn't want, under any circumstances, to turn a great success into a possible failure.

"What do you think about what the pig says?" the prosecutor asked, addressing the notary.

"We will have to think about it," he answered thoughtfully.

Joan Pérez was afraid that the king would be angry with him and wouldn't fulfill his promise to deliver the treasures found in the synagogue. Nor was he interested in emphasizing that ten people had slipped away and they had no idea where, because surely, in the next few days, and after subjecting those they had caught to the corresponding interrogations, they would arrest more pigs.

Each of the three had their reasons for hiding the detail of the ten people.

10 NOWADAYS. MONDAY, SEPTEMBER 3rd

Rebecca left the house at half-past six, heading to the On the Clocks pub, just as she had promised to Tere. She parked her bike at the door and headed to the door of the place.

The things we do for a friend, Rebecca thought, looking forward to a boring afternoon.

She entered the premises and didn't see anyone she knew. She went to a side that wasn't visible from the door of the pub. Suddenly, the silence became a roar.

"Finally!" a bunch of voices shouted at the same time.

Tere pounced over her and smacked her cheek with a kiss.

Rebecca looked up and saw the entire staff of *La Crónica* applauding, apparently to her.

"But what's going on here?" a stunned Rebecca asked.

"Congratulations! It's certainly a huge success."

It's the editor Fornell! Rebecca thought, confused. What is he doing here?

"You really deserve it."

What? Is that really Alba!? She told herself, completely adrift. In the end, she reacted.

"Ladies and gentlemen, I'm grateful for your greetings, but I'm a bit confused. What's the reason for them?"

"I see your colleagues have kept the secret well," editor Fornell said.

"What secret?"

"It took me a lot of effort not to tell you anything this morning. I had a horrible time doing it," Tere said, biting her nails. "Come on, pour yourself a glass of *champagne* so you can toast with us."

"Toast for what?" Rebecca said, who understood less and less what was happening.

"You listen to me and shut up," Tere ordered.

Rebecca obeyed her friend and poured herself a glass of *champagne*. She stared at all her colleagues, waiting for an explanation for that surprise party. Her birthday was still a month away.

"Now that we all have a drink in hand, let's toast to Rebecca."

They all repeated the toast.

"To Rebecca!" It was heard with a great roar.

"Well, bravo for me!" Rebecca toasted, still not knowing what the hell was going on there.

"Rebecca, this summer, you have achieved something that no one has ever achieved in the history of the communication group that *La Crónica* is a part of," Fornell said in a very high-pitched voice.

"And may I know what I have achieved this summer? Has no one from the newspaper ever visited Norway with their aunt? Was I the first one?"

"You're such a joker. Not even in a moment like this can you help it," Tere said.

Not even in a moment like this? Rebecca thought without understanding anything at all.

Editor Fornell rose ceremoniously to his feet, tapping his glass of *champagne* with a pen to capture the attention of the group. For a moment, there was silence amid the general revelry.

"Rebecca Mercader, you have just been nominated for an Ondas Award in this year's edition," he said with solemnity, unlike his grim character.

At first, Rebecca was stunned. Then she started giggling.

"An Ondas Award? What did you smoke? I don't have any radio or television programs! How are they going to nominate me for something that I don't do and have never dedicated myself to?"

"Do you remember the recordings you left us before you went on vacation?" The editor asked.

"The recordings? Are you referring to the series of four articles about the Count of Ruzafa and the Countess of Dalmau, which I left recorded because I didn't have time to write? I did it this way so that they would be transcribed and published during my summer holidays."

"Well, it turns out that this series of articles were never published in our newspaper."

"I don't understand, Mr. Fornell. What have you done with them?" Rebecca asked, who couldn't get over her astonishment.

"The recordings were heard by our colleagues on the radio. They liked them so much that they broadcasted to all of Spain, just as you recorded them."

"With my voice? Please! I recorded them without any care!" Rebecca protested. "Without any kind of means, with my own mobile and not even with a poor microphone."

"That is precisely one of the things they liked the most. The content was very good, and your light-hearted style wowed them. They said that it was difficult to get to disseminate historical issues in such an entertaining and fresh way."

"Please, I'm so embarrassed!"

"Don't be ashamed. Apparently, they had great success, so much that you have been nominated in the category of the best podcast of the year at the Ondas Awards. In little more than a month, they will be awarded, but the fact that you are nominated is already a huge success," editor Fornell concluded. "You know that we are a modest communication group, and these things help us a lot in terms of advertising."

Rebecca was confused. She still hadn't come to terms with what they were telling her, and she couldn't quite believe it.

"This has to be a joke, right?" She asked incredulously, looking at her colleagues. She approached Alba directly. "Come on, tell me!"

"This is no joke," the secretary said in her characteristic impersonal voice. Rebecca thought she had never played a joke in her life, so if she said so, it must be true.

"Well, now I do believe it," she said. "Let's celebrate. Pour me another glass of champagne!"

The party continued. They were all very happy. Rebecca turned to her friend.

"And as for you," she said to Tere, "we'll have a serious conversation. You tricked me like a fool!"

"It was very difficult to hide it, but it wasn't all a lie. Do you want me to introduce you to Fabio? This is the first time he has come to a newspaper party."

"Not now, later. I want to enjoy this moment. It's something that I could never have imagined. I suppose it will be very important for my career and also for the newspaper."

In reality, Rebecca had no idea how important it was going to be, but not exactly for her career.

‖ JANUARY 20th, 1500

"Quick! We must leave this place as fast as possible," Blanquina said. Her nerves were on edge.

Disguised in a corner of the room, there was a tile that could be lifted. Below it, there was a grid, which, once removed, connected to an underground water stream, which passed just below the house.

As soon as the members of the Great Council were safely inside the secret room, they removed the tile and entered the ditch. It was wide enough to fit comfortably. It was in complete darkness, but Blanquina knew how to guide herself.

"Don't worry if you can't see anything. There is a small path next to the stream. Follow that path downstream. I'll go to the back of the group. It empties into the Guadalaviar river, between some hurdles. It's a hidden corner and safe from prying eyes. Start descending right now!"

"We're going blind," Number Seven said, who could only hear the sound of the water from the ditch without being able to see anything.

"It is a safe path, rest assured, but you have to hurry," Blanquina said, kind of insane by the slowness of their escape. She didn't know when the people who had broken into the house might show up. Even though she didn't know who they were, she could imagine it

Before leaving the room, Blanquina March and Castellana Guioret melted into an embrace. They both knew they would never see each other again.

"When we're all out, put the grate back in place and secure the tile on top of it. Nothing can be noticed. Take off your shoes, grab the book, the unleavened bread, and sit in the chair. If they find this room, you know what to do and say," Blanquina said.

"Yes, I'll take this manuscript, sit in the chair and tell them I'm reading a heretic book, barefoot and while eating. It will certainly be a puzzling image for them."

"Exactly. And if they ask about us, don't forget to suggest that they don't need to find out who we are. Emphasize that the discovery of the synagogue is already a remarkable success for them. Also, tell them that it's the last one in town. Be as subtle as you can to see if you can convince them that it isn't convenient for them to investigate more about our group. It's very important that they don't record anything about us in their reports. Also, make sure that Miguel removed the papers of the Great Council that were on the table. Although they were in our language and coded, we shouldn't leave clues around, even if they don't understand them."

"Don't worry. I have it clear. Come on, my little one, go now."

Blanquina descended into the underground watercourse. As she did so, she could see Castellana place the grid and then the tile. *My aunt is a great woman*, she thought proudly. She was sure she could fool whoever the house assailants were, though she couldn't help but shed tears for the fate that surely awaited her.

She joined the queue of the group, which was following the course of the canal, downstream. In just five minutes, they arrived at the end. Indeed, as Blanquina had anticipated, it flowed into the Guadalaviar River. They sat on the ground, covered by the vegetation of the riverbank.

"What has happened?" a voice said.

"What happened was that, in all probability, we have narrowly escaped the Holy Office of the Inquisition, which, as Blanquina had told us, was coming for us," the woman's voice said, who was Number Nine.

"We have managed to flee thanks to the safety measures of Number One. At our usual meeting place, those bastards would have sure caught us," Number Five said. "Luckily, we're all safe."

Blanquina's eyes were wet.

"Not all of them, really. Miguel Vives didn't want to come. He preferred to stay at home with his wife and mother-in-law."

With all the hustle and bustle, they hadn't realized that Number Four hadn't escaped with them through the hidden room behind the closet.

"Miguel isn't here!" Concern was evident in their voices.

"Why did he do that? Without any doubt whatsoever, the Holy Office will burn him alive at the stake."

"I'm afraid that's right," Blanquina said, "but it's what he wanted. He has preferred to remain with his family, even though he knows that certain death awaits him."

"They are your family too, Blanquina. How are you feeling?"

"The truth is that I'm feeling bad. You know that I have suffered too many misfortunes in a very short time. There are times when I think we're all going to end up burned at the stake."

There was silence in the group. They were shocked and disconsolate. Blanquina spoke up, trying to compose herself as best she could.

"They have discovered our existence. Although we can suppose that the Inquisition doesn't know what our true reason for existing is, the fact is that they know who we are and have tried to trap us. This is extremely dangerous, not only for the Great Council as such but for the tree."

"So, are we going to continue with your relocation plan?" Number Six asked

"It was necessary before. Imagine now, with everything that has just happened. In the next few days, I will contact Number Eleven to take care of finding the new location. I will provide them with the strictly necessary information. I will not tell them what happened today or that we are being persecuted. They don't need to know those details. I also don't want to scare them with the mention of the Holy Office. I will take advantage of the fact that the nuns of Saint Christopher's convent are doing some remodeling jobs in the Church, and I will use it as a pretext. I hope they don't ask any more questions and accept the assignment."

Sitting there, between the wattle on the Guadalaviar river's riverbank, all the members looked at each other in complete silence

"This is a disaster," Number Five said.

"It's much more than that. The Great Council is incomplete. Number Four has been arrested without appointing a successor," Blanquina continued.

The flood of events hadn't allowed them to become aware of the tremendous catastrophe they had just suffered. Events had overtaken them.

"And what do we have to do now?" Number Six asked with deep concern.

Here goes the last bomb of the night, Blanquina thought. I would never have imagined this scenario, but it is necessary.

"We must dissolve the Great Council," she said, her voice very serious.

Immediately there was a great commotion in the group, and everyone wanted to speak at once.

"That isn't possible!" several voices said.

"Not only is it possible, but it is necessary," Blanquina answered firmly.

"But we must protect the tree!"

"That is precisely why we must dissolve the Great Council. Our very existence poses, right now, a direct threat to the tree. Number Eleven will take care of its transfer and it will be safer without our presence around."

"Why?" Number Seven said, still incredulous at what he was hearing.

"I've already told you. The Holy Office knows our group and we don't know what information they manage. Therefore, we must disappear now, for our own safety, but above all for the preservation of the tree."

"I mean, you're asking us to improvise another plan similar to *The Twelve Doors*, but more than a century apart, and this time without any prior preparation, aren't you?" Number Nine.

"No, I'm actually asking you for something else. Our ancestors moved out of the city in an organized manner and without breaking the Great Council. Instead, we must undo it. It's a leap of faith, although necessary."

All members were shocked. Blanquina continued speaking.

"After I assign Number Eleven to move the tree, what's left of my family will leave town. We will settle in Elche."

"For how long?"

"I wish I had an answer to that question. At the moment, for an indeterminate period. It will depend on future circumstances."

"This is a real massacre," Number Five said, covering their face with their hands.

You don't really know it, Blanquina thought. And you don't know that, in all probability, this means the final disappearance of the Great Council. In the end, it will depend on what my successors, as Number One, think of my decision, but it could mean the end of the structure created in the 14th century, at least as it was conceived.

12 NOWADAYS. TUESDAY, SEPTEMBER 4th

Today she didn't have to go to the newspaper. After yesterday's party for her Ondas Award nomination, she had been given the day off.

Of course, that was starting September with style, Rebecca thought with amusement. I'm coming back from vacation. I work only one day, they organize a surprise party for me, and they give me the next day off. Let's see who can overcome that. She was ecstatic.

But the start of September also meant that the Speaker's Club meetings were resuming at their regular Kilkenny's pub venue. During the month of June, the activity was interrupted because most of its members had exams, and during the summer, they took the opportunity to rest, so they had been completely inactive for the last three months.

Rebecca had summoned the meeting at seven in the afternoon. All the fixed members of the club had confirmed their attendance, and to a general surprise, so had Carolina Antón, who hadn't attended for a whole year. She had gone to study her last year of International Law at the *Sorbonne* in Paris.

How amazing! Rebecca thought. She wanted to see new faces, especially Carol's. In the past, their parents had been close friends and shared many trips and weekends together. She had very pleasant memories of her.

Carolina Antón, or Carol, as she had always been called, was Carlota Penella's antagonist at school. They competed to get the best grades, although, in most cases, they were tied

59

because it was impossible to get better grades. *Drawing doesn't count.* She still remembered that phrase that came out of Carol's mouth when she was barely ten years old, reproaching Carlota for winning her for that one subject. *Well, learn to draw. You only know how to paint sticks. You seem like a Neanderthal,* Carlota answered.

It had been a long time since that, and now Carolina Antón was a role model student who aspired, like her father, to join the French diplomatic corps. However, she also had that nationality. She had been preparing for years. She was fluent in French as her second language, Spanish and Valencian as her native languages, in addition to being fluent in English, German, Italian, and, surprisingly, Hebrew, even though she had no Jewish roots. She was the only one in the group who was a member of a political party, not Spanish but French, related to the protection of nature, as well as being a Greenpeace activist.

It was customary at the Speaker's Club that the first meeting after the summer break was special. They used to dress more elegantly than usual and, when it was over, they all went to dinner together at a nearby restaurant. After three months without seeing each other, they always had many things to tell the others and the celebration dragged on.

Charly was the joker of the group, along with Fede. At times they were joined by the anti-establishment republican Xavier and the three of them formed the skull trio. They were very dangerous. Almu was her soulmate, they had been together since they were six years old, and both of them had finished their history degree this year. Bonet studied robotics and everyone thought he could pass as one of them. Then there was Carlota, the most unpredictable of all, a privileged mind whose reactions scared even Rebecca herself. To complete the group, Carmen and her boss Jaume, who worked in the town hall's repository, had joined from outside the school. And now Carol Antón would also join them, after returning from her last year of studies in France.

Rebecca was reading the messages on her cellphone.

Charly asked her to wear that tight red minidress that she dared to wear to the club a few months ago with remarkable success. *Not that one, but I will wear a similar one if they fit me after the summer's excesses,* she thought amusedly. Charly was a clown. He complimented her, but at the moment of truth, he disappeared with Carlota. *They make a good couple,* she told herself, with a knowing smile on her face.

Fede had entered Charly's game and proposed a mixed competition to see who would dress sexier. Carlota ran out of time. As soon as she read Fede's message, she wrote: *Admiral, I want you with all your badges, you will win the street contest.* Rebecca couldn't help laughing. She didn't know if the others would understand to whom Carlota's message was addressed. She also challenged Fede to appear with the American basketball team of Los Angeles Lakers' jersey, but with nothing underneath. *The firecracker of Carlota shoots to kill,* she thought with amusement. If what her friend wanted was to end the topic of conversation, she got it right away. Neither Charly nor Fede dared to comment on anything else. They did well. With Carlota, they will always lose. Her quick and agile mind was far superior to theirs.

Now the topic of conversation in the group was the choice of restaurant. After many messages. Xavier's opinion prevailed, who lived in Barrio de Carmen and knew it perfectly. They would dine at 'San Tommaso,' one of the best Italian restaurants in the city, which was on Corretgería street. *Good choice, and also very close,* Rebecca thought. It was a mere five-minute walk from Kilkenny's Pub.

They really wanted to see each other. After the events of the past May, everyone hoped to return to the usual charming tranquility of the club, with its delightful inconsequential conversations.

Not really all of them, but they didn't know that yet.

13 SEPTEMBER 12th, 1508

"There was no mother who loved her son more tenderly than mine loved me."

Without a doubt, today was the saddest day of Luis Vives' life. They were burying his mother, Blanquina March, in Santa Catalina Church's cemetery, in Alzira.

Everything had started to go wrong one night in March of 1500. His mother came home with a face of terror that he still remembered until today, with her clothes made a real mess: wet and full of mud. She summoned the whole family. Luis was barely seven years old, but he remembered all the details perfectly. Their mother told them that they had to prepare to leave Valencia as soon as possible.

Preparations began immediately, but the day after they began, a person who identified himself as Juan de Astorga, the prosecutor of the Tribunal of the Holy Office of the Inquisition, appeared at his house, accompanied by two bailiffs. He clearly remembered that his mother was very alarmed; however, the one who was taken prisoner was his father. They wanted to question him, apparently as a result of the discovery of a clandestine synagogue in the home of the widow of his late brother, Salvador Vives. *They had to arrest me, not my husband.* Luis remembered hearing this phrase from his mother, who was absolutely dejected and desperate. At that moment, Luis didn't understand what she meant.

Fortunately, after being questioned, his father was released. It seemed that the Inquisition had failed to gather any evidence connecting his father to the underground synagogue. The son of his uncle Salvador, his cousin Miguel Vives, with the Jewish name Juseff Abenzaram, had stated that he was the rabbi of the synagogue and that no one else was involved. It was evident that he had lied; besides, he wasn't very sane. They assumed they didn't pay much attention to his statements. He got rid of the fury of the Holy Office, which had punished his family so badly.

They immediately moved to Elche, where they were welcomed by their family in that charming city. Everything was normally going until one night in January 1502. A person knocked on the door of his home. Luis remembered it perfectly because he was the one who opened the door. The visitor asked about his mother. Luis was surprised, so he listened to the conversation secretly. The stranger informed his mother of the inquisitorial process against her aunt Castellana Guioret, his cousin Miguel and against his wife. The Holy Office had condemned them to die at the stake, a sentence that had been executed on December 28th, 1501. In other words, it had been just two weeks since they had been burned by the Inquisition. That was horrible. All their assets were confiscated, even their house was going to be demolished and, in its place, a large cross was intended to be erected, commissioned to Pere Compte, the architect who was building La Lonja. His mother asked the stranger to review the full sentence of the Holy Office, which that person had brought with him. He heard him read it aloud.

«La dita Castellana Vives ensems ab son fill enora en sa casa tenya una Sinoga o scola de oració de Jueus, en el qual tenía llannes, cresols, cresoletes, ciris et altres moltes maneres de llums en nombre de mes de vint e set, que continuament en totes les festes e pasques de Jueus sobredites y en altres díes ardían e allumbrabrauan la vivlia, nomynes ebrayques e altres libres de oracions e cerimonyes de Jueus, que en dita Sinoga estauen en molta veneració posades, en una de les quals dites nomines ebrayques está escrit com la dita Castellana e son fill, de christians se convertían a la ley dels Jueus. En dita Sinoga la dita Castellana Guioret estant descalsa, ab molta devoció escoltava los sermons que lo dit Vives son fill feya en favor de la ley de moyses».

"How many people did they capture in the days after the raid?" Her mother asked the stranger once he had finished reading the sentence.

"About thirty people."

"Who?"

The stranger gave her the names of the people imprisoned by the Holy Office. Luis was scared since he knew most of them. After a brief silence, he heard his mother say that 'Castellana was successful' and that 'the prosecutor had made no mention of the ten.' She seemed very relieved. Luis didn't understand anything.

But they had burned her relatives and arrested thirty friends! He remembered thinking with deep sadness. What was positive about that?

Immediately his mother reunited the family and told them that they could return to Valencia safely. The danger had passed. Luis was a real mess. It seemed that the stranger had been the bearer of good news, despite the burning of his relatives and the imprisonment, with an uncertain future, of many friends.

They returned to their home on Calle Taberna del Gall. Luis continued his studies, and they lived peacefully until February of 1508. A new epidemic of the black plague was devastating Valencia, and, like many nobles and wealthy people, they left the city to seek shelter in the countryside, where they believed they were safe from the plague. Unfortunately, his mother couldn't escape the pestilence, and she fell ill. They took refuge 'al lloch de les rahanes de Xatyva.'

Sensing that death was stalking her, Blanquina called her son to her bed and instructed him about the Great Council and the Kabbalah. She also told him what had happened that fateful night of March 1500. Now Luis understood many things, among them the reason why they had left Valencia so hastily and why they returned almost two years later, after reading that sentence of the Holy Office of the Inquisition, which he didn't understand that day.

Luis Vives saw how his mother was being consumed at times and that was very hard for him. In just two weeks, her flame was finally extinguished. She was the person he loved the most in this life, and she was gone forever, being too young, only thirty-four years old. He was shattered; nothing and no one could comfort him. He could never fill the hole his mother left in his life. He was sure that nothing would ever be the same again.

And now, her memory is, for me, the most sacred of memories, and every time her thoughts storm me since I can't do it physically, I hug her and kiss her in spirit with the tastiest of sweetness.

14 NOWADAYS. TUESDAY, SEPTEMBER 4th

It was time to get dressed and get ready for the Speaker's Club meeting. It was time to choose a dress. It was suffocatingly hot, so Rebecca discarded tight-fitting outfits. *What if I dress up as a hippie?* She thought, amused. She searched the closet for the hippie outfit she hadn't even used yet. She put it on and looked at herself in the mirror. She couldn't help but laugh. All she had to do was show up on the back of a pink van.

She had decided to arrive at Kilkenny's Pub a quarter of an hour before the meeting. She wanted to greet the waiters, especially Dan, with whom she had a good friendship for several years.

She took the bus and showed up at the pub at twenty to seven. She walked over to the bar and greeted everyone. She talked for a moment with Dan, and thus, incidentally, he practiced his Spanish, which was a bit rusty. Rebecca was quite a polyglot; she spoke English, Spanish, German and Italian with some fluency. The holidays were briefly recounted. Dan had spent them with his family in Halifax, in the county of Yorkshire, in England, curiously the same city where Ed Sheeran, one of Rebecca's favorite singers, had been born.

"There are your friends. They arrived more than ten minutes ago," Dan told her.

Rebecca turned around to the usual corner where they met. She was surprised to see three people sitting at the table.

"What are Charly, Fede, and Xavier doing here so soon?"

"I don't know," Dan replied. "They have asked me for a notebook and a pen."

What are they plotting? Certainly nothing good, Rebecca thought.

She walked over to the table, curious.

"Did you move the meeting time?" She asked out of the blue.

All three turned towards her. She had taken them by surprise, as they weren't paying attention to the entrance.

"Rebecca! What are you doing so soon here?" A surprised Xavier said.

"Likewise, what are you doing here before time?"

Rebecca stared at the table. They had torn several sheets out of the notebook and had them in front of them, each in a small pile. *What are they up to?* she thought.

The three of them stared at Rebecca, their mouths open.

"Peace and love," Xavier said, making the peace sign with the fingers of one hand. "It seems that you have become one of mine, 'health and the republic, comrade,' raising a fist in mid-air. Or if you prefer "make love and not war," which is more of the sixties."

"It's incredible. You wear a sack of potatoes with four flowers and you look just as spectacular," Charly said, looking her up and down.

"Thank you for appreciating my dress," Rebecca replied, pretending to be offended.

"No, no. I do love that thing you are calling a dress. It's even smaller than the red one, which is already difficult."

"Isn't it too short?" Fede asked, winking at her as he smiled. "As the slightest breeze blows, the dress will go over your head."

"Well, I'm not wearing anything underneath," Rebecca said playfully. "Someone will have fun."

"Really?" Fede asked very interestedly.

"Idiot!" Rebecca replied, laughing.

The four embraced. Suddenly, Charly, Fede, and Xavier rose theatrically from the table. Each took a piece of paper and exhibited it as if it were the score of a contest.

"A ten, without a doubt," Charly said, looking at Rebecca.

"Me too, a ten," Fede said.

"To not give her the maximum score, I give her a nine," Xavier said.

"Rebecca gets twenty-nine points," Charly said, in that monotonous voice typical of juries. "You have set the bar very high. Let's see who can beat you!"

Rebecca couldn't help but laugh. Now she understood the reason for the notebook and the torn pages.

"What about you? You also have to be scored; you are very elegant."

"When everyone arrives, then we will walk. Don't worry. You're going to laugh. We've rehearsed like Victoria's Secret angels," Charly said.

Just by imagining it, Rebecca laughed again.

"Hello everyone!"

They were distracted by the scores, and they hadn't seen Carolina Antón arrive.

"Long time no see. I was looking forward to it!"

"Carol!" Rebecca said as she pounced on her friend, giving her a big hug.

Charly, Fede, and Xavier were speechless. Carol wasn't a girl who could be considered pretty. Not that she was ugly, far from it, but she was too thin, and her features were too marked. However, this last year they hadn't seen her, it seemed that she had gained some weight, and the change was truly striking.

"A ten, no doubt," Charly managed to say.

"What ten or whatever!" Carol replied. "Come on, give me a hug, you bastard!"

Fede and Xavier forgot about the scores, and together with Charly, they gave Carol a big hug. They had never been so long without seeing each other since the age of six. They were very happy to meet again after a whole year.

"Sorry, Carol, but we see you somewhat changed, and you have left us speechless," Fede managed to say.

"You know I was a vegetarian, but now I've become vegan. Since then, my mind, but also my body, has improved dramatically. I have reached a balance."

"Really?" Xavier said, looking from head to toe in detail.

"Of course not, silly! Well, the vegan thing is true, but as for the body, the credit doesn't go to the vegetables or the balance, but to my plastic surgeon."

"Don't tell me you've had surgery?" Rebecca asked, her jaw dropped.

"Of course! Not everything is natural. Do you think tofu and spinach can do this?" Carol said, pointing to her silhouette.

"Long live the artificial things!" Charly said, who finally seemed to have reacted.

"You didn't need it, but the truth is that the result is spectacular," Rebecca said.

"The one who doesn't need it is you. I looked too skinny. I know it may sound silly, but it makes me feel better about myself," Carol replied.

"Well, that's what's important, and it's certainly not silly."

"Besides, I date more now," Carol said. "Of course, that has never bothered you with that great body you have," she continued, looking at Rebecca and her hippie dress.

Rebecca was about to object when they heard footsteps approaching the corner of the Speaker's Club. They all turned around. They were Carmen Valero and Jaume Andreu. They all hugged. Carmen introduced Jaume since Carol didn't know him.

"You are both very tan," Charly said. There was mischief in his eyes. "By any chance, have you spent the holidays together?"

They didn't answer. Carmen laughed, but Jaume turned as red as a shrimp.

Rebecca tried not to laugh because every time she looked at Jaume Andreu, she saw the face of Harry Potter at the age of sixty, and it was already taking her a lot of effort not to laugh. *It seems that Harry has thrown some magic powder this summer, maybe some floo powder*, she thought, fighting back the urge to burst out laughing.

Meanwhile, Bonet and Almu arrived. Bonet was dressed impeccably in a modern tuxedo, a designer bow tie and all.

"Look out! James Bond has just arrived, licensed to kill," Charly said jokingly.

"In the service of her Majesty," Bonet replied, smiling, as he bowed in the direction of Almu, who was dressed as a true queen.

"Bonet, how elegant! And Almu, how beautiful!" Rebecca said while hugging her dear friend. "You look like a princess of Monaco."

"I thought you were going to say Disney," Almu said, smiling.

Everyone was chatting very vigorously. They had gotten up from their seats, between all the hugging and kissing, and hadn't sat down again.

"Only Carlota is missing. She confirmed that she was coming, right?" Fede asked.

"Yes, she wrote it in the group," Rebecca replied. Carlota used to be punctual, so she didn't think it would take her long to come. On the other hand, it seemed that the skull trio of Charly, Fede, and Xavier, amid all the fun, had forgotten about the scores with the papers. *Thank goodness, because I'm dying of shame*, she thought.

Suddenly, they saw someone approach the table, dressed in a most peculiar suit, deep red, full of irregularly sewn yellow and pink hearts.

When Rebecca saw her, she couldn't help but go to meet her.

"Carlota! You have dared to wear a design by Ágatha Ruiz de la Prada!" She said, between being surprised and amused.

"Didn't we have to dress differently from a normal day? Well, here you go something different!" Carlota replied as she greeted everyone.

"I'm so glad to see you," Carol told her.

"Have you learned to draw yet?" Carlota replied in a joking tone as they merged into a hug.

"Have you noticed? Tonight, we have the flower child and the hippie," Fede said, laughing while pointing to Carlota and Rebecca.

"And the snob," Charly said, looking at Carol, remembering that she was considered an eco-snob at school. She was always defending the importance of climate change and other ecological postulates while traveling in her family's private jet around the world.

They were all crying with laughter.

Laugh, laugh while you can, before I drop the jaw-dropper, Carlota thought, a mysterious smile on her face.

Rebecca noticed it.

15 NOVEMBER 11th, 1508

Luis Vives, along with his father and brothers, had returned to their home in Valencia after burying their mother in Alzira. They had been in the city for two months, and he couldn't get used to Blanquina's thunderous absence. He tried to escape reality by focusing on his studies, but he was barely succeeding. Luis attended classes at the Estudi General, which would later become the University of Valencia.

He was precisely among books when he heard a knock on the door of his house. He opened it and found a well-dressed man asking for Blanquina. He felt a pain in his chest. He informed the person that they had just buried her. The stranger timidly identified himself as the Eleventh Door, and Luis told him that his mother, before passing away, had initiated him and he had become the new Number One. The man apologized for coming to his home address but told him that he couldn't locate anyone from the Great Council.

That man was called Johan Corbera. He informed him that he had been commissioned, eight years ago, to move the location of the tree by his own mother, Blanquina. After many deviations, he had finally managed to extract it from the secret crypt of the Church of Saint Christopher's Monastery, which was the place where the original Great Council had hidden it in 1391. At that time, it wasn't a Catholic temple but the main Synagogue of Valencia's Aljama, which sadly disappeared after its assault and looting. He told him that they had to find a new location for the tree with the utmost urgency. Johan had extracted the tree from its original hiding place but hadn't yet hidden it. They temporarily left it at Luis' house. It was safer than in Johan's home, which was noticeably humbler.

Between the two of them, they hid the Jewish treasure in a place they thought would never occur to anyone to look for it. They created the message that would lead to its location, and Luis promised to distribute a tenth of it among the ten members of the Great Council. They created another message and split it into two, one part for him and another part for Number One.

Johan asked him the reason why he could not locate any member of the Great Council. Luis didn't dare to tell him what happened that fateful night of March 1500. He simply told him that a serious unforeseen incident had occurred without further explanation.

Luis became real friends with Johan. He had to admit that his presence helped him a lot to forget his family tragedy. It was very supportive on an emotional level. He even dared to visit his mother's burial in his company since he couldn't find the courage to visit it on his own.

He still remembered with pain the day they said goodbye at the foot of his mother's grave. It was difficult for them to locate the exact place. The brambles had invaded all the space. Shortly after, Luis Vives left for Paris in order to continue his studies at the *Sorbonne*, safe from the cruel scourge of the Spanish Inquisition.

How fast Mother Earth makes us hers, wrapping us in her sweet green cloak. It almost seems like she doesn't want us to part, getting tangled between our feet. In this place, I leave with deep pain about all that I have been and will never be.

16 NOWADAYS. TUESDAY, SEPTEMBER 4th

"What have you done this vacation?" Charly asked cheerfully. "You start, Rebecca, in which hippie commune have you been?"

"I've spent the whole summer in Ibiza working as a stripper and living in a small cove; that's why I came dressed like this."

"Really?" Fede answered, his eyes open wide.

"What do you think?" Rebecca asked, laughing. "You know that Joanna moved to the United States, so my aunt and I spent three weeks in Norway, disconnected from the world."

Fede seemed to breathe easier.

"The one who went to Ibiza was me," Xavier said. "Two weeks. Can't you see how I look?"

"It won't be tanned. You look like a vampire because of how white you are," Almu replied.

"Tanned? What I got was fat! Ibiza by day is for tourists. I'm a bat. I work and hunt at night."

They all laughed, imagining a bat with afro hair, like Xavier.

"Speaking of tans, what about the archivist couple? What paradisiacal beach have you been to? Because you can't find that tan in a basement...." Charly said, turning to Carmen and Jaume.

16 NOWADAYS. TUESDAY, SEPTEMBER 4th

"We have only spent a week in Punta Cana, in the Dominican Republic. We came back the day before yesterday. That's why our skin tone still lasts."

"Just like me. I came back on Sunday," Carol said. "But I wasn't on any beach with palm trees. For a change, I have spent the holidays in Paris with my father's family."

"Me too! I mean... I wasn't in Paris, but with my father's family. I have met the Black Forest. You know that my father is from there. That area is beautiful, "Almu replied.

"Don't ask me," Bonet said. "I haven't had a vacation. I have been preparing for the start of my Master's degree in Robotics."

"Robotics? But you're already one of them," Fede said, "like *I Robot,* by Isaac Asimov. Does your positronic brain know the three laws of robotics by memory?"

"Very funny," Bonet replied. "Let's see, what have you done?"

"I've been with the whole family for a whole month in Florida. My nephews enjoyed the amusement parks, and I enjoyed fishing in the Caribbean Sea."

"Fishing what?" Charly asked. "What are the natives of Florida called? Cougars? I have read that there are many around the Everglades."

"They're called Floridians. And no, it isn't the name of an extraterrestrial race." Fede answered, anticipating his funny friend.

"And what have you done, Charly, that you seem so happy?" Rebecca. asked

"At the end of June, I was fired from the air taxi company."

Rebecca was surprised by her friend's apparent cheerful response.

"And that's why you're so happy? For being unemployed?"

"Who said I'm unemployed? Actually, I've been working all summer. I have important news to tell you. I passed the courses, and I can now tell you that I am officially a pilot for the Mare Nostrum airline."

"Congratulations, Charly!" They all said in chorus, very happy for their friend.

"You've got what you always wanted," Carlota said. "Now you'll buy a round of beers, right?"

"I said I have a new job. Now I just need to get paid," Charly replied. "What about you, Carlota? How is your mother?"

"It is seasonal, but she's fading little by little. At least I have the help of my two brothers, who have moved to live with us."

"We're really sorry."

"As you understand, I haven't been able to go anywhere on vacation. However, I'm sure I had a much better time than all of you. I'd even bet a round of beers."

"I have met wonderful villages in Alsace. How can you be so sure?" Almu asked, in all her innocence.

"Doing what exactly?" Xavier asked. "I haven't known any wonderful towns, but I assure you that I have been able to enjoy a few international monuments, also in all their splendor. I assure you that it's very difficult for you to exceed my two weeks in Ibiza and that I have blurred memories of many days," Xavier concluded, laughing.

"All in due time," Carlota said, wearing an enigmatic smile on her face. "Don't be in such a rush. We've just started the club meeting."

What could this firecracker have done? Rebecca thought uneasily. *Should I worry?* At least it seemed that Charly, Fede, and Xavier had forgotten about the scores. Naïve, one more time.

17 NOVEMBER 2nd, 1521

"Today, you're going to meet a great person," Luis said enthusiastically.

"Greater than you?" Johan asked.

"Don't be an idiot. I'm not even thirty years old and I still have a lot to learn."

Johan Corbera had arrived just two days ago in Leuven, the great university campus where Luis Vives currently resided, after a heavy journey.

It had been more than thirteen years since they had parted, that sad afternoon in front of Blanquina March's grave. They hadn't seen each other since then, but it seemed like yesterday.

He had kept in touch with Number One during these years through correspondence. He had always hoped that he would return to Valencia as soon as possible, but it seemed increasingly unlikely. The Great Council had been missing for quite some time, although it was none of his business since, as the Eleventh Door, he didn't participate in their meetings. Despite this, he had asked for a small exemption at work so that he could travel to Flanders and speak in person with his friend. There were subjects that couldn't be discussed by letter.

"Who is it? If you talk about him like that, I'm sure he's quite a character."

"You are curious, like me. I like it," Luis mocked him.

During the almost four months that they enjoyed in Valencia, between 1508 and 1509, Johan Corbera and Luis Vives had established a great friendship and there was real complicity between them. Not for nothing, according to the Kabbalah, they were soul mates. Sefirah Daat, Number Eleven, was the consciousness, the hidden, non-material form of sefirah Keter, which was the root, Number One, according to the Kabbalistic tree.

"You know that, according to the Kabbalah, we are two forms of the same thing," Johan replied. "We must resemble by force. Also, your real name is Juan Luis Vives, don't you see it? Your name is like mine, Johan or Juan in its Spanish version."

"Despite being Number One on the Great Council, I have never believed in such nonsense. On the other hand, my mother Blanquina was a staunch supporter and defender of the Kabbalah. I still remember when she started me on her knowledge. I also remember how disappointed she was by my utter disbelief. I refuted it step by step and left her without arguments. She didn't know what to answer me, so she ended up getting mad at me. She was on her deathbed, so I didn't want to discuss it further."

Luis Vives made a small pause. His face seemed to be transmuted.

"You know, Johan? After all this time, I still miss her," he said in a melancholy tone. She died too young. Her memory evoked his childhood and his roots. He didn't want to continue thinking about that, so he decided to change the subject and his attitude. He couldn't allow the sadness of his mother's memories to dominate his life. He had decided to move on long ago.

"Do you mean we look alike? But you are very ugly, and I'm a complete Adonis! Besides our name, I don't see any other similarities between us." He laughed.

"An Adonis? But have you taken a good look at yourself? I suppose it is because of the inner beauty, because of course that on the outside you leave much to be desired," Johan replied, laughing too.

Since the departure of Luis Vives from Valencia, that ugly duckling with ideas ahead of his time had become a great swan. He had received his doctorate from the *Sorbonne* in

Paris in 1512 and then spent a few years in Bruges, being welcomed by the Valldaura family while he frequented the Royal Court of Flanders of the future King Charles I of Spain. In 1517, he decided to move to the Flemish city of Leuven, although he also spent some time in Bruges and Paris. Now he was a great humanist, philosopher, and even pedagogue, a personality of enormous prestige throughout Europe, claimed by nobles and kings. For all this, Johan Corbera was curious to know who he was going to meet.

"Who are you going to introduce me to? Some royal personality?" He tried to make him talk.

"Of course not! With a few exceptions, they are remarkably boring. Consider that Leuven is a city of scholars and students from all over the world, not of kings, especially in the historical moment in which we live. You already know that the Royal Court left Bruges a few years ago."

Flanders had joined the Spanish crown since the marriage of the daughter of the Catholic Monarchs, Joanna of Castille, also known as Joanna the Mad, to Philip of Castile, whose nickname was the Fair. Now, the son of the Mad and the Fair, Charles I, had unified in his name the territories of Castile, including the kingdom of Navarre, and the crown of Aragon, also encompassing the kingdom of Valencia and the county of Catalonia. Additionally, since last year, he has held the title of Emperor of the Holy German Empire, an honor whose origin comes from Charlemagne himself. Consequently, he also ruled half of Europe under the title of Charles V. At that time, Spain was a power.

During his stay at the Court, Luis Vives had been his occasional teacher of the Spanish language. Charles of Austria, current King of Spain, was born in Ghent and was raised in Flanders for the first seventeen years of his life, so he hardly spoke it, and that was a reason for suspicion on the part of many nobles. For his part, Luis Vives was a polyglot since he was fluent in six languages. He was the perfect teacher.

"Don't make fun of me. It's the first time in my life that I have left Valencia. I must look like a small-town man," Johan said apologetically, "especially by your side."

"Valencia is not a small town; it is a great city. Although it has been twelve years since I abandoned it, I will never forget my origins. You don't know how I miss its light and its colors. Everything is gray in here. There, my curiosity for knowledge and reading was born. In addition, you would be surprised to know how many compatriots there are in these lands."

In the cities of Antwerp, Ghent, Bruges, and Leuven, there had been, for some years, an important colony of Spanish merchants who acted as contractors in relationship with the Hanseatic League, the powerful commercial federation of northern Europe. It was no longer as powerful as it had been a few centuries ago. Since the discovery of America and the consolidation of the Dutch and English naval power, it had weakened considerably. In fact, there had already been some military confrontations between them.

In this colony, there were quite a few Valencians, especially in the textile business. Although, at that time, Luis Vives still didn't know that in just three years, he would end up marrying Margarita Valldaura, precisely the daughter of some Valencian merchants living in Bruges, the same ones who welcomed him when he finished his studies at the *Sorbonne* in Paris.

"Don't tell me you're going to introduce me to a compatriot?"

"Of course not. Do you think you made this big trip to Flanders to meet a Valencian? You have plenty of those in our land. You don't need to rub shoulders with more compatriots."

In reality, Johan Corbera hadn't gone to Leuven to meet anyone. He had to inform Luis Vives of a very serious situation, which affected him in a very direct and personal way.

I don't know how he's going to take it. He seems very happy here and leads a very quiet life, Johan thought.

18 NOWADAYS. TUESDAY, SEPTEMBER 4th

"Did you think we had forgotten, Rebecca? Not at all! After telling each other about the holidays, now we're all going to walk the runway before the Grand Jury," Charly said, showing the papers with the numbers written on them.

For general enjoyment, everyone paraded as if they were on a fashion runway, clowning around, each with their own style. The people who were sitting at the tables around them looked at them with amusement. They even participated in the applauses and laughter. Rebecca wanted to die of embarrassment but put up with it. The highlight of the afternoon was when Charly, Fede, and Xavier paraded with fake wings that they had brought from home, simulating a fashion show of Victoria's Secret's angels. They even asked the bartender Dan to play Maroon 5's *Moves like Jagger* song, the same one that was used on that legendary 2011 Fashion Show. It was a real scene.

When everyone finished walking, Charly got up and adopted that theatrical role that he loved so much. He pretended to remove a note from an envelope, calculating the moment.

"And the winner is... Carlota!"

Indeed, the final winner was Carlota, with thirty points, followed by Almu, Bonet, and Rebecca, all three with twenty-nine. Everyone stood to applaud. Not only the members of the Speaker's Club but also the customers at the adjoining tables, to the embarrassment of all participants. They were causing a real buzz in the pub.

Please, how embarrassing! Rebecca thought, although Carlota didn't seem to mind. She even got up and showed off that quirky dress to thank for the award.

"Thank you all very much for this well-deserved award. You have tried hard, but I think that the most different, not to say ridiculous, without any doubt is me."

"Ágatha, I love you!" Charly yelled, crying with laughter, barely able to contain himself.

"I'm going to screw you later," Carlota warned him, making a gesture with her hand, pretending to spank him on the ass.

"Screw it as a sexual connotation?" Fede asked, who couldn't help laughing.

"Fede!" Carlota exclaimed, pretending to be scandalized. "Don't make me talk..."

Rebecca got involved immediately. She didn't like where the conversation could lead.

"Now the winner will say a few words to us," she said hastily the first thing that came to mind.

There was silence in the club, waiting for the winner to speak.

"Do you want me to say a few words? Well, they're going to freak out!" Carlota thought, enjoying what she was going to trigger.

Rebecca saw her friend's bright eyes. She already knew what that meant and couldn't help but become alert. *Maybe it wasn't a good idea to ask her to speak,* she told herself uneasily. *I'm afraid of her.*

Carlota stood up, touched the hearts of Ágatha Ruiz de la Prada's dress, and stared at everyone present. The expectation was at its maximum. *Here I go,* she thought.

"Do you want a few words? Let's see if these are worth it. We are idiots. They have been deceiving us from the beginning. The Great Council of Ten exists nowadays, and the Jewish tree remains hidden."

19 NOVEMBER 3rd, 1521

Luis Vives introduced Johan to his teacher in Leuven. It was part of the cloister in its Trilingual School, so-called because its teachings were taught in three languages: Latin, Hebrew, and Greek, which Vives mastered perfectly, along with French, Spanish and Valencian. The latter was his mother tongue, the one he had spoken since childhood at home.

"Johan, I have the pleasure of introducing you to Desiderius Erasmus Roteradamus, as he likes to be called in Latin," he said as solemnly as he could.

"Erasmus of Rotterdam?" Johan asked incredulously, looking at this impeccably dressed person who, by appearance, was in his early fifties.

Erasmus was the most influential thinker of Europe at the time, which was almost as saying the world. Besides being a precursor of humanism, he was a philosopher, philologist, and theologian. It had been a few years since he had read his essay *In Praise of Folly*, which had been widely publicized, especially because of how transgressive it was for the times in which they lived. It was said that he wrote it with his great English colleague Thomas More in mind.

He really enjoyed the conversation. It was obvious that Erasmus and Luis Vives were great friends, and they professed a sincere admiration for each other. Johan already knew about the somewhat eccentric personality of Erasmus, but even so, he was surprised by the vehemence of his words against the established power and against the abuses of the 'bad religious,' as he himself called them. He said that most educational institutions didn't allow the development of free thought of the individual, with its rigid and, at times, absurd discipline. He also put in the same bag the teaching activity of the Church. According to him, everything had been perverted, and it was necessary to pay attention again to the great thinkers of the Greek and Roman civilizations. He spoke with total sincerity since all his life, he had been consistent with his thinking and criticisms.

Johan couldn't help asking the question that had been on his mind from the beginning of the conversation.

"Hasn't that way of thinking caused you problems with the Catholic Church, which is very vigilant of your activities?" He asked curiously. Let's not forget that Johan Corbera, in addition to being an architect, was also an ecclesiastic. He would never have dared to utter those words, even if he shared them for the most part.

Erasmus answered him immediately.

"Of course. Although they shouldn't doubt my faith, especially after the work that I'm doing with the translated versions of the Bible, I have had to constantly give explanations throughout my life. It's difficult for them to understand that I have never criticized the Church as such, much less God. What I have criticized and keep criticizing is the attitude of some bishops and friars in particular, who make huge amounts of money selling the paradise and who do fabulous business with simony."

Johan, from his religious background, knew what the word simony meant. It was the perversion of faith, the commercialism of the divine for the sole purpose of obtaining material goods and wealth. For example, the ease with which ecclesiastical offices could be bought in exchange for certain sums of money, or the excessive enrichment of some personalities of the Church at the expense of their parishioners, who were certainly needier than they were.

Fortunately for Erasmus, his enormous influence had always gotten him out of trouble, at least until now. It wasn't clear to Johan why he could always get away without being punished. Right now, he even enjoyed the favor of the Pope of Rome, but the situation could change. The extreme orthodoxy of the current Inquisition frightened him, despite his good relations with Adriano of Utrecht, Grand Inquisitor of Spain.

Erasmus and Adriano had met at the Royal Court of Flanders and they professed a sincere friendship.

"Will you be staying in Leuven for a while?" Johan asked curiously, knowing Erasmus' eagerness to travel.

"No. In fact, I have moved my residence to Basel. I don't like Leuven as a city, although, of course, my bonds with Flanders are very powerful, and that is why I visit my friend Luis as often as I can," Erasmus replied. "At the moment, I also maintain my school and it will be so as long as my abilities allow it. We are already getting old and, in the end, I will have to prioritize my activities. Teaching and reading take up a large part of my time."

After a long time, the conversation came to an end. Knowing where Johan came from, Erasmus said goodbye by giving him a copy of his work *Education of the Christian prince*, which he had written in 1516 for the then Prince Charles, when he was only sixteen years old. Now, he was king of Spain and emperor of half of Europe. Erasmus was proud to have influenced his education, even if it had been somewhat limited.

Johan and Luis left the Trilingual School in a good mood, chatting vigorously. *Too bad the fun is ending so soon*, Johan thought to himself, thinking about the real reason for his visit to Leuven.

20 NOWADAYS. TUESDAY, SEPTEMBER 4th

The general hilarity of the catwalk had turned into utter astonishment. The faces of all the Speaker's Club members were hardly describable.

"What's the matter? Don't look at me like that! I already told you that I had fun this summer," Carlota said, who was the only one who seemed entertained.

"Jesus, Carlota!" Almu said immediately. "Are you aware of what you just said?"

"Have you gone crazy?" Fede said. "Everything was very clear before summer."

Carol looked at them with an expression of not understanding anything.

"Can someone explain to me what you are talking about? And by the way, you can also tell me why you have those very disjointed faces. You should see yourself in a mirror. You look like The Addams Family." She turned to Rebecca. "You are paralyzed; you even look like Wednesday Addams."

Rebecca reacted; she had been mentally trapped before Carlota's revelation. She briefly explained everything that happened last May to Carol. The visit of the alleged Countess of Dalmau to her newspaper, which, in reality, was Number Three of the current Great Council, the actress Tania Rives, in disguise. She also told her that she gave her some drawings and how, after various vicissitudes, they had reached the location of the ancient Jewish tree of knowledge, which was a chest buried in the Patio de los Naranjos of Valencia's Lonja. That chest was empty; someone had been ahead of them. Finally, she told her how she had unmasked Number Eleven, who was Joanna Ramos, her aunt's partner.

"How exciting! Now I understand why there was so much activity on the Speaker's Club mobile chat that month. I couldn't keep up with your rhythm. Also, it was during the exam period, so I didn't read practically any message. What a pity not to have been in Spain to have participated! It certainly seems like it was quite an adventure, right?"

Carlota looked like she was shining.

"Don't use the past tense, Carol. It wasn't, it still is, and it will be," Carlota said, with that enigmatic smile that intrigued Rebecca very much. "And most importantly, you arrive at the right time to participate."

Charly, finally, seemed to react.

"Hey Rebecca, have you given your friend some of that hippie joints of some kind?"

"I swear I didn't," Rebecca said, still in shock. *What did she find out this summer?* She wondered nervously.

"Well, then she has been possessed by the spirit of Ágatha Ruiz de la Prada," Charly declared. "The dress has taken over her mind. So many hearts can't be good."

"I have proof of what I say," Carlota said very confidently.

"What proof is that?" Carmen asked. As always, the voice of sanity.

Carlota stared at Rebecca.

"The day you discovered that Joanna was the Eleventh Door, in that meeting, you said something that made me think a lot about it. I'm going to try to remember your exact words, they were something like: 'I had a strange feeling. It gave me the impression that we were simple pawns in someone's game, and we were following the orders of someone else without us realizing.'"

"Yes, I remember them," Rebecca replied. "They were exactly like that. You have a very good memory."

"I remember that, immediately afterward, Fede told you that he didn't understand you, and I said that I had the same feeling as you," Carlota continued.

"That's how it happened. Where do you want to go with that?"

"To a very simple place. I have continued having that same feeling, even after Joanna's confession. Sorry, something fundamental doesn't fit into the whole story we know. I'm afraid we still don't realize we're simple pawns in someone's game."

"What is your basis for such a statement?"

"You should know it better than anyone else," Carlota said, looking at Rebecca.

"Me? Why?"

"To begin with, because one of the two parts of the message, which led us to search and locate the Jewish tree in La Lonja, was completely false. A great lie, yes, a very well-crafted lie."

During the month of May, they had discovered the inscription 'under the star' on a choker of great value, owned by the Count of Ruzafa. Bonet had also deciphered a message hidden in an envelope, which the Count kept in his safe. That message read 'silk lust.' The union of both messages had led them to *La Lonja de la Seda*, and more specifically, next to the star-shaped fountain in the *Patio de los Naranjos*. Now, Carlota claimed that one of the two messages was false.

There was silence in the group. Rebecca was completely shocked, not knowing what to answer.

"Are you going to say it or should I do it myself?" Carlota asked her.

"What if we go to dinner and continue the conversation there?" Rebecca replied, trying to buy time to find an answer.

"Good idea, it's almost the reservation time, and I'm hungry," Xavier said. "We're barely five minutes away from the restaurant, so I think we'll be able to endure the suspense until we get there."

"My stomach is making rumbles," Carlota objected.

"Well, you can eat a heart out of your dress; you have too many," Xavier replied in a mocking tone.

They got up from the table and left the Speaker's Club in the direction of the del Carmen neighborhood.

How the hell had Carlota discovered that the message on the envelope with the Caesar cipher was written by me?

Rebecca told herself in terror. From the way she addresses me, it is clear that she knows. Now that she thought about it, she supposed it wasn't impossible. At the time, she had had to improvise urgently and hadn't paid much attention to the little details like, for example, the calligraphy on the envelope or anything else that she couldn't think of right now. Carlota knew it was false; that was the important thing. She didn't know what to do. She was confused and was about to face a small crisis. She had five minutes to come up with a convincing response to the fake message on the Countess' envelope because when they got to the restaurant, she assumed the attention was going to be on her, and she had to be prepared.

Rebecca was scared.

21 NOVEMBER 4th, 1521

"I have to talk to you," Johan said seriously.

Luis Vives stared at his friend for a few seconds. He didn't seem surprised.

"I figured out you didn't come to Leuven just to visit me."

"You know very well that I really wanted to meet with you, but I also have something to tell you, and it's important."

"Come on, tell me what's so serious that you've kept silent for three days. If you don't let it out, I think you're going to end up bursting."

"Have you noticed?"

"Of course, although I have no idea what it is."

"Actually, it's not just one piece of news; they're two. Which one do you want me to start with, the good one or the bad one?"

"Is there good news? Wow! Now that's a surprise. Lately, they are all bad. As I wasn't expecting it, start with that, with the good news. I'm curious."

Johan made a small pause.

"Although I shouldn't know this, I know that your friends in Spain are making great efforts, so you can return from this exile safely and out of danger from the Holy Office of the Inquisition."

Luis made an expression of obvious disappointment.

"Is that the good news? Well, what a disappointment. I'm very comfortable in Flanders. At the moment, I'm not considering going back."

"Let me finish. You still haven't heard what I have to tell you."

"Go ahead, go ahead," Luis said with some curiosity.

"I have found out that the noble Don Bertrán is in contact with Don Fadrique Álvarez of Toledo, second Duke of Alba, that, as it is well-known, has two grandchildren. It seems that he's looking for a cultured and knowledgeable person to take charge of the education of both."

"The second Duke of Alba and his two grandsons. Besides, you and me together talking about it. Two, two, and two. A Kabbalist would surely see some hidden meaning in your triple-two speech."

"Don't be an idiot, Luis! We are talking seriously about Don Fadrique Álvarez de Toledo."

"I know, none other than the Duke of Alba."

"Exactly, a lord with greatness from Spain, the highest noble rank after the king himself and his direct descendants. With his power, he could place anyone out of the reach of the Inquisition for good, especially if he is the tutor of his grandchildren. I know the Holy Office terrifies you."

Luis nodded.

"Although I don't have bad relationships with them today, in the past, they burned a large part of my family. What they did to them, they also did it morally to me, so the further away from the Inquisition, certainly the better. I simply avoid any contact with them."

"I'm aware of your aversion to the Holy Office; that's why I was telling you."

"Aversion is a very mild word, but has the Duke of Alba specifically asked for me?" Luis Vives said, surprised.

"No, he is still looking for candidates, but I'm relaxed because I know that the noble Don Bertrán, who is quite a personality in the court, and grandson of the former Grand Inquisitor of Spain, Fray Diego de Deza, is doing an important job, as he's a personal friend of Don Fadrique. He's offering your services."

"Are you offering my services without consulting me? It's curious. Anyway, I must insist, I'm very comfortable in Leuven."

Johan got up and looked around, clearly dismissive.

"Do you really like Leuven?" Johan couldn't believe Luis. He had only been around for a few days, and he even disliked the smell of it.

"As a city? Of course not! You may have observed that it is dirty and abandoned, but today it is a true emporium of science and literature. Besides, I work for Erasmus. He even visits me on occasions, which he would never do if I were in Spain. You know that he has rejected multiple invitations to go since he doesn't trust the Spanish Inquisitors, like me. Don't lose sight of the fact that Flanders is the most important cultural center in Europe right now. Here, my mind feels free and safe from stakes."

Johan didn't know how to continue the conversation without hurting his friend's susceptibility. He had to try. *Here I go*, he told himself.

"Luis, you must think very well. I know that at the beginning of this year, your young pupil Guillermo de Croy fell from his horse and unfortunately killed himself. I also know that he was your main patron and that your current economy is very battered. Don't deny that you are in financial difficulties," Johan emphasized. "You have told me that you have just arrived from Bruges, where you have lived for six months in a house given by Captain Pedro de Aguirre and that you have met with King Charles I himself, at his request. I also know that, at those parties, you have met Cardinal Wosley, Lord Chancellor of England. Without a doubt, it's a great honor, but let's be serious, Luis, that doesn't bring food to your table. Prestige doesn't fill the pantries or pay for your roof. You will not be able to stay in Flanders forever if you can't find another stable source of income. If that doesn't happen, you will have to emigrate again, and what better place to return than to your own home."

Luis stared at his friend with some amazement.

"Gee, Johan, you had your speech well prepared. You aren't wrong about my finances, but unfortunately, I don't have a home. I'm a citizen of the world. 'Where I am, I am well,' that is my true nation and my shoes are my homeland. I don't believe in frontiers, and if you put pressure on me, I don't believe in flags either. They have caused more deaths than the plague."

"That's not true, but we'll discuss it later," Johan replied very seriously.

Luis Vives tried to change the course of the dialogue. He didn't want the conversation to go that way.

"The news of the revolt of the brotherhoods that threatens the entire kingdom of Valencia has reached Flanders. Isn't it worrisome? I think that the viceroy was defeated a few months ago by the insurgent leader Vicent Peris, and he had to take refuge in the Villena castle, according to the merchants who came from our land, right?"

"It took you a while to bring up that topic," Johan replied with some annoyance. He knew it was a controversial issue.

"You have to understand me. You're insinuating me to return to my city, which, right now, is in a full military uprising. How do you want me to ignore that?"

"It's not as serious as it may seem from far away. You live in Leuven and I live in Valencia. It's a revolt doomed to failure. Do you think that armed artisans, organized in the form of guilds, have any chance of defeating the nobility and King Charles I himself? It's ridiculous. The bad thing is that they believe it."

"Well, it seems that the Germanies rebels have a lot of popular support, and it's a fact that the king isn't paying too much attention to this uprising."

"Don't forget that just two years ago, we suffered another epidemic of plague in Valencia. At that moment, the nobility left the city, and the guilds seized their control, taking advantage of the power vacuum. At the time, it seemed like a good idea for them to arm themselves to defend us from the incursions of the Barbary pirates, although now it has been shown that it was a great error. But make no mistake, it's a mere temporary illusion. As soon as the king awakens from his slumber, everything will return to normal. He will defeat them with blood and fire, and I don't think it will take longer."

"I would like to remind you that the rebels have conquered important places and won an important battle."

"But they will lose the war, listen to me. They don't form a homogeneous group. They will end up divided and defeated, and it's something that is going to happen sooner rather than later. Also, don't forget that your uncle Baltasar Vives is one of the most significant leaders opposed to the revolt. When it's over, he'll be in a good social position, and that will be good for your family. It could help you."

"Well, believe me, I'm worried about the revolution, even though my uncle fights it."

Johan Corbera tried to redirect the conversation. Now the one who didn't like where it was going was him.

"What should really worry you at this moment is not the German rebels but the offer of the Duke of Alba. Don't tell me you're not curious about what it is? You know that he's a very powerful person but also very rich."

"You're dying to tell me. Come on, what's that offer?"

"None other than two hundred gold ducats a year, apart from all the privileges that a position of that category would entail."

Luis Vives couldn't help being surprised, although he tried to hide it. He didn't want to reveal his reaction to Johan. He was really impressed by the offer.

"Not bad at all, really," he said with feigned shyness.

"Not bad at all? But if it's a small fortune, Luis! In addition, I also know that they are looking for a chair at a university. If you return, you could do what you have always said you would like to do in life, 'learn and teach.'"

"But the Duke of Alba has made no offer to me."

"No, not yet, but I hope Don Bertrán will be able to convince him shortly. Trust me, I've seen him in action and he's taking it very seriously. You already know that he has great power. He even seems superior to his noble rank."

"Then, I can't make a decision now. I must wait for it to occur if it does, and then I'll decide accordingly."

"That's right. I suppose they would communicate it to you through a special emissary from the House of Alba."

Luis Vives was silent, thoughtful for a few endless seconds, looking at his friend Johan Corbera in the eye. In the end, he broke his silence.

"But you really didn't come to Leuven to tell me that, did you, Johan?"

"No. I already told you that I was also the bearer of bad news."

"Well, the time to tell me has come, don't you think?"

"I'm afraid that's correct."

Johan Corbera told him the real reason for his trip. He took his time to narrate all the events with their corresponding details without overlooking anything. It was truly terrible.

Luis Vives paled. He didn't know what to say. He was deeply shocked.

22 NOWADAYS. TUESDAY, SEPTEMBER 4th

They crossed the Plaza de la Reina and walked over Corretgería Street, talking lively. Rebecca tried to stay alone so she could think, but it was impossible. Almu accompanied her.

"What was Carlota talking about in the pub?"

"I really don't know, Almu."

"She said she had evidence of a hoax."

"We deciphered and joined the two messages that led us to the ancient Jewish tree of knowledge. I have no idea which part Carlota thinks is fake," Rebecca lied as best she could.

"We'll get rid of doubts shortly."

That was precisely what Rebecca feared, and she hadn't yet thought of a plausible explanation. Time was running out.

They arrived at the Italian restaurant 'San Tommaso.' A large round table had been reserved for them at the end. They all sat down, ordered something to drink, and several portions of their famous entrance *parmigiana de melanzane* to share, while they looked at the menu.

"Come on, Carlota, tell us what you've done this summer to give us such news," Charly said, who, like everyone else, was expectant.

"You're curious, right?" Carlota replied.

"Don't be mean, Ágatha, don't make us beg you," Fede said.

"It's very simple. As I have already told you, I have discovered that one of the two parts of the message is fake."

"Even if it was true and there was an error in one of the parts of the message, how do you come to the conclusion that the Great Council and the tree still exist?" Carmen asked. "I'm not following you."

"I'm not talking about a simple mistake. I'm affirming that one of the parts is completely fake."

"Still," Carmen continued. "That we have investigated a fake clue doesn't prove the current existence of the Great Council either. I can't understand it."

"I assure you it does prove it. It isn't that we have made a mistake in our reasoning or even that we interpreted some aspects in the wrong way. I insist it's that someone has purposely misled us."

The expectation at the table was at its maximum. They were all waiting for Carlota's explanations. Looking at her friends, she asked a question.

"Why would someone take the trouble of falsifying part of the message in order to direct our search for the tree to the Patio de los Naranjos of La Lonja?"

"Why? That's what I say," Bonet said.

"It's obvious. Actually, that person didn't care if we looked there or not," Carlota replied.

"Now, I certainly don't understand anything," Almu replied.

Carlota tried to explain herself better.

"I mean, they weren't intending for us to go to that particular location. If we solved the fake message, then it would be better because they had prepared a small scene, with an empty chest included, so that we would think that the Jewish treasure had been lost forever. But their true intention was that we wouldn't look in the real location where the tree remains hidden. Don't you realize? What they wanted was to mislead us, and I admit that they didn't achieve their goal."

They all fell silent, thinking about Carlota's words.

"And who would bother to falsify part of the message?" Jaume said.

"Good question. Now I'll ask you another one. I'll return the favor to you. Who is in charge of protecting the tree?"

"The Great Council!" Charly answered immediately.

"Exactly. Don't forget that the only reason for their existence is to be, precisely, the guardians of the tree. Falsifying the track will have cost them a great job; it wasn't easy at all. If you think about it, it is only justified because they were trying to preserve their great treasure, the tree."

"What track are we talking about?" Bonet asked somewhat impatiently.

"I suppose you mean the envelope with those strangely arranged letters," Fede said.

"Hasn't it been a very strange element to you from the beginning?" Carlota asked.

"The truth is, it has," Fede continued, "although not to the point of thinking it was fake. That didn't occur to me."

"Stop thinking for a moment. A blank envelope appears that reveals some letters when held up to the light. Not that they were especially hidden, anyone could have discovered them, as, in fact, Bonet did the first time that envelope fell into his hands. The letters make up an encrypted message, but not by numerological techniques as the Kabbalists of the Great Council did, but by using Caesar's encryption, an extremely simple method to solve. Would you keep such an important secret that way, visible for everyone and with so few security measures?"

Carlota stared at her friend Rebecca, who no longer knew how to act due to how nervous she was. She continued speaking.

"But, on the other hand, put yourself in the position of the Count of Ruzafa. Imagine the scene. He makes an appointment in his palace, specifically in his office, with the Eleventh Door, so they provide them with their half of the message under the pretext of rebuilding the Great Council, which has been broken for centuries. Remember that only the first three doors attended the meetings. The Great Council was split by the fourth one."

"Yes, we already know that," an impatient Carmen said.

"In the Count's office, the Eleventh Door conveys its message orally. It isn't weird that the Count took the first thing he had on his table, for example, an envelope, and wrote the message with a secret code that was easy to remember.

After all, he was going to keep it in a safe that not even his wife, the Countess of Dalmau, knew about. It isn't an unusual situation."

"What do you mean with that explanation?" Carmen asked, who seemed very intrigued.

"Don't you understand? What I want you to understand is that the clue on the envelope is plausible. Actually, I don't have any proof that it is fake. In fact, I think that for its simplicity, it must be authentic."

There was a little commotion at the table. Their faces were all of complete perplexity. Suddenly, Charly burst out laughing.

"You're making fun of us, right?" he said. "You're an asshole!"

Now everyone accompanied Charly with laughter. Fede threw a piece of bread at Carlota's face.

"We all believed it, you idiot! You had us in suspense."

Carlota was laughing too, but at the same time, she was watching each of the Speaker's Club members. That was what she wanted right now, with her little scene. It took her a very short time to realize the person who was out of tune with the whole group. Rebecca was the only one who didn't participate in the general revelry. She was very serious.

How curious! Carlota thought. *From the beginning, she has had a very strange attitude towards this subject.*

23 NOVEMBER 4ᵗʰ, 1521

"Again? Aren't they going to leave us alone ever in our lives?" Luis said, devastated, as he covered his face with his hands.

"Your father was arrested by the Inquisition a little over a year ago. You know it's the second time it has happened, but I'm afraid this is the final one."

"How do you know?" Luis asked, anguished.

"I have my connections; you already know that. The sequestration notary has proceeded to catalog all his assets, which are already at the disposal of the recipient of the Holy Office."

"What assets have they discovered?" Luis asked.

"Judge for yourself. I have the inventory here," Johan replied, handing his friend the list of belongings.

"Family home on Calle Taberna del Gall, valued at 220 pounds. Personal property valued at 327 pounds. Debt certificates are valued at 1,026 pounds. Blanquina March's dowry valued at 10,000 incomes and 380 *arrobas*[1] of stored wool and silk," Luis read aloud.

"Is it complete?" Johan asked.

"Yes, it seems they've figured it all out. They haven't even been able to hide my mother Blanquina's dowry, despite the fact that she was never declared a heretic by the Holy Office.

---

[1] Portuguese and Spanish customary unit of weight, mass or volume equivalent to 25 pounds (11.5 kg) in Spain.

They have no right to keep it. Even some debt certificates also belonged to her."

"That's a very bad sign. You know how the Inquisition works."

"In economic matters, I don't know. Why do you say it is a very bad sign?" Luis asked, intrigued.

Johan stared at his friend.

"I see you don't know how it works."

"This is the second time that my father has been arrested and the previous one, he came out unscathed, after the discovery of the clandestine synagogue in my uncle Miguel's house. What's different about this time?"

Johan had no desire to do it, but he had to explain to him the internal and economic workings of the inquisition so that his friend Luis would be aware of the gravity of the problem.

"When the Inquisition seizes someone accused of heresy with solid evidence, they immediately seize their property. This is what happened to your father. The first thing they do is an exhaustive inventory of assets, which is carried out by the so-called sequestration notary, and these properties are noted in a book known as the *Book of manifestations*. In theory, it should be a preventive system, so that the accused can't embezzle or hide their assets from the Holy Office when there is solid evidence against them."

"Why do you say in theory?"

"Because that is not the case in practice. Since the moment that goods and property are seized, they are controlled by the recipient of the Holy Office."

"And that is bad?"

"And a lot. The recipient is one of the key figures of the Inquisition. He's the economic manager. He's the delegate of the King of Spain's Treasury in each local court. Specifically, Amador de Aliaga, who's the recipient of goods in Valencia, possesses immense power, I would even say superior to the inquisitors themselves."

"So what?"

"Well, the recipient gets the seized assets from the start. He doesn't wait for the conviction of the arrested person."

"And can he do that? Shouldn't he wait for the final judgment of the Court?"

"In theory, there should be a distinction made between seized assets, which are seized preventively, and confiscated assets, which are after a conviction; but in practice, this isn't the case. The recipient of the Holy Office has full powers to dispose of them, even before the sentence."

"And with what purpose does he do that?"

"The main pretext is that the arrested person must take charge of their maintenance cost in prison for themselves. Prisoners pay for their own food according to their financial capacity. Each prisoner has a different menu, but, in reality, it is a simple pretext, as well as the payment of the procedural costs, which are outrageously high. Of course, if they are convicted, they also pay for their *sanbenito*, if any, or even the expenses incurred by their death at the stake. To give you an idea of the macabre of the matter, the condemned even have to pay the wood they use to burn them."

"And what happens if the accused is acquitted after all that?" Luis continued asking. "They have already taken their property."

Johan stared at him seriously.

"You still don't understand the seriousness of the matter, do you? This is the second time your father has been arrested by the Holy Office. You asked me a moment ago what is different about this occasion that makes it that serious. Well, you already have the answer, the sequestration of their assets. That didn't happen in the previous situation, did it?"

"Not that I'm aware of. They only took him as a prisoner to testify, but they released him very quickly, after the inquisitor Don Juan de Monasterio himself took a statement."

"You don't know many things Luis, even who Don Juan de Monasterio really was."

"Why are you telling me that? He was one of the two inquisitors at the city court at the time."

"Let's not get lost in details that lead us nowhere and let's get to the bottom line. Do you know how many arrested people the court of the Holy Office of Valencia acquits after the seizure of their property?"

Luis was silent, looking at his friend and waiting for the answer.

"They don't absolve anyone. Of thousands of prisoners, only a dozen has escaped conviction in more than thirty years of the court's operation. A significant part of them is burned to death," Johan answered himself. "Do you understand the difference?"

Now it was Luis who was left with a serious expression on his face.

"At this very moment, I understand what you wanted to tell me from the beginning of the conversation," he finally answered, saddened. "The sequestration of his assets changes everything."

"I'm glad, and I hope you understand the extreme gravity of the matter."

Luis was still shocked. It was difficult for him to continue the conversation.

"What are my sisters doing?"

Luis Vives had a brother, Jaime, who died at the age of twenty-one. He also had three sisters, Beatriz, born in 1499, Leonor, born in 1503, and the youngest, Isabel-Ana, born in 1507.

"Listen, they're doing the impossible, but your family needs your help urgently. They don't have the influence that you have. The situation is absolutely desperate. They can't do anything to save your father's life. They are focusing on the economic aspect. Your sisters, Beatriz and Leonor, along with the latter's husband, Miguel Dixer, are making real efforts to raise as much money as they can. Her plan is to try to keep the property, at least, of the family home and furniture, in order to have a roof where she can live. I want you to understand the severity of the situation."

"Don't think I don't understand it. You are talking about Beatriz and Leonor, but what about my other sister, Isabel-Ana? She is barely a child."

Johan didn't answer right away. He made a very serious face.

"What has become of her?" Luis asked, looking very distressed.

Everything is so dark and the night covers me, he thought.

24   NOWADAYS. TUESDAY, SEPTEMBER 4th

"You really tricked us there; you are a horrible friend!" Almu said, "Trust me, you really got me worried."

"With that dress, I don't know how we could have taken you seriously," Fede said, pointing to Carlota's quirky heart pattern.

The main courses had already been served, so they began to eat. Charly also noticed that Rebecca was very serious.

"What's wrong with you, that you're so quiet? Is there no peace in the world? So, let's make love!" Charly laughed, addressing Rebecca, the hippie.

"I'm just thinking."

"And what exactly are you thinking, may I ask?"

"I'm thinking about Carlota."

"About Carlota? Don't tell me you like her! Well, today, with the way she's dressed, she has a lot of merits."

Rebecca ignored Charly's comment and turned to her friend. Her expression was still very thoughtful.

"Listen, Carlota, I know you as if you were my own sister, and I think I know when you're being serious and when you aren't. I think our minds are, somehow, connected."

There was silence at the table. They all stared at Rebecca, waiting for her to continue. She did.

"This wasn't a joke, was it?" She said, looking into her friend's eyes.

Now all the attention was directed towards Carlota, who remained silent for a few seconds with a quite enigmatic smile.

"Carlota, for God's sake, will you please answer!" Almu said, who was visibly impatient.

Carlota took her time to answer.

"It's clear that you know me too well; it's true that we are too alike. Obviously, I can't hide certain things from you."

"So, you weren't making fun of us?" Charly asked in amazement.

"Not this time. Rebecca is right. The topic of the fake clue wasn't a joke. I was serious."

"I don't understand anything. So, in the end, it turns out that the envelope is fake?" Almu asked, no longer sure of what to think.

Rebecca anticipated and answered the question.

"The envelope is authentic. Now Carlota is going to tell us a very interesting story, which has nothing to do with that envelope, isn't it right?" She said, looking back at her friend.

Carlota stared at Rebecca.

"Sometimes I forget that you are almost as smart as me," she replied with a smile.

"You can leave out the 'almost,'" Rebecca said, who seemed amused for the first time in quite a while, "and change it to 'more.'"

Carlota stared at her friend.

"Indeed, as Rebecca seems to have deduced, the part of the false message isn't the one contained in the envelope but the inscription on the Count's choker."

Rebecca's mind was blown. The first deduction had been simple. She knew that distinctive sparkle in Carlota's eyes and knew from the beginning that she wasn't kidding about the fake clue. If she wasn't talking about the envelope, then there was only one part of the equation, the choker. What she didn't understand was how the message engraved on it could be fake. She was as surprised as the rest of the group, although she tried to appear confident and calm, although she was barely succeeding.

"How is that possible?" Carmen asked. "Rebecca showed us the photo that the private detective got. The message was there, we all saw it and we could read it."

"That's the problem, that we all saw the message and could read it."

"How can it be a problem that we see the message and read it?" Carmen asked, increasingly intrigued. "Are you pulling our legs?"

"The problem is, we all saw and read the message, but no one actually saw the choker."

Carmen didn't understand anything. She interrupted Carlota's explanation.

"What do you mean by we didn't? The private detective, a friend of Rebecca's aunt, obtained the photograph, which had been taken by the Count's own jeweler. In addition, Tania Rives also saw it on the desk in his office when she sneaked into his palace, the same night the Countess of Dalmau died," Carmen answered in somewhat indignation. "Your statement isn't true. That choker, at least, was seen by two people. That is a fact that you can't deny it."

Carlota didn't answer immediately. She remained silent, smiling with that style that she liked so much and that intrigued and exasperated Rebecca so much. She couldn't bear it.

"Did I tell you that this summer I had a lot of fun?"

"Carlota, please!" Charly exclaimed.

25 NOVEMBER 4th, 1521

Luis Vives was horrified by what he was hearing from his friend Johan Corbera. What had become of his little sister Isabel-Ana?

"Don't tell me that she has also been arrested by the Holy Office? She's only fourteen years old!" He said, scared.

"No, she's free, but I don't know for how long. She's about to marry Luis Amorós de Vera, who is a prominent member of the Jewish community. I'm afraid she is exactly like your mother, Blanquina; even her physical resemblance is amazing. You should see her now."

Luis felt a stabbing pain in his heart. Johan continued with his explanation.

"She's following the same Judaizing footsteps as your mother. I know the Inquisition watches them. Despite my repeated warnings, she's very stubborn and there is no way to convince her. You already knew Blanquina; well, she's the same, both physically and spiritually. I'm afraid both will end up in the hands of the Holy Office," Johan replied.

"This is never going to end!" Luis said, completely dejected.

"As I was telling you, the hopes that your father won't end up at the stake are low. Your sisters Beatriz and Leonor are raising all the money they can to become *capllevadors* of the house and of the personal property, but they need a lot of capital for the guarantee. Right now, they don't have it."

"Become *capllevadors*? What does that mean?"

"I forgot that you were unaware of the economic functioning of the Inquisition. The Holy Office has two ways of converting the seized assets into auctions. The first is the public auction, but it's more common for the recipient of the Inquisition to contact friends and relatives of the prisoner, offering to retain the assets in exchange for bail. For the recipient, it is more comfortable since it's a swift system, and he gets money in a faster way. These relatives or friends are called *capllevadors*".

"And is that why my little sister was left out?"

"Exactly. I have advised your sisters Beatriz and Leonor to put her aside. It isn't recommended that she is listed as the owner of the old family possessions because they could fall into the hands of the Holy Office again if Isabel-Ana is arrested along with her future husband, since everything seems to indicate that could happen."

"You're very well informed; you always surprise me."

"Don't forget that, in addition to being a master stonemason, I am a member of the Catholic Church and have access to a lot of information."

Luis was dejected.

"In short, the inquisition is going to burn us all, and you want me to return to Spain so they can burn me too," he said.

"Your father is in prison and all family assets are sequestrated. If they get the bail money and, at last, your family manages to keep the house, they will run out of resources even to eat. And if they don't get the money they need, they will be homeless. The situation is desperate whatever happens. Don't you understand? Take charge of the tragedy."

Luis was about to burst into tears.

"What can I do? I have almost no resources even to support myself, as you well know, and you remembered it to me a while ago."

"Don't forget who you are, the great Luis Vives, a very influential person throughout Europe. You can return to Spain and accept one of the job offers that will surely come to you, whether they are from the Duke of Alba or a chair at a university. They will protect you from the fury of the Holy Office. Think that they have nothing against you; you have never committed a heretical act."

"I can't do this. My father took me out of Spain thirteen years ago to protect me from the Inquisition as soon as my main teacher Antoni Tristany was arrested. Do I have to remind you that my guardian was burned and that, in all likelihood, I was going to be next?"

"Luis, if you don't help them, they'll end up dead or bankrupt. Your family has always cared about you. They have given you a magnificent education. You have never lacked anything in your life. Don't you think that the time has come to give them back something of all that they have given you so generously and you have received? Think that you are who you are, thanks to them."

Now Luis couldn't take it anymore, and tears escaped from his eyes.

"Is the tree safe?" He asked at last.

"At the moment, it seems so. They don't suspect anything."

"At least some good news," Luis said, trying to fake false relief.

They didn't know how wrong they were. It was going to be like this for a while, but even that wasn't good news.

26 NOWADAYS. TUESDAY, SEPTEMBER 4th

"If you don't tell us now, I'm capable of pouncing on you and tearing apart each of the hearts of your dress by biting them," Charly said, looking at the garment of Ágatha Ruiz de la Prada.

"It's a tempting offer," Carlota answered with a mischievous smile.

"Seriously, don't keep us on edge," Carmen said.

"Come on, tell us the story," Almu insisted.

"That's what I'm doing. Actually, the first red flag regarding the choker came from Tania Rives herself."

Rebecca was visibly surprised.

"Did you contact her this summer?" She asked, clearly curious.

"I tried, but I couldn't locate her. The one I did speak to was Inspector Sofía Cabrelles, the police officer who handled the case of her alleged death, in case she knew her whereabouts, but she didn't know anything either. Of course, she's no longer officially missing, but her resurrection hasn't been advertised. It seems that Tania has chosen a discreet life, away from the media spotlight. Nobody knows where she currently lives."

"So?"

"I was referring to what Tania Rives said in the Patio de Los Naranjos of La Lonja." Carlota paused and turned to Rebecca. "You were with me that day. I don't know if you remember her reaction when your aunt Tote accused her of stealing the choker the same night they sneaked into the palace and took the drawings. Wasn't there anything in Tania's behavior that caught your attention?"

Rebecca was thoughtful.

"It's true. I remember there was one thing that seemed strange to me. My aunt was accusing her of the theft and she, meanwhile, was smiling. I also remember that, at that moment, I thought I didn't know what was funny about the matter. Later it seems to me that she answered that she had nothing to do with that robbery, and my aunt was frustrated by her attitude."

"Unfortunately, I have a memory similar to a recorder. When your aunt asked her for explanations, she literally replied that 'it was normal' for the choker not to appear while smiling, as you well remember. Why was it normal that no one could find it? And what was so amusing to Tania? After all, a police officer was charging her with robbery."

Rebecca remembered another detail.

"Don't forget that the day she visited me in the newspaper disguised as a Countess of Dalmau. She also told me that she had seen the choker on the table in the Count's office."

"You already know she was playing a role, and she was very good with details. She's a method actress. She becomes her character and embellishes her performance with all possible details to give herself greater credibility."

"But she said it; that's a fact, no matter if she's such a method actress."

"On the other hand, isn't it strange that she was the only one who actually saw that alleged jewel?"

"You're mistaken on that. She wasn't the only one. The Count's jeweler, who took care of its repairs and maintenance, also saw it," Rebecca immediately replied.

Carlota made a small pause, taking the opportunity to drink some beer. Her lips were dry from talking.

"Do you know that I have a boyfriend?" She said, suddenly resuming the conversation in a surprising way.

"No kidding!" Rebecca exclaimed in surprise. "You hadn't told me anything."

"I'm doing it now."

"Well, I'm happy for you, but what does having a boyfriend have to do with the choker?" Rebecca asked, somewhat surprised. "I can't understand it."

"Well, actually, he's not a formal boyfriend, far from it. We could say that it is something like a summer fling, do you understand?"

"Carlota!" Rebecca exclaimed. "You're beating around the bush and not answering the important questions."

"Don't be impatient. Everything I'm telling you has a meaning. Do you know his name?"

"The one of your fling? How do you want us to know?" Fede asked, somewhat irritated. "We aren't mindreaders.".

"His name is Álvaro Enguix."

"Enguix? Why does that last name sound familiar to me?" Rebecca asked immediately.

"You may be familiar with Enguix Jewelry, which was where the Count took his famous choker to be repaired," Carlota replied.

"And that Álvaro has something to do with jewelry?" Xavier asked.

"Sure, he's its current manager. It was founded by his father, Sergio Enguix."

"And have you hooked up with the jewelry manager to get information out of him?" Charly asked incredulously. "That's almost master level. I take my hat off to your audacity."

"No, idiot!" She answered indignantly. "One thing came after the other."

"Come on, Carlota, would you mind telling us the story from the beginning? I think we're all a bit lost," Carmen said, as always the voice of reason.

"Sure, forgive me, but I lost track. As I have already told you, this summer I didn't have vacation, so it occurred to me to visit Enguix Jewelry to ask about the Count's choker. I showed up on a Saturday morning, and to my complete surprise, it was closed. On the door, there was a sign with their opening hours, Monday through Friday only."

"To your complete surprise? Why?" Xavier asked.

"Because you'll remember that Tote's private detective friend, Richie, said he visited the jewelry store on a Saturday. Well, it's impossible that he did since it remains closed throughout the weekend."

"During the month of August, it had summer working hours. Remember that Richie visited it in May," Rebecca said.

"That was my question too, so I came back the following Monday. It's a small, family-owned jewelry store that has been open for almost forty years. Behind the counter, there's only one person. I asked him, and he told me that the schedule was established three years ago. Richie couldn't visit it on a Saturday. It's impossible because they don't open that day."

"That's weird!" Rebecca said, surprised.

"But there's more. The inconsistencies in the story told by the detective don't end here. I expressly asked the jeweler about the choker, and he had no idea what I was talking about. He didn't know about the choker, nor did he know anyone named Richie, nor, consequently, did he show any photographs to that detective or anyone else."

The surprise was general.

"Don't they keep any entry records?" Carmen finally asked.

"I also asked him about it. He consulted the archives. No jewel of these characteristics appeared on his records in the last twenty-five years."

There was silence at the table. Rebecca reacted.

"I think I remember that Richie said that he had spoken with a certain Sergio Enguix, who, from what you have just said, is the founder of the jewelry store, Álvaro's father. Is it possible that Richie was taken care of by Sergio and that he didn't say anything to his son?"

"I'm sorry, Rebecca, but that's not possible either."

"Why?"

"Because Sergio Enguix retired three years ago and hasn't been in the jewelry store since. The only one who serves the customers is Álvaro."

Now, the members of the Speaker's Club were speechless. The astonished expression was widespread. They didn't know what to say. Carlota broke the silence.

"Now, it's perfectly understandable why the children of the Counts didn't know anything about that jewel, nor was it insured, nor did it appear in any inventory of assets. Not even the slightest trace of it was found in the palace."

"What do you mean by that," Almu asked, amazed.

Carlota took her time answering, looking at all her friends.

"Actually, the choker isn't missing."

"Oh! No? And who has it?" Almu continued asking.

"Nobody has it."

"Nobody has it and it isn't missing?" Almu interrupted, her mouth hanging open. "Sorry, Carlota, but that seems like a contradiction."

Carlota smiled. Almu's mind didn't work at the same frequency as her own.

"I said no one has it because it just never existed," she said at last.

Now everyone was puzzled. No one dared to refute Carlota. They were becoming aware of her deductions.

"It's incredible!" Carmen finally reacted.

"Unfortunately, it isn't. Do you understand the tremendous implications of the discovery?"

"I do," Rebecca said, who seemed the most shocked of the whole group.

"It would be interesting to be able to speak in person with Álvaro Enguix. What do you think, Carlota?" Fede asked. "I think the issue is very serious."

"For me, there is no problem. I can't meet until Friday, but if you consider it, we could call a Speaker's Club meeting and I'll invite him to join. He's a very interesting person. I assure you that he can contribute a lot to the group. Sounds good to you?"

They all nodded their heads. They were still stunned by what they had just heard.

Rebecca was completely taken aback. *This has turned everything into a mess,* she thought, alarmed. *I have to talk to my aunt as soon as possible.* She still believed that there could be an explanation to justify all this, although right now, she wasn't able to see it.

The worst thing is that Carlota could be right.

27 NOVEMBER 5th, 1521

"The time to say goodbye has arrived," Johan Corbera said.

"Do you have to go now?" Luis Vives asked.

"Unfortunately, I do. You know I asked permission for a few days, and I still have a long journey to our kingdom."

Luis was sad. Their last conversation had been extremely depressing. He was silent.

"Have you thought about what we talked about yesterday?" Johan asked.

"Sure, who wouldn't do it with such news?"

"Have you decided something?"

"I have decided to wait. Although I'm terrified of the Holy Office, and more so with the news you have told me, I don't want to rule out any options. I'm open to offers."

"I would prefer you to return to Valencia with me."

"I've thought a lot about my family's situation. Right now, without a job and without money, for them, it would be one more cause of concern, and, for now, they already have enough. There is no need to add a new one."

"You would never be a burden to your family. They already know that your finances are battered, and they don't expect that kind of help. You have become a very influential person throughout Europe. You even have access to the King of Spain, even to the Pope of Rome himself."

"But I can try to use those influences from here. I don't have to go back to Spain to do that. Also, that ancestry on

117

those characters that you just named isn't as great as you think. I know they will listen to me, but unfortunately for my family, I doubt they will consider any of my pleas."

An awkward silence fell between them.

"You really have no intention of ever going back to Spain, do you?" Johan asked.

"Don't misunderstand me. If any offer you told me about, especially that of the Duke of Alba was to come to the realization, I promise I will consider it. I have already told you that I don't rule out any option, and you know that I miss my homeland, despite the Inquisition."

"You know you won't be able to stay in Flanders much longer if you don't find another patron, and that's not easy to do in the current times."

"You're right, but I also have another possible offer."

"From whom? You hadn't told me anything."

"Because it hasn't materialized yet. Cardinal Thomas Wosley told me, during my stay in Bruges just a month ago, that he might require my services in England. You know that he's a person of great influence on the island. He is Lord Chancellor of the kingdom and Archbishop of York. Although it's the second prelature in order of ecclesiastical importance after the Archbishopric of Canterbury, in practice, it has more authority than he. I would venture to say that after King Henry VIII, he's the most powerful person in England right now. You will agree with me that he isn't a bad ally.

Johan Corbera seemed scared by what he had just learned.

"Listen, Luis, do you know Wosley's reputation? He's a sinister character, drunk with glory and ambition. He's the son of an Ipswich butcher and has been thriving in society through wiles. His character has nothing to do with yours. He is greedy for control and money. I very much doubt that your relationship will ever work."

"That's what rumors say, yet he made a wonderful impression on me when I met him in Bruges. He isn't illiterate as you seem to imply, not in vain he has been a professor of grammar at the University of Oxford, for example."

"I'm not saying he's an idiot. It's clear he's not one to get where he is."

"Then we agree on something, at least."

"Do you know that it is said that he's a candidate for the papal tiara? If he's appointed pope, he would move to Rome and leave you alone again, but this time even further away, in England."

"I haven't heard those rumors," Luis answered, surprised.

"Take my advice, you know I'm a clergyman and I find out about many things. He's one candidate among others, but you should worry about just the possibility."

"And what prevents you from believing that if Cardinal Wosley moved to Rome as pope, he wouldn't take me with him?"

"That is what worries me most about your attitude, your detachment from Spain. You mustn't forget that you are the First Door, Number One, the Keter, the root of the Great Council. You can't keep running away from your responsibility forever."

Luis Vives stared at his friend with a strange expression on his face. He took his time to continue the conversation.

"Johan, you're a great friend of mine, and you have rendered me great services. Also, you are the Eleventh Door, but, as you well know, you don't belong to the Great Council. I can't tell you certain issues."

"You don't have to remind me that, I know it."

"There are two very worrying things that you don't know about and that determine many of my decisions," Luis said, his voice very serious.

"What do you mean by that?"

"The first one, do you know I'm being watched?"

"Are they watching you?" Johan repeated the question, completely scared.

28 NOWADAYS. WEDNESDAY, SEPTEMBER 5th

Rebecca came home very late; it was already past one in the morning. The evening had gone on longer than expected. It was too late to wake up her aunt, so she left a note attached to the fridge with a magnet.

Don't leave without talking to me, it's important.

She set the alarm clock at a quarter to seven in the morning. *Another day of little sleep*, she thought, because who was going to fall asleep with everything that had happened. She couldn't help thinking about Carlota's discovery.

Despite falling asleep late, she woke up the first time the alarm went off. She went out into the kitchen in her pajamas. She didn't want her aunt Tote to go to work before talking to her. There she was, sitting at the table, waiting for her.

"Good morning, Rebecca. I've seen your note."

"Good morning, aunty. I arrived quite late last night and I didn't want to wake you up."

"What happened yesterday?" Tote asked, with a tone of obvious concern.

Rebecca hadn't spoken to her aunt since Monday morning.

"You know we had the first Speaker's Club meeting since June. Carol Antón came."

"Oh! Really? Did she come back from Paris? How is her father? I still see her mother from time to time in Valencia, but I haven't seen him for a long time."

Tote was close friends with Carolina's parents because they had previously been friends with Rebecca's parents. They met more than fifteen years ago in a formal ceremony at the French Embassy in Madrid, and they frequented cultural circles with quite a few friends in common, especially contemporary artists based in the province of Valencia, such as Paco Caparrós.

"He's fine. He's been promoted. I guess you know they broke up a few years ago."

"Yes, I knew that. As I have already told you, I have met her mother a few times. From what she told me, they seem to be getting along."

"Yes, it was a friendly separation, motivated above all because he's no longer at the consulate in Valencia. Now he works at the embassy in Madrid. He's the national cultural attaché, but they have a great relationship, even with their daughter."

"That's why I didn't see him. I'm happy for him. But come on, tell me what worries you. I don't think it has to do with Carol or his parents. To have gotten up before seven in the morning, it has to be something important. You always play it slow."

"Like I was saying, we had a club meeting yesterday. We told each other about the holidays, as usual for the first time we met after the summer and then we went to dinner. Carlota told us that, due to her mother's condition, she hadn't left the city."

Rebecca recounted to her aunt about her friend's activities, how she had visited the jewelry store, and how she had discovered the alleged inconsistencies in Detective Richie Puig's story.

Tote was shocked by everything she had just heard. In the end, she seemed to react.

"Rebecca, I've known Richie Puig for more than twenty years. Half of them have been partners in the National Police Force. I fully trust him. He has never failed me, not even now that he works in a private company. I assure you that I have commissioned him many times, and all to my satisfaction."

"Well, they don't know him in the jewelry store, neither him nor the choker. It seems that this time, he lied to us."

Tote shook his head from side to side, refusing to believe it.

"It can't be," she said in a very firm voice. "There are a few things I'm sure of in this life, but one of them is Richie's honesty. As soon as I get to the police station, I'll call him on the phone. There must be an explanation for all this."

"Well, you'll tell me what it could be because I can't think of anything," a dejected Rebecca replied.

"Don't fall apart. Trust me."

"Aunt, do you know the implications of this whole issue? If Carlota's inquiries are true, that means that we aren't controlling the situation as we believed. You know that I created the message on the Countess' envelope, but I thought the choker was real. If it's also fake, it means that there is someone else, apart from us, interfering in this matter. That is very serious because until now, we had no idea of their existence. It would show that they have been smarter than us and, above all, that they have an advantage over us."

Tote was thoughtful. She trusted Richie Puig, but the evidence presented by Carlota seemed very consistent.

"Really, Rebecca, get this thing out of your mind until I can talk to Richie. Throughout the morning, I will send you a message on your cellphone. Now I have to go to the police station, because, even though I'm the boss, I must not be late. Believe it or not, they look at me badly if I do."

They parted. Rebecca finished getting dressed and left for *La Crónica*. With all the fuss, she hadn't told her aunt or anyone else that she'd been nominated for an Ondas Award. In fact, she didn't even remember it herself. She had buried it in her mind. The feeling that we were following someone's else orders and that she was the pawn was present again. It was very unpleasant, but it was there and it would be irresponsible if she ignored it.

She couldn't help but remember Abraham Lunel and his favorite phrase, 'Nothing is what it seems.' It seems that it was going to haunt her all her life.

29 NOVEMBER 21st, 1521

"What are you talking about!" Johan exclaimed, surprised and scared. "Are you sure they are watching you?"

"I don't have any doubt."

"By whom? Who is interested in you?"

"I don't know. Just two months ago, I received a letter from my great friend Francisco Cranevelt, and I assure you that it was clearly manipulated. It isn't the first time that I have noticed it. Since then, I have watched carefully. Someone spies on all my correspondence, whatever its source. The last time was with a letter from Erasmus himself. It was open and even its contents were wrinkled. Erasmus is especially neat in his ways."

"Could it have something to do with the Great Council?" Johan asked, thinking about the possible scope of the revelation his friend had just confided to him.

"I don't know, but nothing can be ruled out."

"It's certainly a serious matter."

"I told you there were two things you didn't know about. If this first seems serious to you, the second one is even more serious."

"And what is it? You're really scaring me."

"The time for you to know it hasn't yet come."

"And when will that moment come?" Johan asked, intrigued. "Why are you telling me that for?"

"If I decide to return to Spain, you won't need to know, but if, at some point, I decide not to go, I'm afraid we'll have to see each other again."

"Besides being scared, you're worrying me, Luis."

"There are issues that I can't entrust to correspondence, not even using Kabbalistic encryption, not even using the Temurah technique."

"That seems obvious. After what you just told me, I'm afraid we can't trust the mail for certain matters. Let me insist, when will it be time to know that second matter? You got me very uneasy."

"I hope you never forget that you are the Eleventh Door, and in theory, for your own safety and of everyone else, you should not be aware of certain matters concerning the Great Council. This is how it was established in the 14th century, and I assure you they had their reasons. You must stay out of certain issues for the good of all."

"Then why are you telling me? Don't you say that I should stay on the sidelines?"

Luis stared at his friend, who seemed to be searching for the right words.

"Yesterday, you told me that the tree was safe, and that's the most important matter, but things can get complicated. I can't give you more details. I simply ask you to trust me."

"You know I've always done it and will continue to do so," Johan replied, "but understand that I can't help worrying. Your words have caused me great distress. "

They said goodbye with great regret. At least they knew they would see each other again, either in Spain if Luis returned or elsewhere if he decided not to. It was quite a consolation because they professed a sincere and deep friendship, although Johan was concerned about what his friend was hiding. On the other hand, he was right. Johan, as the Eleventh Door, didn't belong to the Great Council. There were questions about him that he was completely unaware of. However, he knew Luis Vives very well and had the intuition that the subject he was hiding from him was something very serious.

Unfortunately for him, he wasn't wrong.

30 NOWADAYS, WEDNESDAY, SEPTEMBER 5ᵗʰ

Rebecca arrived at the newspaper and walked over to her table. Tere greeted her with a smile from ear to ear.

"What did you think about the day before yesterday's party?"

"I'll take you by surprise, you bastard. I took the bait like an idiot. I'm going to get even," Rebecca replied with a smile.

"What impression did Fabio make on you?"

Rebecca met her new co-worker at the surprise party on Monday, when she had already drunk several glasses of *champagne*. Maybe that was why he seemed extremely polite and very handsome. He had an air of Charly, but with longer hair and taller. She chatted with him for a while. He spoke Spanish without an Italian accent since his parents were from Naples, but he was born in Madrid and educated in Spain. In addition to his journalism degree, he was also a doctor in Mathematics, his true passion. A true prodigy at only twenty-five years old."

"You certainly have good taste in candy."

"Good taste? That falls short! What did you talk about with him?"

"That he doesn't have a partner," she answered meaningfully.

"Is that true?" Tere said excitedly.

"Of course we talked about more things and I don't know how that topic came out. We all had one too many drinks, but it's true that he told me that."

"You rascal!" Tere exclaimed, laughing, imitating with her hand the gestures of a gypsy curse.

"Don't worry, I'll leave all the candy for you," Rebecca replied, also laughing. "Right now, I'm on a diet."

"Yeah, yeah, leave something for the rest of us who are not lucky enough to be a Taylor Swift clone."

"For this job, I'd rather be a clone of Eduard Punset. By the way, where is that eye candy, Fabio? I never see him at his table."

"You know he's in the politics section, and since he's the new one, well, they always send him to cover issues outside the newsroom," Tere answered, smiling.

Suddenly, she saw Alba approach her table in a clear collision trajectory.

No, please, she thought.

"Rebecca, the editor is calling you to his office; it's urgent," she yelled over all the tables and their corresponding heads.

Back to the routine in style, Rebecca told herself. I hope it doesn't become a habit again to start the working day in the editor's office.

She walked down the hall and knocked on the door. She heard a voice say, 'go ahead.' She entered Bernat Fornell's office. He was sitting behind his table, unaccompanied. *Thank God, for a moment, I imagined that he would be with another Countess.*

"Have a seat, don't just stand there."

Rebecca sat down and waited for the editor to finish whatever the hell he was doing. It took a couple of minutes to start the conversation.

"First of all, I want to congratulate you in a more formal way than at the party on Monday. You don't know how important your nomination is to our communication group. It's almost manna from heaven."

"Thank you, editor. It was completely unexpected."

"I have called you because our radio colleagues want to continue relying on your collaboration. As you will understand, after the tremendous success, we can't leave the History section without continuity."

"But those recordings were very homemade, with a little script and a lot of improvisation, with a mobile in my hand and without technical means."

"That is precisely what they want. The technical media didn't matter, they fell in love with your sparkle in front of the microphone, and it is clear that it wasn't only them. Otherwise, you wouldn't have been nominated for the award."

"Yes, but now that I know their true intention, I'll get more nervous, and I'm sure they won't turn out the same."

"Try it. I'm convinced that they will turn out even better. Anyway, from now on, you will record them in a studio."

Rebecca thought about the editor's words. They were silent for a moment. Fornell continued the conversation in a somewhat unexpected way. Even the expression on his face, usually stern, had changed. Now it seemed somewhat kinder.

"Have you ever wondered why I hired you when you came to me, at eighteen years old and with no experience?"

"I think you are a friend of Joanna Ramos, who was a professor of mine at the Faculty of History."

Fornell was watching her closely. That behavior wasn't normal for him. He usually ignored his subordinates.

"Joanna is a close friend of mine and she arranged the interview, that's true, but I didn't hire you because you came on her behalf. Do you know how many recommendations I reject each week? If I were to hire all the ones I get, I would need eight editorial departments like this one."

Rebecca was intrigued. There was a part of Mr. Fornell that she didn't quite understand. He had once given the impression that he was playing a role, that his job was not really a newspaper editor. Of course, he was much more intelligent than what he tried to show; that was clear. What she didn't know was why he tried so hard to hide it.

"I hired you because of your eyes."

Rebecca snapped from her thoughts. In fact, she nearly fell out of her chair. She was aware that she had very striking blue eyes, but she had never expected that response from editor Fornell.

"Because of my eyes?" She answered, surprised.

"Don't get me wrong. I'm not talking about their physical appearance, which, by the way, I imagine you have been told countless times that they are precious. I mean what I observed through them, and it's clear that I wasn't wrong. I knew you would end up succeeding. I've always had a special intuition to choose, well, leaving my ex-wife aside. I guess she's the exception to the rule."

"Don't exaggerate, Mr. editor. I haven't succeeded in anything. To begin with, hardly anyone knows who I am, not even in my city. History geeks follow my posts with some regularity, but outside of that small and specific circle, I'm a complete stranger, a completely anonymous citizen."

The editor smiled as if he knew something she didn't. It seemed like he was having fun with the conversation.

"By any chance, have you seen our cover today?" he asked her.

Oh, God! Rebecca said to herself, Please, let it not be what I think it is.

Fornell handed her a copy of the newspaper. Sure enough, there was Rebecca's photo, taking up a quarter of the cover, along with a big, very prominent headline.

"Please, I'm so embarrassed!"

"Embarrassed? Didn't you say that they didn't even know you in your city and that you were an anonymous citizen? Well, from now you are not. It can be said that you are officially famous, at least here."

Rebecca looked scared.

"Do you know something, editor? I haven't told anyone about the Ondas Award, not my friends, not even my aunt. Only you know."

"Well, look at the positive side. Now everyone knows it; you won't have to tell them anymore. They will read it for themselves."

"Very funny," Rebecca said, who was afraid of her aunt's reaction when she read the newspaper.

Suddenly, her cellphone rang. By the tone, it was a message from Tote.

"I think she just found out," Rebecca said.

"Come on; you can go now. This week I will introduce you to the radio fellows. Now it's your turn to deal with your aunt. I hope it isn't that bad."

Rebecca left the editor's office, feeling strange. *Who's hiding behind Bernat Fornell's mask?* She wondered. Maybe it was her imagination and he was simply a brilliant mind in a mediocre job. She remembered the principle of Ockham's Razor. The simplest explanations were usually the most likely. *But in this case, what is the simplest explanation?* She thought, intrigued.

She shook editor Fornell out of her head and opened her aunt's message, expecting to get a good fight. What she read made her nervous: *I'm expecting you as soon as possible at the police station. It's very important. It's Richie's subject.*

Whatever her aunt had found out, it seemed urgent. She was on her nerves. She almost preferred the fight.

31   NOVEMBER 21st, 1521

Johan Corbera returned to Valencia safely. The journey from Flanders was long and heavy, but he hadn't suffered any inconvenience. He rested for two days, and, once he recovered, he went to speak with Beatriz, Luis Vives' older sister. He had arranged to meet her who, on his return, would inform her about the outcome of the negotiations he had made with her brother.

"He's not coming back for the moment," Johan Corbera told her.

"That's a disaster!" a dejected Beatriz answered, who was taking all the responsibility, along with her sister Leonor, for the entire inquisitorial process against their father.

"Not so much. He has promised to take some action with King Charles I. He's going to send him a letter."

"Yes, but from afar from Flanders. It isn't the same to send a letter than to visit him in person."

"He's still very scared of the Holy Office. I think that, deep down, he thinks that if he steps on Spanish territory, he will be arrested."

"He is now a huge personality of European prestige. I don't think they would dare to do that to him. In addition, he's a good Christian, writes books related to the principles of the Catholic Church, and has never committed a heresy."

"I don't think so either, but the important thing is that he does. In any case, he hasn't ruled out a possible return."

"What does it depend on?"

"Right now, the most promising possibility is that the Duke of Alba will claim him as the tutor of his two grandchildren. Negotiations are being made and are quite advanced. It will probably be decided next month. The duke himself will send him a formal letter with the proposal."

"And will he accept it?"

"I think he will. The offer is very generous and would put him out of reach of the Holy Office."

"Let's hope it happens very quickly. I don't know how much time we have."

"Don't worry. I'll keep you posted on the progress."

Johan was silent for a moment, thinking about how to continue the conversation.

"I'm going to ask you a question, and I want you to answer it after thinking it through."

"Tell me," Beatriz said, somewhat intrigued by Johan's mysterious tone.

"Have you noticed being watched in a special way? How about your sister Leonor?"

She was thoughtful for a few moments.

"In a special way? I think not. Of course, the Holy Office keeps a close eye on us, but nothing out of the ordinary. My sister Leonor hasn't told me anything either. Why are you asking me this strange question?"

"Because your brother Luis is being spied on. They examine all his correspondence. Be very careful about what you write to him."

"I'll tell my sister," Beatriz replied, somewhat surprised.

They parted. Now Johan was really worried. If they only spied on Luis Vives and not the rest of his family, it could have something to do with the Great Council. Actually, it was the only logical explanation.

Have they discovered its existence? He thought, alarmed. It was very strange that there was no sign of them. What would be the second serious matter that Luis didn't want to tell me?

Something was happening around him and he wasn't able to see it.

32 NOWADAYS. WEDNESDAY, SEPTEMBER 5th

Rebecca left the editorial department, got up on her bicycle, and went to the police station on Zapadores Street, where her aunt worked. She had to admit that she was nervous. She didn't know what Tote had found out.

She parked the bike and looked at her cell phone. It hadn't stopped ringing the whole trip. She had fourteen missed calls and a gazillion messages to read. She took a quick look at them, in case there were any important ones. Most were congratulations. It was clear that they had seen her photograph on the cover of *La Crónica*.

I've been famous for ten minutes and I'm starting to get overwhelmed, Rebecca thought lazily.

She kept looking at her cellphone. Carlota confirmed that she had arranged to meet with Álvaro Enguix, the jeweler, the day after tomorrow, on Friday. So, she called a meeting of the Speaker's Club at his usual schedule of seven in the afternoon, although she notified that Álvaro would arrive a little later. Curiously, it seems that no one from the club had heard the news because they hadn't congratulated her. *Better, I'll tell them. Personally,* she said to herself, *and thus avoid unnecessary jokes, I know Charly and Fede well enough.*

Rebecca had the habit of always answering all the messages and emails she received, both personal and professional. It was a matter of good manners. She thought that if someone took the trouble to write, she should also take the trouble to reply. What happened is that now she felt overwhelmed by the situation. *I'll still answer all one by one, but this afternoon*, she told herself. Now she had an appointment with her aunt Tote. She put her phone on silent mode.

She arrived at the police station. The policeman at the door recognized her immediately.

"Hi, Rebecca, Are you coming to see your aunt?" He said with a big smile.

"Yes, she sent me a message to come."

The policeman picked up the phone and made a call.

"Go ahead, you can come in; she's waiting for you."

Rebecca walked to her aunt's office, knocked on the door, and entered. She was not alone; there was a person sitting in front of her. She remembered the last time she had been in that same room. Her aunt wasn't alone either. On that occasion, it was Inspector Sofia Cabrelles who accompanied her, but now it was a bald man.

"Come on in, don't stand at the door."

Rebecca obeyed. The office was huge. When she reached the table, she immediately recognized the person sitting.

"Heavens, Richie! What have you done to your head? I didn't recognize you from behind."

"Hi, Rebecca," the detective said as he got up to give her a couple of kisses on the cheeks. "They were already too many years with long hair, so I shaved my head. From time to time, you have to change your image."

"I suppose, but what a radical change. From hairy to alopecic."

The three of them laughed.

"Come on, sit down. Richie just got here," Tote told her niece.

"Your aunt told me the story a little while ago on the phone. The truth is that I found it very strange," Richie said. "I came as soon as possible. I would like to hear the story in your own words."

"I'm going to try to be as faithful as I can to Carlota's own words," she answered.

Rebecca told him everything her friend had found out about the jewelry, trying not to omit any details. Richie listened to her in silence. When she finished, he had a singular gesture on his face.

Why is he smiling? Rebecca thought. What does he find funny?

"I bet that, from that point of view, it seems very mysterious, right?" Richie asked.

"Mysterious?" Rebecca said. "Well, I guess that's one way to put it."

"It's not really that enigmatic because things happened slightly differently."

"Slightly different?" Rebecca repeated, surprised.

"I'm not used to explaining my research methods to my clients. They don't care; I just offer the results. In this case, I'm going to make an exception because I think the situation requires it. Besides, Rebecca, I see you are very worried, even though your aunt has told me that you trust me."

"It's true. If my aunt trusts you, so do I, but you have to understand that Carlota's story made me feel uneasy."

"It's normal, but don't worry, your friend doesn't know all the details. Now, when I explain them to you, you will understand too."

Richie told them how he found the clue to the choker and how he got all the information about it, including a photo. He gave them a little course on the running of the city's back alleys.

Tote was smiling because she already knew some of the information, but Rebecca was amazed. Now that she knew the details of the investigation, she saw things clearer. Her doubts had been completely dispelled.

She considered texting Carlota to call off Friday's Speaker's Club meeting. Richie's explanations made it unnecessary, but she thought better about it. She was curious to see her friend's summer fling. *Let her bring Álvaro to the club, let's see if he passes the skull trio test,* she said to herself, thinking about the jokes Charly, Fede, and Xavier could play on him. *I'm sure they'll come up with something and it will be fun.*

"Shall we go to lunch?" Tote asked, more animated after listening to the explanations of her friend Richie. Although she trusted him, she had to admit that she had been worried.

They went into the restaurant Tote used to go to when she didn't have time to go home to eat, a reality that happened quite often. All three were in a good mood. They sat at the only table that was free.

"Hello, Commissioner," Angela, the restaurant waitress, said. "What are you going to order?"

"I'll have the usual salad and let them order whatever they want."

Suddenly, the waitress stared at Rebecca.

"You're Rebecca Mercader, right?" she said.

Tote was surprised.

"Do you know my niece?" she asked.

"Is she your niece? Well, congratulations! Besides being smart and pretty, she also has a police aunt," Angela answered.

"What are you talking about, if you could tell me?" Tote asked who didn't understand anything.

Angela went to the bar, picked up a newspaper, and placed it on the table.

Fight in three, two, one... Rebecca thought, who seemed to be shrinking like in cartoons.

Tote and Richie stared at the cover of *La Crónica*. The detective looked amused, but the expression on her aunt's face was anthological. She seemed out of her mind.

"And exactly when were you going to tell me this, if I may ask?"

33   FEBRUARY 22nd, 1522

Johan Corbera was enraged. His face was the vivid reflection of anger; it was redder than a tomato.

"How could it happen? You fucking bastard!" He shouted angrily, unaware of his son's presence in the room.

"What's wrong?" Batiste asked, alarmed, who couldn't remember ever seeing his father so upset.

Johan Corbera had had a son eleven years ago and had named him Joan Baptista Corbera. Since he was born in the family, his nickname was Batiste. The name endured, and it was by which he was always known, even when he wasn't so young anymore.

Batiste was extremely intelligent for his age, just like his father Johan and also his great-grandfather, none other than Samuel Perfet. Samuel, through the intercession of the then Fray Vicente Ferrer, canonized and saint since 1455, changed his Jewish identity to become an old Christian with the surname Corbera in order to protect him from the Catholic fury in that hard time against the Hebrews. Samuel was the first Eleventh Door, which played a great role in the preservation of the ancient tree of knowledge when it was hidden in its original location, in the secret crypt of the Ancient Synagogue of the sadly disappeared Jewish quarter of Valencia, after its assault and destruction in 1391.

The intelligence and insight of the last great rabbi of the city of Valencia, Isaac Ben Sheshet Perfet, Johan's great-great-grandfather and consequently Batiste's great-great-great-grandfather, were undoubtedly present throughout the

Corbera family. Isaac had been one of the greatest Talmudic authorities in the history of Judaism, specifically between the 14th and early 15th centuries, and he had left a great legacy behind him. But his secret side was much more exciting than the erudite one. He had been Number Two of that legendary first Great Council completed in 1390, which had been in charge of collecting in a single location all the Jewish knowledge accumulated over the centuries and that they had hidden to preserve it for future generations.

Johan Corbera was educating his son Batiste in a special way, and he was very advanced for his age. He wanted him to follow in his footsteps and, over the years, become a stonemason or master stonemason, as he was. On the other hand, Johan was already older and knew that in a few years, he would have to initiate his son Batiste to take over and become the third Eleventh Door in the history of the Great Council, after himself and Samuel Perfet. It was an honor, but it was also a huge responsibility.

Johan returned from his thoughts and addressed his son. He was still red with the anger that was controlling him.

"Don Fadrique Álvarez de Toledo, second Duke of Alba, has chosen Luis Vives as tutor to his two grandchildren, the children of his first-born," Johan continued.

"And that's why you got angry? Isn't that what you've been waiting for a long time?" Batiste replied, astonished by his father's anger.

"The duke was going to send an emissary to Leuven to personally communicate the order."

"And didn't he do it?"

"A Dominican friar named Severo appeared and told the Duke of Alba that he was leaving for Leuven the next day. Given the coincidence, Don Fadrique asked him to get in touch with Luis Vives and make the offer."

"The friar was very timely, right?"

"Additionally, Don Bertrán, who is the nobleman who interceded in favor of Luis with the duke, was present at the conversation. He also gave a personal letter to the Dominican friar to give to his friend in Leuven."

"And what happened?"

"It was a trap," Johan said, being carried away by the anger. "A vulgar and regrettable ploy."

"So, father, there's someone who doesn't want Luis Vives to return to Spain?" Batiste asked innocently.

His father stared at him in surprise. That possibility hadn't occurred to him and yet it was the first thing his son had thought, at only eleven years old. He saw reflected in his gaze that so characteristic brightness of the eyes of his grandfather Samuel.

I have to take his comments very seriously, Johan thought, who was thoughtful, frightened by the consequences of that reflection.

Actually, it was perfectly possible.

34 NOWADAYS. THURSDAY, SEPTEMBER 6th

Rebecca had gone to bed late, answering all the messages and emails congratulating her on her nomination, so she got up a little later than usual. She went out into the kitchen. There was no one. Her aunt had already gone to work. It was almost better like that. She still remembered the tremendous scold she had gotten yesterday for not telling her anything, although it is also true that she ended up giving her a kiss and congratulating her.

She didn't forget her warning. *Remember well who you are; you can't go around drawing attention; it could be dangerous.* Obviously, the warning had come late, and she defended herself with good reason. She had nothing to do with this nomination.

She had her usual glass of fresh milk for breakfast and went to the newspaper. She didn't know if today would be the day that editor Fornell would introduce her to the people in charge of the radio station. *He told me it would be this week,* she thought. She was hoping it would be tomorrow. She was tired today. Plus, with all the unforeseen events, she was late with her work.

She came to her desk and sat down. This morning she wanted to do her research for her next article, so she hoped they wouldn't bother her too much. Fortunately, she was alone. There was no sign of Tere or Fabio, the candy couple.

She noticed the papers in front of her. It was strange to her. Rebecca had a habit of leaving her table clear when the workday was over. She organized all the documentation she had handled during the day and kept it in the drawer, in its corresponding folders. She was even more surprised when she read them. They were notes that Alba had left her. Apparently, she had received quite a few phone calls yesterday afternoon. They were mostly from other media; they wanted to talk to her. Even a national newspaper asked for an interview for its culture supplement, which was also broadcast on its television channel. That seemed unheard of.

She turned on the computer and accessed the news' highlights of the day, like every morning. *Young Valencian student nominated for the Ondas Awards. La Crónica* wasn't the only one who had published it. The news had jumped to other media. It seemed that even some television programs had broadcast it. This matter had gotten out of hand. *My aunt is going to kill me when she finds out,* she thought. *I have the feeling that the thing about going unnoticed will no longer be possible.*

She had to think about how to handle the situation. For the moment, she decided not to answer anyone until she had spoken with editor Fornell and her aunt. She kept getting messages on her cellphone. She put it on silent mode. She picked up the landline and dialed the secretary's extension.

"Hello Alba, don't transfer any call for me this morning. I'm very busy, thank you," Rebecca said with a very professional tone.

She couldn't help but laugh at herself. She was a simple college student writing short history articles in a local newspaper, and she already behaved as if she were an important executive of a multinational company.

She finished her morning workday and returned home to eat. Let's see how she would explain to her aunt the sudden interest in other media in her person. She opened the door and went to the kitchen.

Tote was opening the oven door.

"I already know it; you don't need to tell me anything," she heard her aunt Tote say in a voice that was truly furious.

"What exactly?" Rebecca said, trying to buy some time. It had taken her by surprise.

"Don't even think about accepting an interview on television. I understand that your boss intends to take advantage of you as an advertising strategy for the newspaper, but everything must have a limit. With the written press, it's enough. Its scope is more limited."

"I haven't answered any requests. I wanted to talk to you and Editor Fornell first."

"Well, now you're talking to me. Whatever your editor tells you, that's the answer you should give him," Tote said. Her voice was very firm. "I don't give a damn about that Fornell."

"You don't know him."

"I don't care what your boss thinks. Otherwise, I will have to take matters into my own hands. This issue can't get out of hand."

Take matters into her own hands? She thought. What does she mean?

Rebecca, deep down, had to admit that she was also worried. Her aunt was right, she couldn't forget her responsibility as the Eleventh Door, and excessive public exposure could be dangerous.

Actually, she had no idea how much.

35 FEBRUARY 22nd, 1522

"Father, don't be silent. You just told me it was a trap. Was the Duke of Alba's offer to Luis Vives false?"

Johan woke up from his thoughts.

"No, it wasn't," Johan replied, answering almost automatically.

"Didn't Friar Severo go to Leuven?" Batiste asked.

"He did."

"What happened? Didn't he look for Luis?"

"Yes, he looked for him."

"And he didn't find him?"

"Yes, he found him."

"So, where is the trap?" Batiste asked who didn't understand his father.

"After meeting with him more than ten times for several reasons, Fray Severo didn't inform him of Don Fadrique's offer, nor did he even give him the letter from the noble Don Bertrán."

Batiste was surprised.

"And why did he do that?"

"The bastard Dominican friar will burn in hell forever. If it were in my hands, I assure you that I would do everything possible to make that happen as soon as possible," an exalted Johan said.

"I still don't understand why he behaved like this. Wasn't he really a friar?"

"Yes, he is. Moreover, from the Order of Preachers, of the Dominicans, of my own order, although I fear he's the devil himself in disguise. He returned from Leuven and dared to inform the Duke of Alba that Luis Vives despised his offer."

"What do you say!"

"Don Fadrique got very angry with Luis for what he considered a disrespect towards him and his dignity. He was so upset that he even vetoed him for other possible jobs in Spain, specifically in university chairs."

"And why did that friar do that?"

"To get the job for himself. Now the Dominican Severo is the tutor of the grandsons of the Duke of Alba."

Even Batiste was outraged.

"What despicable behavior! How did you find out about all this?"

"It turns out that Luis Vives and his friend, the noble Don Bertrán, met recently in Brussels. The latter condemned his behavior for not even bothering to respond to his letter and to despise the proposal of the Duke of Alba, which he had put so much effort into getting it for him. Let's not forget that he had recommended him repeatedly."

"And what did Luis say?"

"Imagine his surprise when he heard the whole story from Don Bertrán's mouth. He had no idea of anything. He told him that Fray Severo hadn't transmitted any message to him, nor had he delivered any of his letters. He was unaware of the offer from the Duke of Alba. In fact, when he received no news, he thought that the duke had chosen someone else."

"And they didn't do anything?"

"You can guess it. They got very angry. Don Bertrán immediately left for Spain with a handwritten letter from Luis himself, explaining to Don Fadrique that he hadn't refused his generous offer, that it had simply not been transmitted to him. Don Bertrán also condemns the friar's improper behavior with the Duke of Alba. He told him that such a person couldn't educate his grandchildren. Here is the note that Luis wrote to

Don Fadrique," Johan said, showing a small page, "so you can see my friend's astonishment and sincerity."

Batiste read it aloud.

How could I despise what you had offered me when I was so eager to find an opportunity to show you the very good intentions that I had to serve you? Thank you for the affection that you have shown me and I'm not sorry for the trick that they played on me, but for the villainous behavior of the friar, and that, if we suffer these things from our brothers, what will we have to suffer from strangers? Not satisfied with attacking our culture, they also rise with our pockets. God will judge them. He finished reading.

"Pretty clear, right?" Johan asked.

"I suppose that after learning of this dirty trick, Don Fadrique would kick the friar out of his palace."

"Well, it turns out he didn't. His reply was that he had been tutoring his grandchildren for a few months and that he could not break the contract. That he had a reputation and that he always kept his word and what he signs."

"Is that what the Duke of Alba said? But he had been tricked! He had no reputation to maintain."

"I suppose he had doubts between Friar Severo's version and what the noble Don Bertrán was telling him and he decided not to do anything. He left things as they were."

"And you didn't do anything?"

"I wrote to the General Master of the Order of Preachers. I have a very good relationship with Fray García of Loaysa, who is also the confessor of our King Charles I and a person of great importance within the Catholic Church, with many influences in all areas, not only ecclesiastic."

"And what did he say to you?"

"He replied that if the main person affected by the alleged deception, that is, the Duke of Alba himself, hadn't complained and had accepted Fray Severo, he had no right to meddle in a particular issue. Deep down, you have to admit that he's right."

"Heavens! And how is Luis doing?"

"According to Don Bertrán, he was very unwell. He would have accepted the offer without thinking twice. He was looking forward to going back to Spain so that he could lend a hand to his family, who you already know is in a very bad economic and emotional situation."

"I suppose that, at least, Don Fadrique will have forgiven him for his nonexistent offense."

"That's right, he hasn't given him the promised job, but at least he has lifted the veto for other jobs in Spain. His influential friends in those circles, especially Juan de Vergara, are looking for a chair at some university for him. His financial situation is precarious, and his family needs him here."

"I'm sure they will find him one," Batiste, who was as outraged as his father, said.

"Vergara says that he expects some offer in the next months. I trust it to be that way."

Batiste didn't seem entirely convinced by the explanation. Something didn't quite fit in the whole story.

"Anyway, father, doesn't it seem very strange to you that a simple Dominican friar behaves this way, deceiving and risking confronting the Duke of Alba himself? It isn't normal. Anyone would say that he was following instructions from someone more powerful than Don Fadrique himself. I can't believe that a simple member of the Order of Preachers behaved like this, without any reason and, above all, without the support of someone with many influences. That brother Severo is a nobody. You belong to the same order as him. Tell me, have you heard of him before?"

Johan Corbera was shocked once more. His son never ceased to amaze him. He had to admit that his words made a lot of sense. Friar Severo was nobody compared to Luis Vives and still much less compared to Don Fadrique, Grandee of Spain. He was thoughtful. His deductions led him to a very dangerous path. Nowadays, who was more powerful than the Duke of Alba? Very few people, you could actually count them with the fingers of one hand. Johan was shocked as he mentally reviewed their names.

His son continued to ask with a cleverness improper for his age.

"And don't you think that the mysterious person, who has managed to sabotage the duke's offer, is not going to also try it with the other offers that could come to Luis to return to

Spain? It's absurd that they manage to stop the first one and allow the following. Make no mistake about it that they will continue to act."

Now he was alarmed. *My eleven-year-old son is giving me a lesson in common sense*, he thought. He would have to take measures to ensure that Luis received the message the next time, although he didn't know how.

He didn't know who could be behind the sabotage, but he was horrified by the reduced list of candidates who were more powerful and dangerous. They were out of his reach.

36 NOWADAYS. FRIDAY, SEPTEMBER 7th

Rebecca had slept badly. She couldn't help being nervous. Editor Fornell had told her that he was going to introduce her to the radio station folks this week. Today was Friday, consequently the last working day of the week for her.

She was frightened by the paradox that she had succeeded in a radio show that she had never heard of. It was absurd, even ridiculous; why not say so. She was a little embarrassed to have to face them. *If it occurs to them to ask me what do I think of their program, what do I tell them?* She thought, scared, at the possible slip-up she could make. *That I don't even know who they are?*

She parked her bike, went up to the newsroom, and walked over to her desk. She saw Fabio and Tere talking, with some papers in hand. She sat in her chair and turned on the computer. Yesterday, she started to research her new article, and today she intended to write it. She was pretending because she saw Alba heading towards her. *I'm sure she's going to say, 'Rebecca, the editor is calling you at his office; it's urgent,'* she thought, amused, as she watched the secretary approach her.

"Rebecca, the editor is calling you at his office; it's urgent."

"Told you!" Rebecca said, making a gesture of having guessed something correctly. It hadn't been that difficult either.

"What are you doing?" Alba asked, surprised.

"Nothing, nothing. That's just me."

"You know? You're very weird."

"The pot calling the kettle black...." Rebecca replied, laughing.

"I don't get you."

"It's a popular saying that means we attribute to others any characteristic that would also be applicable to ourselves."

"You speak with strange words. I still don't understand you."

"Come on, let it go. I'm going to see the editor," Rebecca said with an obvious smile. She didn't want to fight with poor Alba either. After all, she hadn't been very fortunate on the day the brains were handed out. She even doubted she had one set up inside her skull.

As she moved down the hall, her nervousness grew. She was thinking about how she was going to be able to deal with the radio folks. She knocked on the editor's office door and entered. As she expected, Mr. Fornell was accompanied by one person.

"Go ahead; you can come in."

When Rebecca approached the chair, she observed the person who was sitting in front of the editor. She was completely surprised and confused. All adjectives fell short. She was lost for words. In the end, she was able to speak, but barely.

"What are you doing here? Don't tell me you're the person responsible for the radio?" She managed to mumble. It was evident that she was very nervous.

"You seem slightly off balance."

"Slightly?"

"That means you don't listen to the radio often, right?"

It was probably the last person she expected to see sitting in that chair. She had no idea that they were in charge of that section. She didn't know how to react or what to say.

"Not too much," she managed to answer after brooding on it.

The word dumbfounded fell short.

37 MAY 23ʳᵈ, 1522

"What a surprise!" Johan Corbera exclaimed. "Come in, my friend."

The noble Don Bertrán had appeared at his house without warning. He was wearing a small leather satchel and a grin from ear to ear.

"You seem very happy. That means life is treating you well," Johan continued as he offered him a seat at his living room table.

"I'm the bearer of good news, actually, more than good, magnificent news," he replied.

"Have you been appointed to a relevant position in the royal court? You deserve it. I knew you would get it, even if you don't need it. You've always given me the impression that you have a lot more power than all that bunch of boring courtiers."

"I appreciate your words, but you're only partially correct. It's true that I have achieved it, although much of the credit goes to Juan de Vergara. You are mistaken in who's the recipient of the blessing."

"I don't comprehend you," Johan answered, confused.

"The good news isn't for me; I don't need it," Don Bertrán said as he opened the small briefcase he was carrying and took out a small letter. He handed it to him. "Come on, read it."

Johan was surprised. He took the letter and began to read it aloud. It had the letterhead of the University of Alcalá de Henares and was addressed to Luis Vives himself.

"After the death of Antonio de Nebrija, a very erudite man, who rules among us the chair of the Latin School with great praise and to the benefit of our youth, we tried to appoint a new teacher who, in our opinion, could follow with dignity such an exalted man. Juan Vergara wrote us, giving us such an honorific testimony of your person -that you possess such a dogma, such erudition, and practice of human literature- that in his opinion, it seemed that only you would take charge this literary institution with glory and would be of maximum help to our studious youth and that at the same time you would fill the longing for that man that is as wise as he is prudent. The judgment of this wise man aroused in us such an opinion of you that it could only be satisfied by an individual as highly educated and completely similar to Antonio himself. Therefore, although there is no shortage of candidates among us full of wisdom who request to be elected for this position within the time established for the granting of the same, nevertheless, we decided in regard to your person (which happens very rarely between us without the proposal of the voters), to offer you the chair in an extraordinary way and without competition from any other. We have therefore commissioned our friend Vergara to write to you on our behalf about the very nature of the chair, the annual salary, in a word, of the condition under which it is offered to you. Consequently, think that what he writes to you, we are writing to you, and have the conviction that what he advises you, we also advise you. Now it is up to your diligence to ensure that we do not ignore your decision on this matter for long. Goodbye".

After reading the letter, Johan was completely silent.

"What's wrong with you?" Don Bertrán asked, surprised by his friend's reaction. "I expected you to be glad, not to remain with that incredulous expression."

"I'm very worried," Johan said at last.

"Worried? Today should be a day of great joy for both of you. I have just brought you wonderful news for our mutual friend Luis and you receive me with a mournful look."

"Don't get me wrong, I'm very happy for him," Johan replied, still serious.

"Well, I assure you, it doesn't seem like that at all."

"It's not because of that."

Don Bertrán was still ecstatic, despite Johan.

"Juan de Vergara has done it. They have proposed to him the chair that Antonio de Nebrija has left vacant after his death. Finally, Luis will be able to return to Spain in complete safety."

"I'm not sure about that."

"What are you talking about? I don't get it, neither your expression nor your attitude."

Johan shared with him the suspicions he harbored about the mysterious person that he believed existed against the return of his mutual friend. It must be someone very powerful, above the Duke of Alba himself."

Don Bertrán was thoughtful. It was true. There were hardly a few people with such power. In fact, very few.

"Don't worry, Johan. I will personally ensure that this letter reaches Luis, and I will also ensure that his response is heard by the University."

Johan stared at his friend. He had wanted to ask him a question for a long time. The moment had come.

"Bertrán, you have always cared a lot for Luis and me in a very special way and without asking for anything in return, just like Juan de Vergara, who has just resigned from a great job, a whole university chair, in favor of Luis Vives. I know you are both of Jewish descent. You continually achieve what you set out to do and you know that it has always given me the impression that you have much more power than you pretend. You don't seem like a simple nobleman, far from it."

"You flatter me, my friend, although you exaggerate a lot. I just have good connections at the court."

"I apologize in advance, but I must ask you a question that may seem strange to you. If you don't consider it prudent, don't answer it. I will understand."

"Go ahead," Don Bertrán said with evident curiosity.

"What door number are you? And Juan de Vergara?"

Don Bertrán answered immediately. He stared at his friend with an expression of not understanding anything.

"What number of what? What kind of weird question is that? Am I supposed to have an answer for that nonsense?"

"Understood," Johan replied with an uncertain smile on his face.

In fact, he hadn't understood anything, but he still had a long time to come to understand it.

38 NOWADAYS. FRIDAY, SEPTEMBER 7th

"Come on, shut your mouth. Flies are going to get inside."

"Don't tell me you have something to do with the radio section?" Rebecca repeated the question, who hadn't yet come out of her astonishment.

"Well, of course. You didn't know?"

"And why didn't you tell me anything?"

"And why do I have to tell you everything I do? Do you do it?"

Rebecca turned to look at editor Fornell, waiting for an explanation for all this. She saw a small smile on his face. *Is my reaction funny to him?* Although she then thought better of it. Strange, Fornell never laughs at anything.

Her world suddenly fell apart. *What an idiot I am!* She thought, not sure what to say.

"You two are kidding me!" She exclaimed.

Fornell couldn't hold back anymore and laughed hysterically; his mouth was wide open.

"How could you think that I have something to do with the radio?" Tote said while she also laughed at ease. "That was the only thing missing in my complicated life."

Rebecca was completely flushed, mortified by embarrassment. She tried to explain herself, although she had it downright difficult.

"I don't know, I went into the office hoping to find someone in charge of the radio station and I didn't know how to react. I was very nervous," she said as an apology.

"Don't worry. It's an anecdote that I'll remember every time I want to laugh at ease," Tote said, still with tears in her eyes. "You made me cry of laughter."

"Do you know each other?" Rebecca asked, still distraught from seeing her aunt in editor Fornell's office with an apparent degree of complicity.

"Now we do, and in style," Tote replied, still laughing. She couldn't stop, just like the editor.

"Stop it!" Rebecca exclaimed, somewhat annoyed. "You're having a great time at my expense."

"The truth is we are," Tote replied, trying to get serious without quite succeeding. "Don't be mad; it's just that it was very funny. You should have seen the shocked expression you had. Too bad I didn't take a photo of you with my cellphone."

Editor Fornell took a handkerchief out of his pocket to wipe away his tears.

"I've never seen him so happy," Rebecca said. "At least I'm glad I was the reason for it."

"Believe it or not, I have a life outside of this office, and sometimes I can even laugh," Fornell said, who was also having a hard time getting serious.

"Now, really, what are you doing here, aunt? You didn't tell me you were coming to the newspaper this morning."

Tote made an effort and tried not to think about how funny and absurd the situation had been.

"I have come to thank editor Fornell for everything related to your Ondas Award nomination. It is well-mannered to be grateful. It seems to me that I had to come to *La Crónica* for it."

"Your aunt has been very kind. I had heard a lot about her, she is quite a leading figure in the city, but we didn't know each other personally. We had never met in any event."

"You have been kind enough to agree to meet me without an appointment."

"Don't think I'm as busy as you must be. We're a very modest media group," Fornell said. He loved repeating that phrase. It was like a mantra.

"And that's it?" an incredulous Rebecca asked. The situation seemed strange at best.

Tote looked at her, still amused.

"No, it's not really all. I have invited Mr. Fornell and the department heads to our house for a bite as a thank you for the excellent treatment they are giving you. You've been working here for more than three years and we didn't even know each other. In addition, we now have the honor that thanks to the editor's efforts, you have been nominated for the award. It seems to me that we should be polite."

Rebecca was amazed. Really? She thought. My aunt has gone crazy. What was all the sweet-talking about? It's not like her."

"Of course, I have accepted. It will be an honor for all of us to accept the invitation," Editor Fornell replied in an exaggeratedly gracious tone.

Rebecca couldn't believe what she was hearing. *There's something fishy going on here,* Rebecca continued thinking. Not just a fish, it smelled like the whole ocean, and they all were splashing in front of her eyes at the same time.

Of course, I do not buy that thing of being polite. What is my aunt up to?

She couldn't even imagine it.

39   MAY 24th, 1522

"Father, why did you ask Don Bertrán what door number he was?" Batiste blurted out without hesitation. "What does that mean? Is it a riddle?"

Johan almost choked on the food. He started coughing loudly and had to take a sip from the glass of water to avoid running out of air.

"What are you talking about?" he managed to ask, with barely a tiny voice.

"By chance, I overheard the conversation you had yesterday with Don Bertrán."

"But weren't you supposed to be at school at that time?" He asked while he was still clearing his throat.

"The teacher was ill and they sent us home. Didn't you hear me come in?"

"Obviously not, and I didn't realize you were eavesdropping on a private conversation between two adults," Johan replied in a scolding tone, already recovered from the sudden choking.

"I wasn't spying on anything. I already told you it was by chance. I was in the kitchen, and you were talking in a very high tone of voice. It was impossible not to hear from you, even if I covered my ears."

Johan hadn't taken any precautions; he thought he was alone at home. Nor had he imagined that his son was listening to them.

"Did you say door number? It was nothing; it was an inconsequential question," he answered the first thing that occurred to him, trying to downplay the matter.

"Well, to be an unimportant question, you were quite nervous, and the most curious thing, Don Bertrán was even more nervous than you. It was even funny."

"How do you know that?"

"Also, by chance, I leaned out the door and could see his face. Our eyes met for an instant. I saw his eyes and his face."

"Too many coincidences, right?" Johan asked, who right now was surprised because Don Bertrán hadn't told him that he had seen his son at home. *How weird!*

"I suppose you would realize that he blatantly lied to you."

"He lied to me about what?" Johan asked, surprised.

"I don't know. If you don't tell me what the doors mean, I can't know why he lied to you, but he was nervous. It is clear that, at that precise moment, he wasn't being sincere. About what? Well, I don't know because you're hiding information from me."

"Hey, do you know that you're becoming a very rude and nosy kid for your age?"

"Maybe, but don't trust that nobleman one bit. His eyes hide something, and I'm not sure what."

Johan had already learned not to belittle the opinions of his son. He was only eleven years old, but he had inherited the extreme intellectual sharpness of the Perfet family. He sometimes looked like an adult, and not just a common one.

"He has always treated us very well," Johan said by way of justification.

"Perhaps, but he isn't what he appears to be, I assure you."

The truth is that Johan had the same feeling, but he didn't know if that was good or bad. Does he belong to the Great Council, or is he from the group of saboteurs? He thought uneasily. Or it was both our imagination, and he was simply a nobleman with sympathy for the followers of Erasmus of Rotterdam and he was eager to help altruistically. It could also be. In fact, perhaps the latter was the most likely explanation. He had always seemed to him that he had a certain inclination for him on an intellectual level.

Batiste suddenly pulled his father out of his thoughts.

"Will you tell me about the doors one day?" He said, like someone asking for a glass of water.

Johan, on the other hand, was shocked by the question. *Surely my son, at his age, seems more intelligent than myself,* he thought, overwhelmed. He feared the day he initiated it and transferred his responsibility as the Eleventh Door, he would reply, 'you're late; I already knew everything.' It wouldn't surprise him, and that scared him. He was still very young. Although, in reality, if he thought about it, he was the same age as Samuel Perfet when he assumed his commitment back in the year 1391.

It's enough for this afternoon. I've upset my father enough, Batiste though, meanwhile. He didn't understand why his father was frightened, but it had been amusing.

40 NOWADAYS. FRIDAY, SEPTEMBER 7th

It was six o'clock in the afternoon, barely an hour before the extraordinary meeting of the Speaker's Club. Rebecca showered, got dressed, and rode her bike to Kilkenny's Pub. After Wednesday's conversation with Richie Puig, she no longer harbored doubts about the authenticity of the choker, but she had a real interest in meeting Álvaro Enguix, the summer fling of her friend Carlota. That was the only reason she hadn't canceled the meeting. She had to admit that her curiosity got the best out of her.

What Rebecca was unaware of was that another meeting was taking place at the same time, not far from Kilkenny's pub. Two people were sitting discreetly on stone benches in a small garden nearby.

"Is everything ready?"

"As planned."

"I want you to record everything."

"Don't worry. I have installed several cameras in different positions. We will not miss any details of the meeting. We will have several angles."

"It's very important."

"I know; you've already told me several times."

"I want to know everything about the attendees, and when I say everything, I mean everything."

"What do you hope to find out?"

"To begin with, I want to know who they are."

"Do you have doubts?"

"I assure you that I have more than doubts. I want to know them one by one, up to what's their shoe size."

41 MAY 29th, 1522

Batiste went to school and was a good student. He wanted to follow in his father's footsteps and be a master stonemason. He was aware that to achieve that goal, he had to work hard in his studies. The truth is that he found it very simple to do. With little effort, he managed to stand out, even in front of students older than him. At first, he wasn't aware of his gift, but little by little, he realized that he wasn't the same as the others. He understood things and memorized them with a different facility than other students. He was constantly looking for challenges that would keep him entertained since, in the end, he would end up getting bored in class.

He had just arrived at school and saw how his teacher, Pere Urraca, was heading towards him.

"Batiste, from today on, you will have a new tablemate. You are my brightest student and I have a special interest in you taking care of this person, who has just arrived in our city."

At last, a new challenge, for a change, Batiste thought immediately, rejoicing visibly.

Professor Urraca opened the classroom door and Batiste's new classmate entered. His joy ended there. He was small, shy-looking, but that wasn't the worst of it. He looked only six or seven years old.

"Batiste, this is Jerónimo. He will be attending our school on a regular basis starting today."

"Jerónimo, it is a pleasure," Batiste said, annoyed, thinking that, in reality, what Professor Urraca wanted was for him to babysit that shrimp. There was too much age difference between the two of them.

"For your information, I'm not a shrimp," Jerónimo said by way of introduction.

Batiste couldn't help but slightly jump in surprise.

"How do you know I was thinking just that?" Batiste asked, frightened. "Can you read minds?"

"Do you think you're the first one? All of you think the same when you see me," Jerónimo replied.

"All of you?"

"You're not my first tablemate, you know."

From that moment, Batiste knew that this child wasn't normal.

"I'm sorry, Jerónimo. I didn't mean to offend you, but you must understand that I was expecting a partner the same age as me," Batiste said by way of dismissal.

"Don't worry; I'm used to it. Apology accepted. Also, you're right; I'm a shrimp."

"Where do you come from?" Batiste asked to break the ice and change the subject.

"From Seville."

"And what are you doing in Valencia?"

"I don't know."

"Why don't you know?"

"It's true; I don't know. I was studying in Seville and, suddenly, they told me that I should move to Valencia from one day to the next, and here I am."

"Did your family have to come to live in the city?"

"I have no family. I came alone."

Batiste didn't understand anything.

"And how did you do it? Where do you live?"

"At the Royal Palace."

Batiste jumped. Now it turns out that he was dealing with a deranged or a phony, and he didn't know which was worse. The Royal Palace was the headquarters of the Valencia Holy Office's court, and Batiste knew that it was only inhabited by

Valencia's inquisitors, Don Juan de Churruca and Don Andrés Palacios. No one else resided in it. It was something of public knowledge. He decided that it wasn't worth explaining it to Jerónimo. For what? What was he going to clear up by uncovering his lie? *If that is his illusion, why am I going to screw it up?* Batiste thought.

Illusion?

42 NOWADAYS. FRIDAY, SEPTEMBER 7th

Rebecca entered Kilkenny's pub and headed for their usual corner. Charly, Fede, and Almu had already arrived. They were having a lively conversation.

"Good afternoon," Rebecca said. "You look like magpies."

"Hi, Rebecca. Charly was showing us his flyway for this month," Almu said.

"This is the first time they have given me a monthly flight schedule. It's really exciting," Charly said.

"It'll be exciting, but you're going to miss a lot of Speaker's Club meetings. To begin with, look at next Tuesday," Fede said, pointing to a spot on the paper. "You start in Valencia and, after four jumps, you sleep in Malaga."

"I hadn't realized that it's true," Charly replied. "It has already lost its initial charm."

"When the others come, we'll discuss that. If there is no problem, we could change the day of the meetings," Rebecca said. "I have no problem."

Carmen and Jaume arrived at the table. They greeted each other. Bonet also arrived with two books under his arm.

"Where are you going with those blocks?" Fede asked.

"I need them for the master's degree. I took the opportunity to buy them before today's meeting," Bonet replied.

"A computer and robotics technician, and you still carry paper books?" Charly said jokingly. "And you probably listen to music on a Walkman with cassette tapes."

"You think you're very funny, right? Let's see, in what format are the manuals for your super modern CRJ-1000 airplane?" Bonet replied defiantly.

Charly couldn't help laughing. Bonet had hit him with a joke of some importance, and that was unusual. It used to be the other way around."

"I deserve it for being a smart ass," Charly conceded.

They saw Carlota and Carol coming through the door, along with Xavier. They all greeted each other.

"At what time will the fling arrive?" Xavier asked.

"Don't even think about calling him that. I will kill you!" Carlota exclaimed.

"Is hook up better?" Charly corrected.

Carlota tossed a coaster at his head, laughing.

"He closes the jewelry store at half-past seven. From there, it takes about ten minutes walking, so he will still take a while."

"Perfect then, because I have important news to tell you, and I want to do it before Álvaro Enguix arrives," Rebecca said.

"Before? Why?" Carlota asked, surprised.

"Don't be impatient. You'll understand right away."

"Well, do it now, don't keep us on edge," Xavier said.

Rebecca took a sip of her beer before starting to speak.

"You are going to let me start the story from the end. It is not to take away the emotion, but I think it will be easier for you to understand the full explanation."

"Or from the middle, but start now!" Fede exclaimed.

"Here I go. The choker of the Count of Ruzafa actually exists, with its message included. This was not a fake clue. It's authentic."

"So, Álvaro lied to me?" Carlota snapped at once.

"No, Álvaro told you the truth," Rebecca replied with a smile.

"Are you trolling me?" Carlota said, somewhat pissed off.

"Trolling? What is that?" Jaume asked with a puzzled face.

Wow, Harry Potter isn't keeping up with youthful slang, Rebecca thought with amusement.

"It means Taylor Swift is having a fool's day and is trying to pull my leg," Carlota replied, looking at her friend.

"I'm not trolling you, as you imply. I am telling the truth."

"So, you want to tell me that the private detective visited Enguix Jewelry on a Saturday, which was closed, they informed him of a jewel that they don't know, and that doesn't even appear in their archives, they gave him a photo that they don't have and, to top it all that the only jewelry store clerk has never seen or talked to that detective or anyone else?" Carlota asked, with a tone that denoted anger.

"That's exactly what I mean," Rebecca replied, with a smile on her lips.

"And despite that, you reiterate that the choker exists?

"That's right. You have nailed it."

Carlota's face was noteworthy, like those of the other club members. Disbelief was reflected on the faces of everyone present who didn't understand Rebecca.

For once, I have an advantage against Carlota; it's fun, Rebecca thought, enjoying the situation. I'm going to enjoy it because it's so unusual, she told herself.

43 SEPTEMBER 12ᵗʰ, 1522

"He did it! It is something extraordinary!" Johan yelled helplessly, sitting at the kitchen table while he read a missive he had just received.

"It seems from your reaction that, whatever it is, it's good news," Batiste's son replied, somewhat surprised by the high tone of his father's voice, which was unusual.

"And it is! You will remember the last conversation I had with Don Bertrán, in which he informed me that the University of Alcalá de Henares had proposed Luis Vives for the vacant chair of Antonio de Nebrija because you were spying on us."

"I didn't spy on you! I just listened to you because you were speaking in a very high tone of voice," Batiste protested.

"Yes, of course, I remember that pretext. Well, Don Bertrán went in person to Leuven. Apparently, he was seriously concerned about the possible existence of a mysterious person that would block Luis' return to Spain. He decided to bring him the invitation letter from the university in person, without relying on any mail."

"And what did Luis say?"

"That he accepted the offered chair, that it was an honor for him to be able to continue the work of the great Antonio de Nebrija."

"Yes, that is good news indeed," an excited Batiste said. "When is he going to return to Spain?"

"Don Bertrán tells me that he will begin preparations to leave Leuven as soon as possible."

"Great. Now let's hope that there is no problem that prevents his arrival."

"What are you insinuating?"

"What you are hearing. Much trouble has been taken so far to prevent his return. Why are they going to stop now?"

Johan smiled as if he had already foreseen that possibility.

"Don't worry about it. Don Bertrán himself will stay with Luis during all the preparations for the trip. When he is ready, both will travel together accompanied by the entire entourage and the nobleman's armed escort for added security."

"For greater security?"

"Do you doubt it?" Johan asked, surprised. Don Bertrán has promised me that Luis' safety is, at this moment, the most important thing for him.

"Of course, I doubt it. That noble is hiding something. Doesn't it surprise you all the trouble he's taking? He can be a good friend of Luis, but his behavior doesn't seem normal to me. A person of his high social position traveling over half of Europe to deliver a simple letter? That is done by the lackeys or servants. You will not deny that he's a somewhat unusual nobleman."

Johan was silent. Don Bertrán's behavior had only one possible explanation, that he was from the Great Council, and he was trying to help his Number One return to Spain and thus be able to continue his work to protect the tree. But he couldn't tell his son all of this. He hadn't yet reached that moment.

It is clear that my father is hiding something from me, Batiste though meanwhile. I don't know if he's going to tell me one day, but of course, I'm going to find out first.

Although it was most likely that Johan was right, what was truly worrying was that Don Bertrán's behavior could have more than one possible explanation, and Johan didn't seem to notice it. He was blinded by the noble's glare.

44 NOWADAYS. FRIDAY, SEPTEMBER 7th

"You're pulling our leg. Álvaro is telling me the truth isn't compatible with the fact that the Count's choker exists. Both things can't be true at the same time," Carlota said, looking incredulous and also surprised.

"I assure you that it is perfectly possible if you let me continue with the explanation," Rebecca replied.

"Go ahead and let's see how you get out of this," Carlota said defiantly. "You have it very difficult, if not impossible."

"After the meeting last Tuesday, I spoke with my aunt about what Carlota had told us. She was very uneasy, and she summoned Detective Richie Puig to the police station on Wednesday at noon. He was also concerned about what my aunt had anticipated him on the phone."

"Of course, he should be! His big lie had been discovered," Carlota exclaimed.

"Not at all. Richie hadn't lied to us about anything."

"And what pretext did he give you for all the inconsistencies in his story?"

"Actually, more than excuses like you say, he gave us a course on how the city's back streets work, how the police and private detectives usually work in cases like this."

"Lying and making up stories?" Carlota insisted.

"You're so annoying. Come on, let me continue and you will understand everything."

"Go on, go on," Carlota answered incredulously.

"The detectives don't usually explain their work system; they only limit themselves to offering the results to their clients. This time, Richie made an exception and told my aunt and me all the ins and outs of his investigation. Considering they like to reveal neither their sources nor their methods."

"Come on, don't think twice; get to the point," an impatient Fede said.

"Do you know what they do when the case of a missing jewel comes up? Do you think that, from the beginning, they are dedicated to visiting, one by one, all the jewelers of the city?"

"I suppose so, to see if a jeweler has seen it," Charly said.

"Wrong answer. The stolen jewels move through different circles, don't expect to find them displayed in the windows of the jewelers in the city center, nor registered in an official entry book."

"And which are those circles?" Almu asked.

"The vast majority of jewelers are honest people, but there are some illegal sellers who are not. Both the police and the detectives know the usual suspects. The first thing they do is go to them and ask them. This is exactly what Richie Puig did that Saturday in May."

"What are you insinuating?" Carlota asked with a serious gesture, thinking that Álvaro could be one of those illegal sellers.

"Not what you're imagining. It turns out that Sergio Enguix, Álvaro's father, is an old acquaintance of the Police. In fact, many years ago, he even spent a month locked up in jail, convicted for possession of stolen goods."

"Possession of stolen goods? What do you mean?" Charly asked.

Fede anticipated Rebecca's explanation and showed off his legal knowledge.

"She's talking about the statutory offense in our Penal Code. It more or less means that a person acquires or hides stolen property, knowing it was obtained through an act of a crime against property in which they haven't intervened as an author or an accomplice. In short, what I suppose Rebecca is trying to tell us is that Sergio Enguix was caught buying stolen jewelry, right?"

"That was exactly what I mean, Fede. Thanks for the technical explanation. Álvaro's father was part of that group of unscrupulous jewelers with stolen goods. Notice that I say 'was' because it seems that his brief time in jail reformed him, and since then, his business has been perfectly legal. He even collaborates with the police force."

"Is he a snitch?" Almu asked excitedly.

"Something like that, I guess," she replied. "I'm not aware of his exact role."

Carlota was still unconvinced by the story of her friend.

"I'm sorry, Rebecca, but I don't understand what everything you just told us has to do with the detective's lies and the Count's choker," she said, unable to hold back.

"How impatient! Let me continue with the story. There are two types of jewelers, those that only sell jewelry and the traditional ones, where the jeweler also has a workshop and can manufacture them. Sergio Enguix, before his retirement, was an artisan jeweler. His son is not one. In fact, there are fewer and fewer artisan jewelers. It is a profession on the way to extinction."

"It's a shame. So what?" Carlota asked.

"Artisan jewelers need a lot of space to carry out their activity. You have to consider that, among many other things, they need a metal smelting furnace. Rent downtown is very expensive, so it's common for them to have, on the one hand, the jewelry in the best location they can get, and on the other hand, the workshop in the suburbs where the rents are cheaper. Sergio Enguix has had his workshop for more than thirty years, through Burjassot Avenue, far from downtown and closed to the public. It is a workspace, not a store."

"Do you mean that the detective actually visited Sergio Enguix in his workshop and not in the store?" Jaume asked.

"Exactly, that's why Álvaro was telling the truth when he claimed that he didn't know him at all," Rebecca replied.

"But Álvaro also said that his father retired and hadn't been in the business for three years," Carlota said.

"He probably won't have been in the jewelry store since then and he's retired too, but it seems he's still working in his artisan workshop. His son told the truth, but he left out some details," Rebecca replied.

"It's understandable that he did it. The retirement pension is incompatible with continuing to work, even behind closed doors in a private workshop," Fede said. "If the Social Security found out, he could lose the financial benefit. It isn't something to tell everyone."

Rebecca finished her story.

"As you may already guess, Richie Puig visited Sergio Enguix in his workshop, not in the jewelry store downtown. That's where he keeps and repairs the jewelry. It seems that he hasn't completely reformed; he still commits some small illegalities. Although he no longer buys stolen merchandise, he repairs jewelry without asking where it came from and even without including it in any entry book, as it is his obligation. The Count of Ruzafa came to him precisely for that reason. He expressly insisted that he didn't want the choker to appear on any record. Now we know why it contained half of the message that led to the location of the Jewish tree, and he didn't want to leave unnecessary clues lying around. What he couldn't foresee is that the jeweler would take a photograph of it, that a detective would visit him later, that he would have to deliver it to him and that after all this journey, that photograph would end up in our hands."

"So, Álvaro didn't lie about anything. He doesn't know that this jewel exists. He doesn't know Richie at all, nor did he give him any photo, nor does the choker appear in any official jewelry book record. It's true that he concealed that his father was still working in his workshop, but that part is understandable," Fede said.

"Now I understand why you wanted to tell us this whole story before Álvaro arrived," Carlota said.

"Sure, we already know the truth, but we shouldn't tell Álvaro about it. We have no idea if he knows his father is a police informer. We don't even know if he's aware of his criminal past," Rebecca said. "Let's not create a family conflict. Also, I don't feel like explaining to a person I don't know the whole subject of the Great Council and the Jewish tree. I'm already a bit saturated with that matter. The subject is closed."

"We won't be able to tell him all that, but we can discreetly ask him a few questions to confirm the detective's story," Carlota insisted.

Rebecca was somewhat alarmed.

"Let's see what you tell him, don't go overboard. I know you. No way he's going to admit that his father works secretly from the Social Security to collect his retirement pension," Rebecca said. "It's absurd to ask him about that matter."

"I'm not an idiot. I'm not going to ask him that," Carlota said, who was clearly annoyed. She believed that she had made a great discovery and that the Great Council still existed. She had taken a piece of candy from her, and she didn't like it.

Carlota was not the only one who was upset.

"Now that I had begun to like the conspiracies, it turns out there are no more," Carol said. "What a bummer. I arrived a few months late!"

Rebecca was very surprised by all the members of the Speaker's Club. How was it possible that no one had asked the most important question?

45   SEPTEMBER 16th, 1522

"First of all, I want to deeply thank you because someone in your position took the trouble to travel to Leuven to hand-deliver this letter to me."

"You know how much I care about you, Luis. I didn't want the unfortunate incident that occurred with the Dominican friar Severo to be repeated when he didn't convey the offer of the Duke of Alba, and you were unable to return to Spain. He didn't even give you my letter."

"That bastard! I still remember his wicked deed."

"When I found out that the University of Alcalá de Henares was offering you the vacant chair of Antonio de Nebrija, I visited Johan Corbera to give him the news. I knew he would be glad."

"A great friend, without a doubt."

"He was very worried about you."

"Worried? Did he also tell you about my finances?"

"Your finances?" No, he didn't tell me anything about that. Do you have problems?"

"Some, but that's irrelevant to the point. So why was he worried?"

"From now, don't worry about economic issues." Don Bertrán said. "I will take care of the part that is within my reach."

"Thank you," Luis replied, "but then, why was Johan worried about me?"

"He felt uneasy about Fray Severo."

"About that bastard? Why?"

"Because he thinks that a simple Dominican friar of the Order of Preachers would never, on his own initiative, have risked snubbing the Duke of Alba himself with such a deception. He believes that there must be some more powerful person who gave him instructions."

Luis was thoughtful.

"More powerful than Don Fadrique? Only a few people enjoy that grace. With what purpose?"

"You don't understand it? To prevent you from returning to Spain!"

Luis was thoughtful for a few moments.

"I don't understand it. Who wouldn't want me to return to Spain? I can't think of anyone."

"Seriously? Well, I do, for example, the Holy Office of the Inquisition."

Luis almost choked with laughter at the glass of water he was drinking.

"Look, you're a joker! And precisely, you tell me that! Actually, I should be the one who doesn't want to go back, not the other way around. They would be delighted to welcome me, with the wood and the stake prepared."

"Johan Corbera thinks there is a mysterious person behind this whole affair," Don Bertrán affirmed.

"Johan always worries too much about me."

For a moment, there was silence between them.

"Luis, the truth is that I didn't come just to deliver the letter in person. In reality, there is another reason more important that I haven't told you."

Luis Vives waited for his noble friend to continue the conversation, although it seemed that he was choosing the right words.

"I have to help you organize your trip back to Spain," he said at last. "It will not be easy. You know that Spain and France are at war right now. It is a problem since it isn't safe to travel by land. We will have to weigh the maritime option, and this leads to serious organizational complications. I promised Johan that your safety would be above all else."

"By boat? But that must be very expensive."

"Money is no problem, I already told you. Don't worry about that."

Luis was worried, but not because of the financial issue. He knew that his friend was rich. He didn't know why, but Luis had the strange feeling that the organization of his trip wasn't the real reason for Don Bertrán's arrival in Leuven. It was clear that he was hiding something from him. He had known him for many years, from the time of the royal court in Flanders, when he finished his studies at the *Sorbonne* in Paris and lived a season with the Valldaura family in the Flemish city of Bruges. He knew what his real activity was in that city, and that was what he was worried about.

If Johan Corbera has doubts, I should have them too, Luis thought, who trusted in the good sense of his friend. He is much smarter than he seems, and he has always been very intuitive. His claims, almost always, had ended up being true.

He was uneasy, and he had reasons for it.

46   NOWADAYS. FRIDAY, SEPTEMBER 7th

"I'm going to go to the bathroom before Álvaro arrives," Rebecca said.

"I'll seize the opportunity and I'll go with you," Carlota answered immediately.

They went up the stairs to the toilets at Kilkenny's Pub. It was exactly half-past seven.

"Are you nervous about your partner coming to the club in just a few minutes?" Rebecca asked. "I would certainly be; I would be so ashamed."

"First, he's not my partner. That we've been fooling around and something like that in the summer doesn't make him my spouse. Second, I'm very comfortable, just like you by being single. I don't want to complicate my life, and more so now with my mother's dependency. My brothers help me, but she still requires almost twenty-four-hour assistance."

"Has her health improved?"

"No. Although it is horrible to say it, we are awaiting her death. She is suffering, not only because of her illness but because she sees all of her children looking out for her. She has always been very independent and she's handling it awfully. Besides, you know what she has, the damn bug. It is terminal; there is no hope."

"Terminal?"

"She isn't going to return to the hospital. The last time they sent her home to die in peace, surrounded by her family. That is why my brothers have come to live temporarily at home, rather than to help me, which they do. The real reason is to accompany her in her last days."

"It's heartbreaking. I'm really sorry. I had no idea."

"Although we have been getting used to the idea for a long time, it doesn't hurt any less."

They went downstairs just as they saw a person approach the club's table. Carlota went to meet him and accompanied him to their corner.

"Guys, this is Álvaro Enguix, the person I've been talking about these days."

Heaven's firecracker! She has good taste, Rebecca thought. He had tanned skin with dark eyes, a short beard, and long hair tied up in a ponytail. He was impeccably dressed, even with a vest. *I suppose it's normal; he comes from working in a luxury jewelry store,* she told herself. He wasn't tall, but neither was Carlota, so they made a good match. He seemed to be in good physical shape.

Each member introduced themselves, shaking hands with him. They officially welcomed him to the Speaker's Club with the traditional pint of Murphy's Irish Red. Cork's Irish Beer was an institution at the club. Everyone who was attending a meeting for the first time had to drink one of them, and Álvaro was no exception. He already knew the pub and the beer, so he didn't find it too strange either. They all toasted with him.

When the initiation ritual of the new member of the club ended, suddenly and inappropriately, Charly asked everyone to be quiet and took a paper from his pocket. Rebecca was horrified. *Have they prepared a trap for Álvaro on his first day?* She thought, frightened. *He wasn't going to come back anymore.*

"Ladies and gentlemen, today we celebrate a singular event," Charly began to say, "because precisely today we have among us a prominent person from the Valencian society."

What a butt kisser! Rebecca thought.

"Their presence at the Speaker's Club is a source of great pride and satisfaction for us, even if we only found out two or three days ago."

Now, he's talking like Emeritus King Juan Carlos, Rebecca told herself. He's going to embarrass Álvaro.

"As a small token of appreciation, we're honored to present you with this modest trophy, lovingly crafted by all the members of our club. We know it falls short, but each piece of it contains a portion of our heart."

What nonsense is this cheesy maniac saying? Rebecca thought, surprised by Charly's speech, considering she was used to his out-of-place actions.

Suddenly, the lights in the corner of the Speaker's Club went out. Rebecca watched as Dan, the waiter, walked slowly towards them with an object in his hands. She turned to look at Carlota, to see what expression her friend had on her face, with the joke they were playing on her fling. She was strangely laughing. *Is she in the loop of this scene and doesn't care?* She wondered. She couldn't believe it.

Dan finally reached their table and lit a few sparklers that were embedded in the object he was carrying. When it was illuminated, Rebecca could see that he was carrying in his hands a very old indoor television antenna, the one with horns. It was also half battered, one of those that used to be placed on top of televisions in the last century, before the arrival of the digital age. It was an ancient artifact.

Oh, God! Rebecca thought, completely embarrassed when she understood what it all meant. Her world fell apart from embarrassment.   Once again, she had been naive.

"Rebecca Mercader, we are proud to grant you the Rabbit Ears Antenna Award to the most famous person in our club," Charly said, with that solemn voice that he knew how to imitate so well, while he handed her that junk.

Everyone broke into applause. Not only the members of the Speaker's Club but also the other customers of the pub, which was completely packed on a Friday afternoon

"I will kill you all!" Rebecca exclaimed.

They got up to hug her.

"When were you planning to tell us about your Ondas Award nomination?" Almu said. "We found out from the press. Are you not ashamed?"

"I am ashamed of this spectacle you have organized for me, you bastards," she replied, still blushing.

"You deserve it for keeping that news from us. For once, I have a famous friend, and I didn't know it," Fede said.

"Let Jimmy Kimmel tremble. Rebecca is coming to the world of entertainment!" Charly exclaimed, laughing.

"You are all so mischievous."

"Actually, we did it to get you to buy a round of beers because you must have been hiding the news from us to get away from it," Xavier said.

"I'll pay for the round if you leave me alone and you all sit down; even that Japanese group is taking pictures of me," Rebecca said, pointing to some Asian people in the corner of the pub with cameras in their hands. "I don't know who they think I am."

"Taylor Swift," Charly said, breaking into laughter. "I wouldn't be surprised if they came shortly to ask for an autograph."

They all listened to their friend and sat at the table. Rebecca kept her word and ordered Dan another round of beers.

"It's a very important nomination, Rebecca. I don't know if you are aware of what you've achieved. Whatever happens, your professional career will never be the same again," Carmen said, with that slow tone that characterized her.

"Nothing will ever be the same again. What group was that song from? From the extinct group *El Canto del Loco*?" Bonet asked, who was very fond of music.

"Yes," Charly replied, "With Dani Martín as the lead."

"Don't think I'm not scared, especially because I wasn't expecting it. I assure you I don't like it at all," Rebecca admitted.

She decided to change the subject; she was done talking about her. Deep down, she felt great embarrassment.

"But today, the protagonist of the meeting should be our new addition, not me. You have known me for many years," she said, looking at Álvaro.

"Exactly," Xavier said.

Carlota took the floor immediately, almost without letting the others react.

"Do you have a workshop apart from the jewelry store on Calle San Vicente?" She asked, just like that.

I'm going to kill her! Rebecca thought. What the hell does she understand by being discreet?

Álvaro was surprised by the oddity of the matter.

"Why do you ask me that?"

"Because I have visited your jewelry store and it's very small. I don't think there's room for a workshop," Carlota replied.

"You're right. We have a rented premise that my father used before he retired, where he repaired and manufactured jewelry near Burjassot Avenue."

"Do you still have it?"

"Yes, although no one uses it now."

"And why do you pay rent for a place you don't use? Do you have money to spare?" Carlota continued asking with the subtlety of a flying brick.

"We don't have much money to spare; it's more of a sentimental matter. This is where our current jewelry business was born almost forty years ago. They were very difficult times. Even my father had a minor problem with justice in the early days. It is now an abandoned warehouse, but we keep it with some devotion. From time to time, we visit it".

Goal accomplished, Carlota thought. Richie Puig's story is confirmed. She went silent.

Luckily, Álvaro doesn't seem to have suspected anything about this blunt examination, Rebecca thought, relieved. It's clear that she doesn't know the meaning of the word subtle.

They both remained apparently calm, although the main issue remained unspoken.

It was strange.

47 NOVEMBER 18ᵗʰ, 1522

"Everything is set up now, Luis. The ship will depart from the Port of Antwerp on January 3rd. You must pack all your belongings and prepare for the trip."

"That'll be quick. I hardly have anything to take with me."

"You have a little over a month to say goodbye to your friends."

"It will also be quick," Luis answered with some melancholy. "I haven't cultivated that many either."

"Unfortunately, I have to leave Leuven immediately and will not be able to travel with you on the ship." Urgent matters demand me in Spain, and I can't delay it."

"Didn't you say it wasn't safe to travel by land?"

"And it isn't. The war between Francis I of France and our King Charles is getting worse at times, but I can't wait for the ship's departure date. It's too late for me."

"But you are a recognized personality. The French king would be delighted to capture you," Luis insisted.

"Be calm, don't worry about my safety. I'll take measures to match the threat. I'm not an idiot."

Luis decided to change the subject and tackle a thorny issue. He had the feeling that his important friend hadn't told him something important.

"I must ask you a question," Luis said, "and I want you to be honest in your answer."

"Go on," the nobleman said curiously.

"What is the real reason for your presence in Leuven?"

"That's the question? What nonsense to give you the letter from the University of Alcalá de Henares in person, to avoid it getting lost along the way, as it happened with the offer of the Duke of Alba."

"I already know that. I mean the other reason."

An awkward silence fell between them.

"The other reason?"

"Are you going to repeat my question or answer it?"

Don Bertrán made a small pause, looking into the eyes of his friend, before continuing to speak.

"I'm afraid I must answer you with another question, does Johan Corbera know my true identity? I also expect a sincere answer from you."

Now the surprised one was Luis.

"I've never told him anything. Why are you asking me that?"

"Because that is the real reason for my presence in Leuven. Now you know it."

"What are you talking about!" Luis exclaimed, frightened. "I have never told him anything! You shouldn't have any doubts about it."

Still, that was really worrying.

48 NOWADAYS. SATURDAY, SEPTEMBER 8th

Rebecca had convinced her friend Carlota to work out with her. Rebecca was a magnificent runner. She had trained frequently for years. She used to compete in all the trials that she could on the running circuit and she wasn't badly classified. However, Carlota was the opposite. She wasn't fond of exercise at all and even less of running. *Besides being boring, running is for cowards*, she liked to say. She also had an old injury on her left wrist that bothered her a bit after exercising. Rebecca insisted and ended up convincing her on the pretext of her mother's illness. They had agreed to meet in the riverbed at five in the afternoon when the sun was a bit more merciful.

"Are you sure running is good?" Carlota said as soon as she met with Rebecca. "I'm still unable to see it clearly. I'm in very bad physical shape."

"Running is a sport of the mind," Rebecca answered, trying to cheer up her friend.

"Well, then it's clear because I'm kind of crazy," Carlota said, laughing.

"Do you know what Jimmy Carter said, the one who was president of the United States?"

"Yes, that the world had gone crazy."

"No, idiot, not that," Rebecca replied, laughing too. "I think his exact phrase was 'everyone who has run knows that its most important value lies in removing tension and allowing a release from whatever other cares the day may bring.' Do you understand? It will help you to relax from your mother's illness, you'll see."

"The only thing I know for sure is that it will help me to have some tremendous aches and pains tomorrow. Luckily, it will be Sunday."

"Come on, let's start. If we keep talking, it will get dark. Don't worry; I'll go at a slow pace. As soon as you get tired, you tell me, and we stop."

"I'm already tired just by thinking about it."

Rebecca grabbed her friend from behind and pushed her while they both laughed. They started running. The truth is that Carlota responded better than expected. She didn't ask for a break until half an hour later.

"Without a doubt, you have an athlete inside you," Rebecca said, trying to lift her friend's spirit.

"Well, I must have eaten her because even my eyelids hurt," Carlota said, who could barely articulate a word.

Rebecca couldn't help but laugh.

"That's a good sign. You haven't lost your sense of humor."

"My sense of humor? I'm on my way to even losing my dignity."

"Come on, don't be a crybaby. Now we turn around and go back. To be the first day, it's not bad."

"Running?"

"Well, of course! If you've already made the run here, you will crush the one back," Rebecca replied as she opened her backpack and handed Carlota a bottle. "Come on, hydrate yourself a bit, and we'll be back in five minutes. As soon as you are ready."

"Did you bring beer? What a good idea!" Carlota said as she took a long sip from the bottle. "What is this? It tastes horrible!" She exclaimed, grimacing in disgust.

Rebecca couldn't help but laugh when she saw her friend's disgusted face.

"How are we going to drink alcohol while exercising? It's a sports drink. It improves water absorption; it also contains potassium, magnesium, and calcium, among other minerals."

"Well, those minerals taste very bad. It's like sucking a stone. I hydrate myself more comfortably with a toasted beer, very cold."

"If you feel like it, when we get back, we'll stop by my house and have one of those," Rebecca said, trying to stimulate her friend.

"Now you've really encouraged me to run. I bet you can't catch me." Carlota said as she ran off.

They continued along the riverbed until they reached the starting point. They also did it in one go, non-stop. When they arrived, Carlota couldn't keep standing and sat down on the grass, panting.

"I'm exhausted. Can you take me to your home on a piggyback? Also, every time I exercise, the injury on my left wrist suffers, and you can't imagine how it hurts!"

"But you did very well! Do you remember Jimmy Carter's phrase? Running allows you to free yourself from any other worrisome issues the day may bring."

"I would strangle that guy right now with my bare hands. I'm sure he never ran in his entire life," Carlota replied. "After such a beating, your only concern for the rest of the day is to recover and go back to breathing like a normal person, not like Darth Vader in Star Wars."

"I am your father," Rebecca repeated the famous phrase from the film, which had gone down in history.

"I don't know if you are my father, but right now, I'd like to be Luke Skywalker to kill you."

They laughed with joy, although they didn't know how wrong they were -Rebecca, Carlota, and even Jimmy Carter himself. The worries hadn't even started.

A good surprise awaited them around the corner.

49 JANUARY 3rd, 1523

Luis Vives was in front of the ship that had to return him to Spain. He had mixed feelings. It had been more than thirteen years since he had left his city, Valencia, urged by the fury of the Spanish Inquisition, which had condemned half of his family to the stake. He didn't know what to think. He didn't even know what he really felt. Was it joy or sadness? Was it hope or skepticism? And, above all, what was he going to find in his country? He longed for his city, its weather, and its colors, but he was a citizen of Europe, and Flanders had been his home for far too long. He had developed as a person and as a humanist between Bruges and Leuven. Ultimately, his feelings seemed like a messy puzzle. He felt that his homeland was the whole world. He didn't even want to put some order in that mess of mixed feelings.

"Luis Vives?" a scruffy-looking person in a uniform that looked like it hadn't been washed in a long time, asked.

"Yes, it's me."

"I'm Captain Francis Drammer of the ship Saint Nazaire. I have direct instructions to make sure that you have a journey as comfortable as possible to Santander's port."

"Thank you very much, Mr. Drammer."

"Francis is fine. Do you have any luggage?"

"Just this trunk."

"We set sail in two hours," the captain said as he climbed onto the ship. "Come with me."

Luis took his luggage and followed the captain. They got on board the ship. The deck was freshly flushed and appeared to be in a decent state of sanitation, though some strong smells quickly permeated Luis' nostrils. Francis noticed the look of disgust.

"Don't worry. You'll get used to it in just a few hours."

The captain accompanied him below deck and pointed to a small bunk.

"You can leave the trunk underneath. If you don't want it to end up on the other end of the ship, secure it with the straps. We're expecting a storm."

Luis looked around. It wasn't the first trip he had taken by boat, and this wasn't bad at all. He had slept in worse places.

Suddenly, he heard a voice behind him.

"Good morning, sir. Who are you?"

Luis was startled. He hadn't noticed the presence of anyone else around him.

"Hi, good morning. I'm Luis, and you?"

'I'm Richard Foxe, an English merchant, although I reside in Bruges. I buy wine and sell luxury fabrics in Spain. I frequently travel on this route; for me, it is routine."

"It's a pleasure to meet you, Mr. Foxe," Luis answered, still surprised.

"What do you do? I had never seen you on this ship or in these waters."

"I'm a teacher and I write books. I have been teaching in Leuven and Bruges, so I don't usually travel by sea."

"Luis? Is it not by chance Luis Vives?"

"Yes, do you know me?"

"Not personally, but your fame precedes you. I'm a friend of Bernardo Valldaura."

"What a coincidence! I was living in his house in Bruges for a good time ten years ago."

Coincidence? Luis thought. He was getting a little paranoid. How many people live in Flanders? And I get someone who knows me on the bunk next to mine? How likely is it?

"Don't get offended, but you don't look like a merchant," Luis told him, carefully observing his companion with rather pronounced spherical shapes, to say gently that he was fat as a barrel.

"Do you say it because of my age or my belly?" Richard replied, laughing, as he looked at Luis' face. "From the expression on your face, I can see that both."

Luis flustered a bit. He shouldn't have thought that. He supposed his face conveyed his thoughts.

Richard Foxe seemed like a person in a good mood.

"Don't worry; I'm not offended. I'm used to that phrase. I like to eat well and I don't know how to do anything else, so I'll be a merchant until I die," he replied.

They both settled in, and before fastening their luggage to the straps, Luis took a book out of the trunk. He went up the deck.

He observed the maneuvers of the sailors, preparing the rigging, the ropes and checking the condition of the sails and rigging to be released from the bollard, which held the ship to shore. Without a doubt, they were starting preparations to sail from the port of Antwerp in a few minutes. He didn't think they would take any longer.

He sat where he could, on top of a barrel, and tried to clear his mind by reading any book. He didn't want to think about the mess of mixed feelings, nor where he was going; it caused him deep uneasiness.

Actually, he didn't even imagine it.

50 NOWADAYS. SATURDAY, SEPTEMBER 8th

"Come on; we're almost there," Rebecca said. She lived on the Paseo de la Alameda, just a few meters from the riverbed where they had run.

"The only thing that keeps me on my feet is thinking about that cold beer that awaits me at your house," Carlota said, who was finding it difficult to walk.

"I have two missed calls from my aunt from half an hour ago," Rebecca said as she looked at her cellphone. "I don't know what she wanted, but we'll see her anyways in a few minutes. I'm not going to call her back."

"What if she ran out of beer," Carlota said.

"That never happens in my house, don't worry," Rebecca replied while she smiled at her friend. She was proud of herself. She had achieved almost the impossible to get Carlota to run, and she also had behaved better than expected.

They went home, and Rebecca opened the door. As soon as they entered, they heard several voices from the room.

"Hey, your aunt seems to have guests," Carlota said. "What if we turn around and leave?"

They didn't have time to react.

"Rebecca! I've been trying to reach you for more than half an hour!" Tote said as she turned towards Carlota. "How are you, darling?"

"You better not ask me," she answered. "Your niece has subjected me to an intense and savage torture session."

"Who are the people in the living room?" Rebecca asked, surprised. "Do you have guests?"

"Have you forgotten? I imagined it; that's why I had called you."

Rebecca was confused.

"What exactly have I forgotten?"

"Come in and see it with your own eyes," Tote replied. "And you too, Carlota. Don't just stand there at the door."

They peeked into the living room.

What a horror.

Almost the entire editorial department of *La Crónica* was there, around a perfectly organized catering. Rebecca didn't know where to hide.

What was my aunt thinking making us come in looking like this, sweaty and with tights? she thought, scandalized, as she looked at her bosses and colleagues, all elegantly dressed.

"We thought you had forgotten about us!" Tere said, giving her a couple of kisses.

Rebecca looked surprised. She reacted immediately.

"I apologize. It's that every Saturday I go out for a run, I don't spare a single one, and I was running late. I'm sorry I wasn't on time. I ask you to pardon me for my mistake."

Carlota looked at her with the face of a serial killer, a serial killer from any Quentin Tarantino's movie.

"I introduce you to my friend Carlota Penella. She came to run with me today."

They all greeted each other and introduced themselves. The editor Bernat Fornell and his secretary Alba Pajares, the head of the local political section, Ernest Ballester, along with his young pupil Fabio Astolfi were there. Also, the head of the national section, Jaime Talens, Javier Puchau from the international section, Pere Devesa from events, and Tommy Egea from sports. Her friend Teresa Fabregat was also there. The deputy director and head of the economy supplement, Carmen María Peris, the one who ran the latest news section, Herminia Camacho, and the layout editor, María Jesús Rubio, were missing. Besides the rest of the subordinates, such as the driver, Adolfo Serrano. She supposed they were working. They couldn't leave the editorial department completely alone.

"Now that we are all here, I propose a toast to Rebecca, the new star of historical disclosure," editor Fornell said as he raised his glass of *champagne*. Rebecca and Carlota took one from the waiter who was passing with the tray of drinks. Everyone toasted.

"Where can I buy tobacco?" Alba asked. "The vice is calling me."

"There is a tobacco shop right in front of our portal," Tote replied, "but we don't allow smoking inside the house. You'll have to go out onto the terrace. I'm sorry, Alba."

"Don't apologize. It's the logical thing to do. I never smoke indoors."

"Your aunt was very kind to invite us this afternoon," editor Fornell said to Rebecca as they had an inconsequential conversation. Rebecca thought that, in this relaxed atmosphere, it was a good opportunity to try to extract something from the editor that had been on her mind for a long time.

"After the reorganization of the tables in the main editorial department, who is going to sit with Tere, Fabio, and me? There is one free chair."

Fornell laughed.

"It's too soon for you to know that; you'll find out. Keep in mind that their incorporation is not going to happen yet. There are about three weeks left if all goes well."

"Has him or her been already chosen?"

"It's close, but it has been more difficult than I expected," Fornell answered, with a smile on his mouth that Rebecca couldn't interpret.

The conversation between everyone was very lively, although Carlota felt out of place. As soon as she could, she took Rebecca's arm and led her out onto the terrace.

"What an ambush! And moreover, we are dressed in tights, come on! We must look so ridiculous in front of all these dolled up people."

"I promise you I didn't know anything."

Carlota was surprised by the answer and also by the expression on her friend's face.

"What do you mean? If you just admitted that you were late and you apologized," she scolded her, surprised.

Rebecca had no recollection of her aunt telling her about today's meeting. It's true that she, the day she was in the editorial department talking to the editor, had invited them to have a snack at home, but she was sure that she hadn't told him the day or time. *Besides being ridiculous, it was very weird*, she thought.

Rebecca explained herself to her friend.

"I said it so I wouldn't put my aunt down in front of all the guests. I assure you that she didn't tell me anything. If she had, she would have told me when she saw that I left the house dressed in sportswear to run, like every Saturday. I tried to find a pretext in front of all the people so that my total surprise wouldn't be too obvious. It's impossible that neither my aunt nor I forget. I'm worried."

"Early-onset of Alzheimer's? You're too young. I don't think it's that; stay calm."

"No, you idiot, I don't mean me. My aunt is extremely organized. She would have never forgotten to tell me such a thing. I can only find a logical explanation for her 'forgetfulness,' to call it some way."

"Oh! Really? Which one?"

"That my aunt had no interest in me coming to this meeting."

Carlota made an expression of not understanding anything.

"Does that seem logical to you? How could she not want you to come to a party organized precisely in your honor? It is so absurd."

"I don't know why, but this is all very strange. I've been working at the newspaper for more than three years, and my aunt has never taken the slightest interest in my colleagues. Now, all of a sudden, she invites all the bosses over and she doesn't tell me anything. Something is happening in front of our noses, and we are incapable of seeing it."

"Don't forget that you're nominated for an Ondas Award. It's not something that happens every day. I think that detail justifies this little party, don't you think?"

"Trust me, from the beginning, when my aunt visited editor Fornell at the newspaper, I had the feeling that something was up, and now that feeling is even bigger," she said thoughtfully.

Carlota changed the subject; it was enough of worries. It was a party and she had to try to have fun.

"Hey, that Fabio is impressive. Do you think the girls in ridiculous tights that are half sweaty could handle him?" Carlota asked with a mocking smile.

Rebecca couldn't help but laugh.

"I don't know, but don't go near him. He's a private hunting pray for my coworker Tere."

"What a pity! I was going to propose to him if he wanted to run twenty kilometers with me, now that I've gotten the liking of exercising," Carlota said, feigning despair.

"Don't get cocky, champ. Now you are thrilled by how well you did, but tomorrow you will have some aches and pains, and you will regret it, even just a little bit."

"Tomorrow will be another day. I enjoy the present."

"Well, just enjoy the view if you aren't looking to get me in trouble at work."

Carlota seemed distracted, looking in all directions on the terrace. At that precise moment, Alba came out, carrying a cigarette in one hand and a glass in the other. She put it down on the table so he could light her cigarette. Tere also came out. *Good thing we're done talking about Fabio*, Rebecca thought. *They come out a moment earlier and they catch us.*

"I see it only took you a few minutes to find the tobacconist," Rebecca said to Alba, trying to break the ice.

"It was simple. I just had to cross the street. I'm clumsy but not that much," Alba answered with apparent good humor.

"I didn't know you smoked," Tere told her, "you never told me."

"Sure, and besides, you've never seen me. I can't do it in the editorial department." Alba replied.

194

"By the way, Rebecca, you have to congratulate your aunt. This punch she made is great," Tere continued as she took a sip from her glass.

Alba gestured at her head.

"Just in case, since I went to buy tobacco, I'm not going to keep drinking anymore. I'm not used to it and I'm already a little tipsy from alcohol."

"You do very well. And you, Tere, be careful. My aunt's punch is legendary for knocking down elephants," Rebecca replied.

"Are you subtly calling me fat?" Tere asked with her arms on her hips.

"She's not being subtle," Alba replied, smiling broadly.

"Hey!" Tere exclaimed, pretending to be offended.

"But the four of us are drinking the same thing!" Rebecca protested.

They laughed at ease. Alba is being nice. Let's see if she's going to act as stupid as she seems at work," Rebecca thought. The truth is that they didn't know each other outside of *La Crónica*. She was dressed very cute and now she had put on a pink hat that covered up to her ears and matching gloves, nothing like the impersonal clothes she used to wear in the editorial department. *I'm misjudging her. People change in their job, and then outside of it, they are different,* Rebecca told herself.

After a brief, inconsequential but pleasant conversation, they joined the party with smiles on their faces. *This short time on the terrace was wonderful for me*, Rebecca told herself, because if she thought about the situation, she would start crying. All her bosses gathered at her house and she arrived late, dressed in ridiculous tights. Of course, she didn't give the best image in front of her superiors, no matter how many nominations she had.

Rebecca served them all with the best smile she could under the circumstances. The party continued without major news until nine o'clock, which was the moment when all the guests left the house.

"I have the latest news; we'll talk on Monday," Tere told her excitedly as she said goodbye at the door and left, along with the rest of her coworkers. Alba also said goodbye with a big smile. *It turns out that she does know how to smile. I thought she lacked some facial muscle,* Rebecca thought wickedly

"I also have the latest news," Carlota said, imitating Tere's excited voice and her schoolgirl gestures. They were alone in front of the elevator.

"You are such a buffoon!" Rebecca replied, laughing.

"I'm not kidding; I'm serious."

"You have never been serious in your life. I think that even if you tried, you wouldn't succeed."

"Well, now I'm doing it. I propose you a riddle. Can you figure out what was hugely out of place in this little party?"

"Hugely? You made it very easy for me, the two of us in tights!" Rebecca replied, laughing again. "It was very simple."

"No, no. There's another thing. Think, for example, on a Kinder surprise egg."

"Those that are made of chocolate?"

"Yeah, sure. A lifelong Kinder egg."

"But you don't like chocolate!" Rebecca exclaimed, surprised.

"See, you've already discovered the first clue," Carlota answered with a vague smile on her face.

"Come on, go home now. My aunt's punch went to your head and you're talking nonsense."

Carlota insisted.

"If you don't guess for the rest of the weekend, I'll tell you on Monday, but think about it, it's very curious and at the same time strange," she said, by way of farewell, with a mysterious tone.

She can't help being the center of attention until the end, Rebecca thought, who was tired, not so much from exercising because the pace at which she had run this afternoon had been too slow for her, but rather from the stress she had been through in the party, and also the embarrassment, why not say so. The situation had been somewhat uncomfortable.

She took a shower. Since she hadn't been able to do it before, she said good night to her aunt and went to her room.

Despite Carlota's funny jokes, Rebecca was still worried. Something didn't fit in this whole show. That was the right word, show. The feeling that she had witnessed some kind of theatrical performance was very intense, and her instincts did not often fool her.

She put on her pajamas and went to bed. Despite the fact that Carlota had intrigued her with this strange riddle, it didn't take her long to fall asleep.

51 JANUARY 3rd, 1523

"I don't recommend that you stay on the deck," the captain said. "We expect a somewhat bumpy start of the trip."

They had just set sail from the port of Antwerp, and the waters were calm. The ship sailed the sea in complete tranquility.

"Well, it doesn't seem like it at all," Luis answered.

"Wait until we get out to the open sea. You'd better lie down on your bunk. It's not going to be pleasant for a person not used to travel by boat like you."

"And how do you know that I don't usually travel by sea?"

"Because of your friend, the one who paid me generously to make the trip as pleasant as possible for you. Among my obligations with him, I have to ask you from time to time how you are doing, in addition to providing you with everything you need, anything."

"I relieve you from those duties," Luis said immediately, imagining the captain bothering him relentlessly. "Don't worry about me; if I need something, I'll ask you for it. For now, I'll stay on deck; I want to feel the sea breeze hitting my face."

"As you wish, but soon that breeze will turn into a gale and it will no longer be pleasant that it hits your face," the captain concluded the conversation, returning to his tasks.

Luis continued reading the book that he had started at the beginning of the trip. He wanted to clear his mind and not think about the final destination of his journey. He was nervous.

"You can never stop reading, can you?"

Luis turned around to see his bunkmate, Richard Foxe, sitting next to him. *It is obvious that they aren't going to leave me alone today*, he thought.

"I'm trying to distract my mind," Luis said.

Suddenly the ship yawed very hard. Although all the sailors were at their posts and looked professional, they appeared somewhat nervous.

"Looks like the captain was right; the sea is starting to get rough," Richard said.

"It doesn't seem extreme either, does it?" Luis asked, who, although he had little maritime experience, had sailed through more turbulent waters than the present ones.

"If the sea is in these conditions at this point, wait half an hour. Actually, we aren't out on the open waters yet. We are passing in front of Vlissingen."

Every time, the ship was moving more and more. The waves hit the hull hard, and foam splashed the deck. The sky was completely cloudy and black, even though it was the early hours of the morning. In just fifteen minutes, a strong storm began to unleash over their heads, with a large amount of lightning on the horizon.

"It seems to me that the time has come for us to retire to our bunks," Richard said. "This doesn't look good at all."

Luis wanted to stay on deck, but in those conditions, it was absurd. He couldn't even read and the heavy downpour was even soaking his underwear.

"You're right; it's time to leave," Luis agreed.

At that moment, a wave swept the deck of the ship and threw them against some barrels. The ship rocked like a round-bottomed doll. It seemed at the mercy of the elements.

"Are you okay?" Richard asked.

"I think so; I look to be in one piece," Luis answered. "And you?"

"In one piece too. My belly protects me."

Another wave washed over the deck. The constant swings of the ship made it practically impossible to stand.

"We should find a safe harbor. This gale seems too strong an intensity to deal with," Richard said, looking scared.

"A safe harbor?" Luis asked incredulously. It was a major storm, but it didn't seem that bad either. The ship was solid, and he was sure it could weather it.

The captain approached them.

"Gentlemen, you shouldn't be here; you could fall overboard."

"We were going to retire to our bunks in this instant," Luis said.

"We're going to find a safe harbor. We can't continue sailing with this gale," the captain stated, contradicting Luis' opinion.

"It doesn't seem like a big deal either, does it?" He asked, concerned.

"We haven't really entered the storm yet. We are simply on the outer edge of it. Later the conditions will be quite worse."

"I agree with you, Captain," Richard said. "What are the alternatives?"

"We're heading to Dover."

"Dover? That's in England!" Luis exclaimed, terrified.

"It is the closest safe harbor for our current location," the captain replied.

"Is it completely necessary?" Luis asked, who couldn't believe they were going to dock in an English port.

"I assure you it is. With these conditions, the most responsible thing is to seek shelter immediately. My first responsibility is the safety of my passengers, my sailors, my cargo, and, of course, my ship."

"Look how I'm going to return to my country without intending to; what a surprise," Richard said.

Luis couldn't help but think about the mysterious person that, according to his friend Johan Corbera, seemed to want to prevent him from returning to Spain at all costs. *I don't believe that the God Neptune is behind this supposed conspiracy*, Luis told himself.

Not Neptune, but perhaps other minor gods were. And some humans too.

52 NOWADAYS. SATURDAY, SEPTEMBER 8th

Now is the right time, they told themself as they accessed the editorial office of *La Crónica*. The main room was completely empty. They only saw light in the office of the deputy editor, in the office of the head of latest news, and in the one of the layout designer. They knew that they weren't going to encounter anyone, since at that very moment they were all at Rebecca's house, celebrating. The editor used to stop by the editorial department before closing time, but he would do it later today. Consequently, they had plenty of time.

They went to Rebecca's table, carefully opening her chest of drawers. They extracted all her folders and spread them out on the table. They opened them and read each of the files, without any haste, with the peace of mind that no one was coming for several hours. They took pictures with their mobile of all the documentation with absolute calm.

There's nothing interesting here, they thought in frustration after taking their time. They checked the table from top to bottom, in case she might have a hidden place, and even checked the legs, which were hollow. *There's nothing at all*, they told themselves with some frustration. So much trouble for nothing.

They collected all the papers and put them back in their proper folders. *I can't make progress. Maybe the time to take a step forward has come*, they told themself as they opened the briefcase they carried with them. They searched inside until they found what they were looking for. The device was tiny, but it was going to do its job perfectly.

With the same calm that they entered the editorial department, they left. They had been there for more than two hours and no one had noticed them. A very simple job, although, unfortunately for them, unproductive. *Not quite*, they told themself with a small smile on their face. Things were going to change.

This is definitely going to get interesting, they thought.

53 JANUARY 3ʳᵈ, 1523

The ship docked with difficulty in the port of Dover. The sea was very rough, and the mooring tasks took longer than usual.

"England, my homeland," Richard said.

"I hope it's a short stopover. I must return to my country as soon as possible," Luis Vives said. "They are waiting for me there."

The rain was heavy. The captain provided them with a kind of waterproof sailor ponchos to protect them from inclement weather.

"We must leave the ship. We'll spend the night ashore and see how the weather conditions evolve first thing in the morning," the captain said.

"Have you ever been to my country?" Richard asked, turning to Luis.

"Never, and I've had nice invitations."

"Let's get off the ship," Richard said.

They crossed the catwalk carefully. Despite the fact that the ship was firmly moored and the port was sheltered from the inclement weather, it still moved with some violence. At last, their feet touched solid ground. Luis was secretly relieved, although he hoped to resume his trip to Spain as soon as possible.

"Don Luis Vives, it's a pleasure to finally see you on English ground."

Luis observed a strange entourage waiting at the end of the catwalk. The weather was terrible and he wasn't expecting any welcome. There were five people dressed in sailor ponchos with the same style he was wearing; their large hoods didn't allow them to identify the people who were wearing the ponchos. They were addressing him personally.

"Don't you recognize me?" the interlocutor insisted.

Luis was in front of the person who was speaking to him. He winced. He had just recognized his face out of the curtain of water that was falling between them.

"Monsignor Thomas Wosley! What a surprise! What is a person like you doing in Dover with such a storm?"

"Wait."

Richard Foxe walked down the catwalk and stood next to Luis, who was confused with everything that was happening.

"Richard, this is Cardinal Thomas Wosley," Luis said while his mind was trying to find an explanation for that.

To his surprise, the cardinal and Richard hugged each other warmly.

"We already know each other. Richard Foxe is my bishop in Winchester. I sent him to the ship to take care of you," Wosley replied.

"I was sure he didn't look like a merchant!" Luis exclaimed.

"I'm sorry I lied to you, but it was necessary," the bishop replied by way of pretext. "I couldn't reveal my true identity."

"So, you already knew the ship was going to dock at Dover?"

"Let's say it was a correct supposition. We knew about the storm and suggested to the captain that he should find a safe harbor. You know the rest," Wosley said.

Suddenly, one of the five people from the welcoming committee addressed Luis Vives.

"And you aren't going to say hello to me?"

He immediately recognized the voice.

"Thomas!" Luis said as they embraced. "What a joy! What a surprise you have all given me."

Thomas More was the most famous English humanist. He had met Luis a few years before, and they professed mutual respect and appreciation, almost like Erasmus of Rotterdam. The three were great friends.

"In this solemn reception, the only one missing is King Henry VIII," Luis said jokingly.

"He sends you warm greetings along with his wife Catherine," Cardinal Wosley replied.

Luis was overwhelmed. He hardly knew how to continue the conversation.

"And what is the purpose of all of you being together in Dover today?" Luis asked, who hadn't yet come out of his astonishment with such a welcome. "And don't tell me it's because of the storm. I don't believe in coincidences."

"Let's go to a place out of the rain and continue the conversation," Wosley said.

The surprises hadn't started yet.

54 NOWADAYS. SATURDAY, SEPTEMBER 8th

All the people from the party she had organized at her house had already left. Tote stared at what had to be cleaned: glasses, plates, and food scraps in every corner of the room. *Luckily, I've hired a staffed caterer and he'll take care of everything*, she thought lazily.

She sat comfortably in an armchair and addressed the waiter.

"You can start collecting everything now, please."

"Do you mind if I take some pictures before touching anything?"

"Go ahead, no problem, whatever you need."

The waiter took out his mobile and took photos of the whole room from different angles. When he finished, he walked over to a sports bag that he had taken from a room, took out some gloves, and put them on so he wouldn't get his hands dirty. He grabbed some bags and began to put away the plastic cups and plates, first tossing the food and trash into the garbage can. He seemed very organized. He was clearly separating the plastic from the organic waste, just as he had been instructed.

Tote was looking at him apathetically.

"Be very careful, please."

The waiter nodded and continued his work in silence.

Tote turned on the television without intending to watch it, just to be distracted by its background noise. It had been a very stressful afternoon, and she wanted to unwind for a while whilst the hired waiter took care of his work.

She was worried about her niece. It was clear that she had figured out the situation. She was not an idiot, rather the opposite. Tote pretended to be alone with her coworkers without Rebecca being present. She hadn't told her about today's party, hoping she wouldn't be on time. She had made a couple of missed calls as a pretext, just in case she showed up, as she had had. She knew she was meeting her friend Carlota to run, and she mistakenly assumed that after exercising, they would go for a beer at any bar. The presence of both almost ruined her plans. In fact, she still didn't know if she had managed to save the situation.

I hope she doesn't ask any problematic questions tomorrow morning, Tote thought. She wouldn't know what to answer her. I'll have to come up with something.

"I'm done," the waiter said.

"Great, have you separated everything into its corresponding bags?" Tote asked.

"As you ordered, ma'am."

Tote got up and looked into Rebecca's room. She was asleep. The noises the waiter had made picking up all the remnants of the party hadn't kept her from sleeping. *Much better*, she thought. She returned to the living room.

"What do you want me to do now, ma'am?" the waiter asked.

"First, take off your latex mask and wig. My niece is already asleep. And the second thing is that you stop calling me ma'am. That makes me laugh."

"Thank goodness, I was getting very hot," he said, pulling off the fake latex mask that hid his real identity and taking off his wig.

"You did very well, Richie. No one noticed your costume."

"When I saw your niece walk through the door, I was almost shocked. I thought that at any moment, she was going to recognize me, despite my characterization. She's very perceptive."

"Well, that's because you don't know her friend Carlota, which is even worse. I saw you gave her the drinks and the canapé almost with your back turned, but it wasn't necessary. Your characterization was fantastic. I didn't even recognize you myself, even though I knew it was you."

"Even so, I preferred to be as far away from her as possible and not talk in her presence. What do we do now?"

"Let's see the recordings and label the bags containing the individual glasses for each of the guests."

Richie went to the pantry and pulled out a computer. He had hidden three cameras in different positions in the room in order to have clear images of all the guests and to be able to identify the glasses that each of them had used. They watched the videos, saw the pictures he had taken before picking up anything, and labeled the individual bags with their respective names with a marker."

"Now extract the fingerprints of each person. I also want a complete DNA analysis. When you have everything, send it on to me."

"You know that the tests are going to cost time and money."

"Don't worry about the money and about the time, do it with the greatest possible urgency. Once you give me the results, I will check them against the official databases."

"And why don't you send the tests to be done at the Scientific Police? You would save yourself some good money."

"It isn't ethical. It's a personal matter, not a professional one. I already feel quite uncomfortable accessing the official databases. You know that everything leaves a computer trace, and I could have to give explanations I don't have. I shouldn't do it either, but at least that doesn't cost the taxpayer money. It is a venial sin."

"What are you hoping to find out that you don't already know?"

"My niece has always suspected she was being watched in the newspaper. She eventually had documentation disappearing. The papers that she was keeping in her drawer appeared to be disorganized from one day to the next and she wasn't keeping anything important, but of course, the spy didn't know that. She was worried, so she decided to put a rudimentary trap for the nosy person by means of strips of cellophane attached to her folders. The ploy worked, and she gave them to me to extract the fingerprints."

"And who was the spy?"

"I got two fingerprints, but one of them was incomplete, and the system wasn't able to identify it."

"And the other?"

"That was the strangest thing of all. When I gave her the name of the person, it turned out that they didn't work at the newspaper. Rebecca didn't know them at all. It's something unusual."

"That's strange."

"There are only two possible explanations for that mystery, and I don't know which one worries me the most."

"What are the two options?"

"The first one is obvious. Someone from inside the newspaper regularly facilitates access to a stranger. It's not possible that someone outside the staff can enter on a regular basis if they aren't receiving help from the inside."

"I agree, and the second one?"

Tote stared at Richie, worried.

"That's what I expect to find out with this scene I did today. I have a hunch that doesn't allow me to sleep. If it's confirmed, that would mean problems."

55 JANUARY 3rd, 1523

"Was it all a plan for you to land in England? And why didn't you ask me directly?" Luis Vives asked, surprised, who didn't come out of his astonishment.

"I did it the last time we met, a little over a year ago in Bruges. By the way, in the presence of your King Charles," Cardinal Wosley replied.

"But that wasn't a formal offer; it was simply an invitation to visit your country. It was also part of a quite carefree conversation between friends quiet," Luis said. "I didn't take it seriously."

"That was the impression you got from our offer?" Thomas More asked.

"The truth is that I did. I have just accepted the chair left vacant by Antonio de Nebrija at the University of Alcalá de Henares in Spain. As soon as the storm lifts, I will continue the trip to Santander."

Both Thomas Wosley and Thomas More looked at the speaker with a mixture of affection and indulgence.

"Listen, Luis, the destination of the ship you took in Antwerp has never been Santander but Dover. You have reached your final destination," the cardinal said.

Luis made didn't understand anything.

"This ship was never going to reach Spain? But they are waiting for me there!" He protested.

"The only ones waiting for you in Spain are the bloodthirsty members of the Inquisition of your country, with the bonfire ready to burn you," Thomas More answered.

"I have given my word, and a letter of acceptance from me will have already reached the university through a mail I sent by land."

"It will not; we've already taken care of it. That letter hasn't arrived, nor will it ever reach its destination."

Luis was amazed. He didn't quite understand the conversation. He felt out of his element.

"And what do you want from me?"

"The first thing to save you from the fury of the Holy Office against your family. Believe it or not, you have very powerful friends in Spain who don't want you to come back for your own safety. Secondly, on behalf of our King Henry VIII, we offer you a professorship at the prestigious Oxford University, but above all, a quiet environment where you can 'learn and teach,' which you have always wanted, plus you can continue to write with total freedom," Thomas More said, "you already know us."

Luis remained silent, looking at his illustrious companions.

"Do I have a choice?"

"Of course, you do," Wosley said. "This isn't a kidnapping. If your wish is to return to Spain, we will charter a boat so that you can return to your country. We will guarantee your safety during the journey, although we will not be able to do so once you have disembarked in your country."

Luis was thoughtful. Everything was happening too fast, and now he had a decision to make that affected his immediate future. Wosley tried it again.

"Think about it, Luis. How did you get to Dover? Who has organized the trip for you? Who has been one of your best friends? Who has watched over you in recent months and supported you financially? Well, thanks to him, you are in England and not in Spain. He has always wanted the best for you. Think why. You know perfectly well who he really is."

Now Luis went pale. He understood everything. Not even his notable friend trusted the Inquisition to leave him alone. Considering who he really was, he had to take his opinion very seriously.

"If you know so much about me, you will know my financial difficulties. I need to send money to my family in a discreet way. You already know that my father is being processed by the Inquisition and all his assets have been seized, including the family home. My sisters are going through a lot of financial problems. That was the main reason for my return to my country, to help my family."

"Don't worry about that; we are perfectly informed about it. Unfortunately, we can't interfere in the inquisitorial processes of the Holy Office in Spain, but we can in everything else. If you decide to stay with us, we will advance your college fees and that funds will be received by your sisters Beatriz and Leonor, so they can keep their home and furniture," Wosley said. "Everything has been agreed upon and prepared for a few months. Only your will is missing."

Luis was a little scared. They knew all the details of his life, and that could only come from Spain. He realized that his great friend had made some kind of pact with Wosley without saying anything to him for fear that he might reject him. He was sure he had done it for his sake. He surely was handling inside information, given who he really was.

He was tormented by not being able to do anything for his father, but that was out of his hands even if he was in Spain. However, if he accepted the cardinal's offer, he could help his sisters immediately, and that, right now, might be the most important thing within reach.

"Is the weather on the islands as bad as they say?" Luis asked.

56 NOWADAYS. SUNDAY, SEPTEMBER 9th

The next time we meet, I'll kill you, Rebecca read on her cell phone. It was from her friend Carlota. She laughed to herself in her room. It was ten in the morning, and her message had been sent at seven-thirty. It was clear that the firecracker had not slept much.

Why exactly? Because of the meeting in tights at my house with all the newspaper's staff? Rebecca replied.

She went to the bathroom and took a shower. Today she wanted to go running again, but this time by herself.

On the way back from the bathroom, she found Carlota's reply on her cellphone, *What have you done to my body? I can't move; it has rebelled against me and refuses to obey me.* Rebecca laughed again, thinking about her friend.

She put on her sports clothes and went out to the riverbed. Today it was her turn to go fast after yesterday's light training. She spent a couple of hours running at a good pace and she returned home. She went into the kitchen and met her aunt, who was preparing food.

"Umm, that smells good!" Rebecca said. "What are you cooking?"

"Grandmother's cannelloni," Tote replied.

Rebecca immediately remembered Joanna, her aunt's ex-partner, her ex-history professor, her ex-twelfth door, and her ex-guardian. Many 'exes' and a lot of pain. The wounds that her departure caused weren't yet healed. She was surprised that her aunt decided to cook Joanna's characteristic dish. It didn't seem normal to her.

"Have you dared to cook Joanna's cannelloni? I didn't even know you knew the recipe."

"And I don't know it, but I saw her doing them so many times that I've tried it. I apologize in advance. I don't guarantee a good result."

On second thought, Rebecca was delighted deep down inside her. The fact that her aunt was cooking cannelloni meant that she was beginning to overcome Joanna's departure.

"If they taste the way they smell, the success is guaranteed," Rebecca said.

Tote hadn't chosen that food by chance. She didn't want to remember Joanna at all, her emotional injury was recent, but she didn't want to talk about yesterday's party with her niece's work colleagues. She told herself that, by cooking cannelloni, she would have Rebecca thinking about Joanna, at least for a while, and would be a topic of conversation. *Right now, I prefer pain to inquisitive questions,* Tote told herself as encouragement.

So it was. The cannelloni were more than acceptable, even though it was the first time she had cooked them. The proof was that they left the plates empty.

"Do you know anything about Joanna?" Rebecca asked at last.

"No. When she said goodbye, she told me that she would be two months without communicating. I suppose that she will also want to heal her wounds. I look forward to hearing from her in the next few days. She made that commitment with me."

"She said something similar to me too, though more enigmatic."

"Enigmatic? What did she say?"

"She didn't actually say anything to me. She told me that she had something important to tell me but that it could wait until September. The truth is that she left me very intrigued."

"How curious! She didn't mention any of that to me."

"More than curious, it's strange," Rebecca reflected. She remembered that it was a somewhat unusual farewell. Saying that you have something important to tell and, at the same time, commenting that there is no rush to talk about it... the truth was that it didn't make much sense. It seemed like a contradiction in its highest form.

Well, it's September already. I guess it won't be too long to be sure, Rebecca thought.

She didn't have to wait as much as she thought, and in a way, she couldn't even imagine.

57 JANUARY 15ᵗʰ, 1523

"And you have no father or mother?" Batiste asked.

"I suppose so, but I only know my father," Jerónimo replied.

"Didn't you live with them in Seville?"

"No, I lived in a convent."

"And your father also lived in that convent?"

"No, he went to see me once a week."

Batiste was amazed by Jerónimo, his deskmate. Despite being a child and leading a completely unstructured family life, he was puzzled by his serene intelligence.

At first, he was angry with Mr. Urraca, his teacher, because he didn't understand why he put such a young boy as a table companion at school, but now he understood it. It reminded him of himself when he was seven or eight years old. It's true that Jerónimo was a bit phony. For example, when he claimed that he lived in the Royal Palace, Batiste supposed it was a way of taking refuge from his problems in an imaginary world. He didn't blame him for it. He hadn't brought up that topic again, either. For what reason? He wanted to say that because Batiste didn't care.

"And who is your father?" Batiste, who was genuinely curious about the boy, kept asking.

"He's a very important person in Seville, one of those who have the most power."

"What is his name?"

"Alonso."

"Alonso, what else?"

"I don't know."

"You don't know your father's full name?"

"Everyone in the convent called him Don Alonso, with great respect."

"If they called him that, he is an important noble. What lands and possessions does he have?"

"I don't know. He has never told me what his title is, if he has it."

"You don't really know anything about your family," Batiste said.

As soon as he finished the sentence, he regretted saying those words.

Jerónimo began to sob, his hands on his face.

"I didn't mean to offend you," Batiste tried to console him in vain. "I'm really sorry."

Jerónimo was disconsolate.

"Do you know what the hardest thing in my life is? When you finish school, you go home and have dinner as a family with your father and mother. In Seville, I had to go alone to the convent and I also had dinner alone in my little cell. I have never known what a family is. I have never lacked anything and I know that I'm receiving a good education, but nobody cares about me. Nobody asks me how I am or how I feel. People assume that I should be happy because I don't lack anything. Sometimes I would rather be a beggar because they are with their parents, even if they have nothing to eat and live off charity by sleeping in the streets. At least they are a family. Surely, they are happier than me. I'm alone in this world."

Batiste didn't know what to say to that emotional stream. That child managed to disarm him with his sensitivity. He tried to change the subject. He didn't have answers to all those questions.

"Forgive my silence, but I don't know what to say to you," Batiste answered honestly.

"Don't worry. I just thought out loud," Jero said. "Maybe I shouldn't have done it, but I don't have anyone to talk to, and sometimes it helps to vent."

"Why have you come to Valencia?" Batiste asked, changing the subject.

"I don't know either. One day in May, my father visited me, and he told me that I had to move to Valencia."

"And he didn't tell you why?"

"No, he never explains anything to me or asks for my opinion on any matter. After all, I'm just a brat turning seven tomorrow."

"So, you haven't heard from your father for a long time?"

"The last time I saw him was in September. He has only come to Valencia twice."

"I'm sorry," Batiste muttered, not being sure about what to say.

"At least in Seville, he visited me every week. I suppose that his residence will be there, and it should not be so easy for him to travel to Valencia to see me. What I don't understand is what I'm doing here."

"Well, you are coming to our house to eat tomorrow, and we will celebrate your seventh birthday. I don't have a mother either, she died a long time ago, but you will eat in the company of my father and me. We aren't your family, but I assure you that you will feel good."

Jerónimo just smiled, grateful.

58 NOWADAYS. MONDAY, SEPTEMBER 10th

"I don't understand. Then, does the Count of Ruzafa's choker exist or not?" a voice asked.

The spy from the Speaker's Club was meeting with the person who controlled them.

"At first, we thought it was a fake clue since Carlota explained to us that the current manager of the jewelry store didn't know Rebecca's detective friend at all, nor had he given him any photographs."

"Then it doesn't exist, and the message is false."

"No, wait, then Rebecca showed us that, in fact, the detective had interviewed the founder of the jewelry, Sergio, the father of the current manager, in his own artisan workshop. That is why his son Álvaro didn't know the detective at all because he had not visited him at the jewelry store."

"What a mess! So, does the choker really exist?"

"It seems so. It's authentic, including the message."

"This matter is getting more and more complicated."

"Of course. Tomorrow, Tuesday, we will have a regular meeting of the Speaker's Club, now with the new member, Álvaro Enguix, who's the manager of the jewelry store, incorporated full-fledged. The initiation ceremony was on Friday."

"Have you invited him to join? Without knowing him?"

"Yes, Carlota proposed it, and we all agreed."

They were silent for a moment.

"You're doing a good job. Keep reporting to me, and only to me. Remember that these meetings have never happened."

"Don't worry."

"Actually, I do get worried. This thing about the jeweler gives me a bad feeling. I don't know why."

"In what do you base on?"

"There are so many people in that club of yours, and has no one ever thought of asking the most important question of all?"

"I don't know what you mean."

"Well, I think it's very clear."

"What is that question?"

"If the choker actually exists, where the hell is it? Have any of you seen it?"

59 JANUARY 16th, 1523

"Father, this is Jerónimo. He's my table partner at school."

"My name is Johan Corbera. Nice to meet you."

"Thank you very much for inviting me to lunch on my birthday; you have been very kind."

"You know what? You're very polite for only being seven years old," Johan said, surprised by the boy's manners.

"That's the only good thing about my life, manners," he answered with a certain melancholy.

"Batiste has already told me that you are from Seville."

"I've lived there since I can remember. I don't really know where I was born. No one has deigned to tell me."

"Well, then you're from Seville," Johan said, trying to give a more pleasant tone to that conversation. "They are good people."

"Yes, I'm from Seville," Jerónimo said, smiling. It was unusual to see him laugh.

They sat around the table. Today they had prepared a special meal. They usually ate a pot of vegetables and similar foods, but in honor of the guest, Johan had baked lamb. He even took out the cutlery, which they had barely used three or four times when some illustrious guest visited them.

"The lamb is delicious, Mister Corbera," Jerónimo said.

Johan gazed at the child, captivated. It was a lot of manners and knowing how to behave for only being seven years old. What surprised him the most were his manners at the table. He knew how to use a knife and fork like a nobleman. He did it with an unusual naturalness.

"Don't call me Mr. Corbera. Johan is enough."

"Thanks, Johan," Jerónimo replied.

"Batiste told me that he's very happy that you sit next to him at school."

"Oh! Really? Jerónimo asked incredulously.

"Why do you doubt it?" Batiste said.

"Because it's unusual. I'm almost always partnered with someone older than me. They tend to despise me or hit me, which is worse."

"I've never done that," Batiste protested.

"No, but you thought I was a shrimp on the first day of school. That offended me very much," Jerónimo said indignantly. "When I remember it, it still hurts. It is something that I have rooted in my heart."

"I told you I was sorry, but you have to consider that it was normal. I was expecting a partner of my age," Batiste tried to excuse himself.

Jerónimo smiled again.

"It was a joke, silly. You're the only one who has always treated me with respect. You're very kind to me and I really appreciate it. You are the best partner I have ever had."

"I believed it," Batiste said, laughing, while he pretended to hit him on the head.

Suddenly, they heard a knock on the door.

"Excuse me, they're knocking; I'll be right back," Johan said, rising from the table.

"Now that your father is gone, I must tell you something surprising," Jerónimo said with a very mysterious tone.

"Come on, you're taking too long," Batiste said, feigning false interest.

"I've heard your father's name before."

"And that seems a surprise to you? Many people have heard of him, he's the master stonemason of the city, and he works or has worked on all the important buildings that have been built, including, for example, La Lonja."

"I haven't heard it in Valencia."

"Oh! No? And where it was?"

"In Seville, my father talked about him. They know each other, they are friends. Our parents are colleagues."

At that precise moment, Johan entered, his face completely contorted.

Horror and anger.

60 NOWADAYS. MONDAY, SEPTEMBER 10ᵗʰ

Rebecca woke up refreshed. She had slept well, after the strange weekend, with an unexpected party at her house included. Yesterday, she didn't bring up the subject to her aunt since they were talking about Joanna, and she didn't consider it appropriate, but she still had the feeling that the party was a whole sham. What she couldn't understand was why. Why gather all her colleagues from the newspaper? That made no apparent sense.

She had a message from Carlota on her cellphone. *Did you guess what the Kinder surprise egg was?* She hadn't even remembered that kind of riddle her friend proposed to her as she said goodbye at Saturday's party. *I'm not going to reply,* she thought. *She will tell me when she feels like it.* Overall, she hadn't thought about it and, consequently, she had nothing to say to her.

She went out to the kitchen. It was deserted. Her aunt must have gone to work. She drank her usual glass of fresh milk, got on her bike, and headed to *La Crónica*, like every morning.

She entered the editorial department. She glanced at Alba, who was sitting behind the counter, with her usual grim face. She didn't even say good morning to her. *It seems that her pretended sympathy on Saturday was a mirage*, Rebecca thought, remembering the pleasant time they had spent on the terrace of her house on Saturday afternoon. She came to her table.

"I had a great time at your house!" Tere said as soon as she saw her.

"Well, I was somewhat embarrassed, dressed in that outfit," Rebecca replied.

"What are you talking about! If everything looks great on you, including sports tights. I wish it was the same for me! Did you forget about the party?"

"No, what happened is that I got confused and was running late," Rebecca lied as best she could.

"You know what? I took advantage of the meeting at your house to speak with Fabio. It's true; he doesn't have a partner. We're meeting tomorrow after work to go out for a drink," Tere said, completely excited.

"The two of you alone or one of those afterworkings?"

"The two of us, without any company."

"I'm so happy! It seems that, in the end, you are going to eat the chocolate."

"Don't say that. It makes me laugh!"

Rebecca opened her chest of drawers, and her facial expression changed immediately. Tere noticed her friend's expression."

"What's wrong, Rebecca? Are you okay?"

"No," she answered very seriously. "Someone has been rummaging through my papers."

"Again? I remember you already told me a few months ago."

"Before summer, all the folders in my chest of drawers even disappeared one day. I asked editor Fornell and he told me that he had no idea what I was talking about. He seemed sincere."

"We all know that he likes to fiddle between the papers, although he always denies it. He usually does it with those responsible of events because he loves them and he is a bit nosy. The strange thing is that he would rummage through your notes, which don't seem to interest him at all."

"That's what I thought," Rebecca replied as she took out all the folders and spread them out on the table. She extracted all its contents from inside.

"What are you doing?" Tere asked.

"They haven't only looked at my notes and my documents, they have also taken them out of each of the folders. They're disorganized. I never leave it like that. It wasn't a mere glance. The person who did it spent a lot of time spying."

"But that's very difficult. There are always people in the editorial department..." Tere began, suddenly interrupting her sentence. "Wait, wait! On Saturday afternoon, we were all at your house, at the celebration organized by your aunt. Only Carmen, Herminia, and María Jesús stayed in the editorial department, and they rarely leave their offices. This room was empty for at least three hours."

Rebecca stared at Tere. She was right, it was the most appropriate time to peek at her table, but all possible suspects were at her home. She remembered the fingerprint she took and the identification her aunt had made. It didn't correspond to any worker at *La Crónica*."

"The moment could have been superb, but who from outside the newspaper could be interested in my notes? They don't matter!"

"Well, it's clear that for someone, they do," Tere said.

61 JANUARY 16th, 1523

"The mysterious person did it again!" Johan exclaimed, completely out of his mind. "They have tricked us again!" He said as he sat down at the table again with his son and his guest from school, Jerónimo.

"What happened?" Batiste asked.

"Luis Vives is in England right now!" Johan shouted.

"In England? And what is he doing there? Didn't the noble Don Bertrán go to Leuven to personally organize his return trip to Spain?" Batiste asked, surprised.

"And he did. Don Bertrán decided that it was safer to travel by sea since France and Spain are currently at war, and the trip by land involved many risks. He was right about that. He had promised me that he would do everything possible to protect him, so he bought tickets on a merchant ship that was leaving Antwerp and was due to reach Santander. Apparently, a strong storm diverted them to Dover, where it docked to protect themselves from inclement weather."

Batiste looked incredulous.

"And where is the intervention of the mysterious person? I don't see it. Everything you are saying is normal. When there is a gale, the ships usually take refuge in the nearest port and then continue their journey when the sea is calmer."

"I haven't finished my story. Do you know what happened when the ship docked in Dover?"

"No, how am I supposed to know?"

"It was a rhetorical question. The Cardinal and Archbishop of York, Monsignor Thomas Wosley, was in the harbor, waiting for him."

"Wosley! He already knew that Luis Vives was going to get to Dover in advance!" Batiste exclaimed, who now understood the indignation of his father.

"Exactly! Before leaving Antwerp, the cardinal must have already known that the ship's destination was England, not Spain."

"And what did Don Bertrán say when he noticed that they were in England with Wosley in front of them?" Batiste asked curiously.

"That's the strange part of the matter. Don Bertrán wasn't on the boat."

"I don't understand. Didn't you tell me that he would accompany him to Spain with all his entourage and personal guard for the greater security of Luis Vives?"

"That's what he said, but apparently, he left Leuven to return to Spain by land a few weeks before the ship left Antwerp."

"By land? Didn't he say it was dangerous due to the war?"

"And it was. Don Bertrán was right."

"Don't defend him! I already told you! From the beginning, I had the feeling that this nobleman wasn't what he claimed to be. He's certainly mysterious. He must have arranged everything, according to Wosley. Right now, he must be laughing at our innocence," Batiste said indignantly.

"I highly doubt it," Johan replied.

"Why do you insist on defending him? I understand that he's a friend of yours, but the evidence is overwhelming."

"What I said is that I doubt very much that he is laughing at us right now,"

"How can you be sure?" Batiste asked incredulously.

"Trust me, I know it for sure. When he left Flanders, something happened which you don't know. Besides, I don't think Don Bertrán was a mysterious person. If it was him, he would have accompanied Luis to England, and he wouldn't have risked crossing France in the middle of the war. It makes no sense. If it wasn't safe for Luis, it shouldn't be safe for him either," Johan explained. "He took too many risks. If he had been working with Wosley, he could have arranged a safe boat trip for him without taking any risks. England has great maritime power. It can't be; it doesn't have any logic."

Batiste was left thinking about what his father had just said. He was possibly right, but he always had a strange feeling about Don Bertrán. He gave him the impression that there was some deception with this man.

Meanwhile, Jerónimo had listened to the entire conversation in silence, hardly understanding anything. *I have to tell Batiste something when we are alone. I don't know if it will be important, but now is not the right time*, Jerónimo thought, seeing how upset his hosts were.

62 NOWADAYS. MONDAY, SEPTEMBER 10th

Rebecca put all her notes back into the folders. That was frankly strange. She didn't understand who could be interested in her documents that had no value, besides someone outside the newspaper staff.

She looked up and saw Alba approaching her table. She already knew what she was going to say to her, although this time, strangely, she didn't yell over all of her colleagues. She came up to her side.

"Rebecca, the editor wants to see you in his office," she said in her customary impersonal tone. "It's important."

Rebecca walked, once again, to Bernat Fornell's office. She knocked on the door, waited for the editor's reply, and entered. There were two people sitting in the chairs across from Fornell.

"Hi Rebecca, go ahead. I present to you Javi Escharche and Mar Maluenda. They are the presenters of the radio program that has launched you to fame."

She was astonished.

Rebecca knew them. Well, not them personally, but their show. Every morning they went on air with their *Buenos días* show. She had no idea that it was on that show that her recordings had been aired. Now her nomination for the Ondas Award had a better explanation. It was one of the most listened to in its time slot in all of Spain, and it had a very loyal and large audience.

"It's a pleasure to meet you. I love your show," Rebecca said, still impressed.

"It's not our program; it's your program, too," Javi answered while he got up to give her two kisses on her cheeks.

"The real pleasure is ours," Mar said, also greeting her.

"You are going to excuse me; I'm a bit excited." Don't take it the wrong way, but I had no idea that the program on which my recordings had been broadcasted was yours. I hear you whenever I can."

"You are the one who has to excuse us. We should have gone to your house party on Saturday, but the radio station sent us at the last minute to a promotional event in a shopping mall and it got too late," Mar said.

Luckily, they didn't come. I would have died of shame if they saw me with sports tights and kind of sweaty, Rebecca thought, relieved.

"But, don't you broadcast from Madrid?" She asked, surprised.

"Yes, but this morning we did the program from the studio in Valencia. Now that we've just finished, we stopped by to meet you and talk to you," Javi said. "As soon as we finish, we will take the AVE bullet train and return to Madrid."

Rebecca was overwhelmed by the attention she was receiving. That seemed too much to her, and she hadn't yet heard everything.

"We want you to come to our main studios, so we can introduce you to the rest of the team. They're already looking forward to meeting you," Javi said.

"Sure, I'd be delighted," Rebecca said, who was on cloud nine, "but editor Fornell will have to give me permission."

"That's already set up. Before you arrived, we already convinced him to borrow you for a couple of days," Mar said, winking at her.

"Of course, Rebecca, you have my permission," the editor confirmed. "We will arrange it as soon as possible."

"Now, we must go. We have little more than an hour to take the AVE. It has been a real pleasure. See you in Madrid," Javi said while he got up from the chair, giving her another two kisses. Mar even gave her a little hug.

As they walked out the door, Editor Fornell addressed Rebecca.

"Come on, shut that mouth. Flies are going to get inside."

Rebecca was stunned.

"Does that radio station belongs to *La Crónica*'s group?" She asked, confused. "But it's so important! Don't you always say that we are a very modest communication group?"

"It doesn't really belong to us, but our radio stations are associated with it and broadcast much of its programming, so you could also say that it does," Fornell replied. "Think that our modest radio station belongs to a larger group."

Rebecca left the editor's office and returned to her desk. She was on cloud nine. She received a message on her cellphone. She looked at the screen; it was from Carlota. *How annoying is she with that damn Kinder surprise egg!* She thought. *Let's see if she tells me once for all and leaves me alone. I don't feel like thinking.*

She opened the message. What she read took her down to earth immediately.

She answered right away, with tears in her eyes.

63 MARCH 3ʳᵈ, 1524

"Children, I present to you Amador. He is joining the school today," Professor Pere Urraca said, addressing the rest of the students.

They all welcomed him. Batiste thought that he should be the same age as him, although he was shorter and thinner than he. He sat at the table right behind Jerónimo. He seemed very shy.

When they went out to the schoolyard, they saw him sitting alone. No one came to greet him or chat with him.

"Jero, let's talk to the new one," Batiste said.

More than a year had passed since Jerónimo's incorporation into the school, and now Batiste addressed his young friend by the diminutive of Jero. He didn't seem to care. Actually, he didn't seem to care at all.

They approached and greeted him.

"Hi, Amador. I'm Batiste."

"And I'm Jerónimo, although Jero it's fine. Everyone ended up calling me like that."

"Hello to both of you. I'm Amador."

"Why isn't anyone coming to play or talk to you?" Jero asked him.

"You don't know who I am?" Amador answered with another question.

"The truth is we don't. Why should we know?"

"I'm Amador de Aliaga, from the Aliaga and Medina family."

Batiste and Jero stared at each other.

"Are we supposed to know you or your family?" Batiste asked, puzzled.

"Everyone else does; that's why they don't come near me."

"Well, we have no idea who you are or who your family is," Batiste said.

"My uncle is named after me, Amador de Aliaga, and my father is Cristóbal de Medina y Aliaga."

Batiste and Jero continued with confused expressions regarding what he was telling them.

"Well, greetings to your family. Who are they?" Batiste asked.

"My uncle is the current recipient of the Holy Office's goods, and in a few months, my father, Cristóbal de Medina, will take the position, replacing my uncle," Amador said at last.

Now Batiste understood, although Jero continued with the same expression of not understanding anything.

"Of course, that's why they avoid you. You are the ones who keep the goods of those accused by the Inquisition."

"We don't keep the goods; that's what people think about us. We're simply the tax collectors, always under the king's orders," Amador replied with an offended tone.

"And why are they going to relieve your uncle and appoint your father to the position?" Jero asked.

"Well, we just meet each other and you seem a bit insolent," Amador said, still offended.

"Excuse us; we didn't mean to bother you. If we make you uncomfortable, we will leave," Batiste said.

"No, no. You're the only ones who have come to talk to me. Forgive my rudeness, I thank you for your attention, but to answer that question, I must give you some rather boring explanations," Amador said.

"It surely is more entertaining than listening to Professor Urraca," Jero said.

"I have warned you. Now you will have to listen to me for a while," Amador insisted.

"Go ahead; we're ready," Batiste said.

"I quite doubt it, but hey, you guys wanted it."

64 NOWADAYS. MONDAY, SEPTEMBER 10th

"Carlota, mother is calling you to her room," her sister Rocío told her.

"Is something wrong?" She asked uneasily.

"No, she just told me to let you know. She looks like she wants to talk to you alone."

Carlota hurried up the stairs and into her mother's room.

"How are you, mom? Rocío told me that you wanted to talk to me."

"Come on, grab a chair, and sit next to me."

Carlota listened to her mother and sat down next to her, next to the bed.

"You know I'm dying. I have very little time left with you in this world."

"That's what you've been saying for over a year, and here you are, talking to me right now, as always."

"Not as always. This morning Don Ricardo Tur came."

"I know, your oncologist. He has also spoken with us. He has already told us that there is no noticeable change in your state of health."

"That's what I asked him to tell you. Unfortunately, the truth is a bit different."

"What are you talking about?" Carlota asked, alarmed.

"I have twenty-four hours to live at the most. Even though you see me fine now, they gave me a good dose of painkillers. I will probably lose consciousness before night and no longer wake up. This dropper that I have by my side is going to leave me sedated little by little," she said while she pointed at it. "That's how I'm going to spend my last hours. Before that happens, I want to say goodbye to you."

Now, Carlota couldn't help the tears in her eyes.

"Why are you telling this only to me? The whole family should be here, by your side, listening to your words."

"There will be a chance later for that. First, I must talk to you. We have a pending conversation since a long time ago. I shouldn't have left it to the last minute, and maybe it's too late."

Carlota was confused.

"I don't know what you mean, mom. I don't understand you."

"First of all, go to the cabinet. Open the first drawer and find a double bottom. It is easy to open; press on the back and the lid will lift. Inside is an old leather wallet. Bring it to me."

Carlota was amazed, but she obeyed her mother without asking the meaning of it all. She followed her instructions and found a very shabby wallet. You could tell it was used a lot. She gave it to her mother.

"You know? This wallet belonged to your father."

"You've never shown it to me."

"Neither you nor anyone else, but the time has come for you to know certain things that you don't know about your family."

Carlota was lost. She didn't understand anything. She was silent, waiting for her mother to continue the conversation, while she watched as she opened the wallet and extracted some kind of book in very bad condition.

"First, this book belongs to you. It belonged to your father, and his will was that you inherited it when I died," she said as she handed it over to Carlota.

What does this mean? It was a very large book. It looked very old, at least three or four centuries old. It was stitched.

"Now I'm going to ask you for an important thing. Let me speak without interrupting until I finish the story I'm going to tell you. I know you will have many questions as you listen to me. You keep them. I will try to answer them in the end, whatever I am capable of."

"Go ahead," Carlota said, who was absolutely stunned.

Her mother began to speak. That story she was hearing was completely surreal. She thought for a moment that her mother wasn't lucid, that the strong painkillers they had administered were working on her. She didn't know if she should interrupt her story or not.

She stared into her eyes and knew in her heart that it was all true.

When she finished, they both began to cry while hugging. She had never suspected anything of all this. Of course, her mother had kept her secret very well throughout her life.

"Don't tell anyone what you just heard, not even your siblings. I don't want them to know anything; it's unnecessary. After my death, I want you to have the same good relationship as now. Nothing must change. Now call them and let them come up. Remember the most important of all, join what's separate," her mother said in a small voice. She closed her eyes. She ended the conversation with a phrase, barely audible, something like drinking wine. It was clear that the painkillers were working on her quickly. Her mother had always been very fond of good wines, but she certainly did not plan to bring her a glass now, even if it was her last wish.

Given her condition, she didn't dare to ask her anything about the conversation, despite the fact that she had a thousand questions and doubts in her head. She didn't know what some phrases she had heard meant; she would have time after her death to think about it.

She left the room shattered and watery-eyed. When her brother and her sister saw her, they already imagined that something very bad was happening.

"Come on, come upstairs to see mom before her flame goes out forever," she managed to tell them as they hurried into her room.

Those were the last words she heard from her mother's mouth.

65   MARCH 3rd, 1524

Batiste and Jero stared at Amador, waiting for him to begin his explanation.

"Well, as you wish, I've already warned you. The inquisition is like a company or any business. It has sources of income and a series of expenses. In the end, it makes its balance and has to generate profits."

"Well, it's a way of putting it, like any other business..." Batiste began. "Businesses aren't used to burning their customers."

"I mean from an economic point of view."

"I wouldn't think of looking at the Inquisition from that point of view," Batiste insisted.

"I'll give you a quick summary so you don't get tired. The income of each one of the courts of the Holy Office comes fundamentally from four concepts. The first is the so-called penalties or fines so that you have it clearer. In the beginning, when the Grand Inquisitor was Fray Luis de Torquemada, they were sometimes collective."

"Collective fines?" Jero asked, not understanding the concept.

"Yes. For example, at the beginning of the Inquisition, in 1491, the Jews negotiated with Torquemada the payment of five thousand ducats in exchange for the exemption of the hypothetical heretical acts committed."

"Funny," Jero said. "Preventive sanctions, just in case they were bad..."

"Yes. something like that."

"Come on, continue," Batiste said.

"The second method of income is the so-called certificates or authorizations."

"And what is that? Do they give you permission for something?" Batiste asked.

"No, they actually give it back to you," Amador replied. "Take into account that many verdicts are accompanied by denying you the exercise of certain jobs. People pay to be reinstated in their jobs. It is often simply honorary."

"Now I understand," Batiste said.

"The third way of income is the withdrawal of habits and *sanbenitos*."

"What does that mean?" Jero asked immediately.

"The habits or *sanbenitos* are a kind of garment, generally woolen sacks with symbols drawn, that the convicted must wear, sometimes even with corozas, which are a kind of caps or hoods. They are a form of public humiliation; people know that those who wear them have been convicted by the Holy Office. It is a way of showing shame."

"And people pay not to wear them?" Jero continued.

"Exactly. You give a certain amount, depending on the crime committed and the person, and they redeem you from that penance."

"So, everything is arranged with money," Jero said.

"Like everything in this life," Amador replied. "And I have saved for last the most important source of income for the Inquisition."

"Which is?" Batiste and Jero asked in unison.

"The seizure of property. The arrest of a defendant with solid evidence of heresy entailed the preventive sequestration of all their property. An exhaustive inventory of assets was made by the so-called sequestration notary, and then they were made available to the recipient of the assets, that is, my uncle and soon will be my father."

"Now I understand why you don't have many friends. What a disgusting job," Batiste said.

"Hey! There are even worse."

"I don't doubt it."

"But you still haven't answered my question. Why are they going to relieve your uncle and appoint your father?" Jero asked.

Amador stared at him.

"I have already told you that the Inquisition is like a company, it has incomes and expenses, and in the end, it makes a profit. If the income falls, the person in charge of obtaining them is removed, and another one is appointed. Well, that's what happened. The receiver of goods is responsible for the income, and they have decreased significantly, so they have decided to appoint a new one, in this case, my father," Amador explained.

"And why has the income dropped?" Jero kept asking.

"You know what? You are a very curious child. The answer is simple; the Inquisition is running out of clients," Amador replied.

"Of course, you've already burned most of the Jews. You're the only company in the world that is running out of customers because it kills them. Now you'll have to start with the Moors," Batiste said. "Until they run out too."

"Something like that, there are fewer and fewer heretics left, and consequently, the Inquisition receives less income," Amador replied. "However, their expenses don't stop growing because their structures are increasing."

"It's curious to hear about the Inquisition in these terms as if it was just any business," Batiste said.

"It really is. Do you know that sometimes their employees get paid badly and late because there is no money?" Amador asked. "I tell you with knowledge of the facts."

"If you want me to pity you, you're not succeeding," Batiste replied.

"By the way, Jero, your face looks familiar. Haven't we met before?" Amador asked, who had been looking at his face for a while. "You remind me of someone."

"I don't think so. Have you ever traveled to Seville?"

"Never."

"Then I doubt we have met. I have lived in Seville since I can remember, until the beginning of last year when I came to Valencia. I've never seen you."

"Well, your face sounds familiar to me," Amador insisted.

It was so familiar to him and he couldn't even imagine why.

66 NOWADAYS. TUESDAY, SEPTEMBER 11th

Carlota's mother passed away on the night from Monday to Tuesday, just as she herself had announced. Obviously, they called off the Speaker's Club meeting, and they all stayed to pay a visit to their friend at the funeral home that afternoon. Rebecca asked for the morning off in the newspaper and went to visit her friend at her house, along with Almu, who wanted to accompany her.

Although everyone expected it, her passing had caused a deep shock in the family. They were all very disturbed.

"I'm so sorry, Carlota," Rebecca said, giving her friend a big hug. "When I read your message, the world fell apart upon me."

"Something like this always hurts, even if you are expecting it," Carlota said while she hugged her friend Almu.

"How are your siblings?" she asked.

"Worse than me. The truth is that I haven't finished reacting. I still can't believe it. The last few days have been especially intense."

At that moment, Carlota's siblings entered the room. They all melted into a hug without saying a word between them.

"If you need anything, you just have to ask for it," Rebecca said, "you know I mean it."

"Thank you very much, Rebecca and Almu. We really appreciate you coming home. In a while, we will go to the funeral home," Rocío said, "as the funeral home has informed us."

"I don't like those impersonal places like the funeral homes and even less the cemeteries; I prefer to go to a private home," Rebecca continued. "You will excuse me and Almu's absence. My aunt Tote will visit you this afternoon."

"Don't worry," Rocío said. "We already know that you are here for us. In fact, you always have been all these years."

As soon as Rocío was silent, Carlota took Rebecca's arm and led her aside.

"When this is all over, I have to talk to you. Believe me; it's very important. What am I saying! More than important, it's amazing."

Rebecca stared at her friend. She had a very strange expression; it wasn't pain what she saw in her eyes. It was more of a mix of fear and surprise. *Is she still insisting on the Kinder surprise egg?* She thought. *Not even the death of her mother is able to stop the frenzy of her brain.*

"Now, focus on what you have to do, and there will be time to talk about whatever that is later," Rebecca replied.

There is something else besides the death of her mother that worries her, she told herself. In fact, it seemed to her that her head was elsewhere.

67 APRIL 4ᵗʰ, 1524

Batiste, Jero, and Amador had a good friendship from day one. They took advantage of the free moments to talk. Jero was very curious, and he loved to ask Amador questions about the Holy Office.

"You were telling us that the Inquisition now has an even larger structure," Jero told Amador.

"You have no idea how it's organized?"

"Should I? Do you think they tell me those things? I'm an eight-year-old boy!"

"And why are you so interested?"

"First you tell me, and then I'll tell you," Jero replied.

"People believe that the Inquisition was created by Isabella of Castile and Ferdinand of Aragon, known as the Catholic Monarchs; however, that's only a half-truth."

"What do you mean half? Either you are right, or you are wrong," Jero answered immediately.

"I mean that the Inquisition was already known in the Crown of Aragon since the end of the 12ᵗʰ century, several hundred years before the Catholic Monarchs. It was the so-called 'medieval Inquisition.' Isabella and Ferdinand created the so-called 'Modern Inquisition' in 1478 by a bull from Pope Sixtus IV, first only in Castile and a few years later also in Aragon. The first Tribunal of the Holy Office that was constituted was in Seville, although in a very short time, they spread throughout Spain. For example, in Valencia, although cases have been known since 1420, it was definitively established by the Catholic Monarchs at the beginning of 1482."

"And who is in charge of its organization?"

"People believe that it was the Catholic Church. However, the Inquisition is under the control of the kings of each country. In Spain, King Charles I is the head of all nominations."

"So, who's boss?" Jero asked curiously.

"The Spanish Inquisition is strongly hierarchical. Throughout Spain, there is the so-called Council of the Supreme and General Inquisition, or Council of the Suprema, even sometimes known only by the Suprema, which is the highest body within the organization. At its head is the Grand Inquisitor of Spain."

"So, an entity is in charge?" Jero continued asking.

"No. Despite the fact that, as I was telling you, the Suprema is the highest entity of the Inquisition, the one that has the highest power is the Grand Inquisitor of Spain himself, who has full power, although later, there were many local courts with their own inquisitors and their own structure. The first Grand Inquisitor was Fray Tomás de Torquemada, who was very famous and well-known."

"What about the local courts?"

"The structure of the Inquisition may vary slightly from one place to another. If you agree, I will tell you how Valencia's court is organized, which is the one I know, and it is also very similar to the rest."

"Go on," Jero said cheerfully.

Batiste looked at him strangely. Amador was right. What was the reason for this interest in the Inquisition by a child as young as eight years old, even if that child was Jero, who was very intelligent? It was remarkable and also somewhat surprising.

"In our city, there are two inquisitors, who are Andrés Palacios and Juan de Churruca. They are responsible for the highest rank in Valencia's Court, although their functions are purely administrative. Above them is the Grand Inquisitor of Spain, who is the one who truly commands all the local courts."

"So, they don't do anything?"

"I didn't say that. They are the highest representation of the Inquisition in the city. How can they not do anything?"

"And why two inquisitors?"

"The reason there are two people is that one must be a theologist and the other a jurist, so they complement each other. It was established by Fray Luis de Torquemada himself in his regulations at the end of the last century, and they are still in force today."

"I understand its logic," Jero said.

"Then, there is the figure of the instigator or prosecutor, who's the person who makes the accusations. For you to understand me, he is the complainant, investigator, and interrogator."

"It's clear," Batiste said.

"There are also three notaries," Amador continued.

"Three? For what? Then you complain that you charge late and badly. I'm not surprised with that waste," Jero said.

"Don't go so fast; each one has a specific function. The Notary of Sequestrations, as his name indicates, is in charge of inventorying the sequestrated assets until their confiscation is decided. The Notary of the Secret is the one who records the statements of the witnesses, the defendants, and in general, of all the participants. Think that the entire procedure must be a secret, and this notary is responsible for guaranteeing that. We are missing The General Notary, who is a kind of secretary, that is in charge of registering sentences, edicts, minutes, autos-da-fé, and other paperwork generated by the court, which is a lot. A few years ago, the king appointed another notary, called of penances and sentences, only for the court of Valencia, due to its special characteristics. In reality, this notary is not part of the common structure. It's perhaps a provisional figure. We don't know for how long his position will be in force. It will depend on the royal will."

"I get it," Jero said.

"Then there are less personnel, such as the bailiffs, who are in charge of the arrests, the persecutions, and even feeding the prisoners. Sometimes their duties are a bit confused with those of the jailer. There is also the *nuncio*, who is a kind of messenger, the doorman, the executioner, the doctor, and the surgeon. You can imagine what his functions are."

"You are too many," Jero said. "Surely, half of you is useless."

"And I haven't told you about the relatives yet," Amador said.

"Yours?" Batiste asked.

"No, man! The relatives of the Holy Office."

"What does that mean?"

"How do you think the Inquisition discovers cases of heresy? A great majority are due to private complaints and accusations of the so-called relatives, who are a kind of collaborators of the Holy Office. They don't get paid, but in return, they get some social benefits."

"In other words, informants or confidants," Batiste said.

"What I was saying, there are too many of you," Jero insisted. "How do you want a business with such a structure to work out?"

"Well, it does," Amador replied.

"And your father?" Batiste asked.

"I didn't mention him in this explanation because you already know his function. The receiver is financially responsible for the court, including paying the wages to the rest of the workers. He's a very important figure, perhaps the most important after the inquisitors themselves," Amador said, showing off a little. "He even sometimes has more responsibility than they do. After all, he responds personally to the king, unlike the inquisitors, who do it before the Council of the Suprema or the Grand Inquisitor of Spain, who is their boss."

"You are too complicated," Batiste said.

"Do you remember the figure of the notary of penances that I mentioned to you before?"

"Of course," Jero replied.

"Well, actually, it's a position created on purpose by the king to help the receiver of Valencia; that is, in theory, my uncle, but now it is dedicated to my father to be able to make the transition to the receiver in an organized way."

"So, your father is quite the personality of the Inquisition," Jero said.

"Locally, yes, of course. Nationally, there are many other receivers, one for each local court," Amador replied.

"Funny," Jero said.

"Well, I've already told you the structure of the Inquisition. Now it's your turn to tell me why you are so interested in this whole issue," Amador said, addressing Jero.

Jero made a strange expression, although he spoke with all the tranquility of the world.

"Because I live in the Royal Palace, headquarters of the Court of the Inquisition, and I don't know why," he said.

Amador's jaw dropped.

"Do you really live there?" He asked, surprised.

"Yes."

Amador got up from his seat.

"Wait, wait. Now that I think about it a little better, that can't be possible. Only the two inquisitors reside there. No one else lives in that palace. You're pulling our legs. Not even my father, when he becomes a receiver, and you already know the importance of his position, will have the right to live there. And you are trying to tell me that an eight-year-old brat like you does?"

"Jero has been trying to convince me that he lives there for more than a year," Batiste said. "Ignore him; those are his fantasies."

Jero looked angry. And a lot.

"You don't believe me, just as Batiste doesn't believe me, but I can prove it to both of you."

"How?" They asked in unison.

68 NOWADAYS. WEDNESDAY, SEPTEMBER 12ᵗʰ

Rebecca was at the Joaquín Sorolla station to take an AVE train towards Madrid, although her mind was on the cemetery, where, at this precise moment, they would be burying Carlota's mother. She was very worried about her friend. She had noticed a very strange behavior when she visited her yesterday. She supposed she still hadn't assimilated it. Maybe her slump would come after her burial when she returns home without her mother.

She was lost in her thoughts when she suddenly heard a familiar voice.

"Hi, Rebecca! What are you doing here? I suppose taking a train, which is what is usually done in the train stations."

She turned around immediately and saw her friend Carolina Antón.

"Carol, what a surprise! Are you going to Madrid to visit your father?"

"Yes, I'm going to see him. They have organized a tribute tomorrow for an old friend of the family, who is very ill. My mother is already there; she left yesterday. And where are you traveling?"

"I'm also going to Madrid, but to meet my new radio colleagues."

"Then we'll share the train, let's see if it's not full and we can sit together. So, we can take advantage and chat during the trip. Although the journey takes less than two hours, we will be more entertained."

They settled on a terrace inside the station, drinking a coffee, while they waited for the announcement of their train track. At last, it appeared on the screens, and they got up and marched together to the platform. They passed the security checks. The train wasn't full, so they were able to sit together.

"Who are the radio colleagues you are going to meet?" Carol asked as she sat down in the armchair.

"It's the show *Buenos días*, by Javi Escharche and Mar Maluenda. I don't think you'll know them," Rebecca replied while she put her bag in the upper compartment.

Carol looked surprised.

"Are you kidding me? Is that your program? Rebecca, it's very famous! We listen to it every morning at my house. And are you going to meet Javi and Mar in person?" Carol said, completely excited. "All my family are big fans of them, especially my mother."

"Actually, I already know them. They were at *La Crónica* on Monday to introduce themselves."

"Did they come to Valencia just to introduce themselves? You must be quite a celebrity!" Carol said, still impressed with her friend.

"Well, tomorrow morning, don't miss the show. They want to interview me live. I'm going to have a dreadful time. Imagine, I've never spoken on the radio."

"Rebecca, almost two million people are going to listen to you! To give you an idea, that's their average daily audience."

"Thank you for soothing me," Rebecca replied, who was nervous just thinking about it.

Carolina changed the subject.

"What are you going to do tomorrow night?" She asked. "Do you have a plan with your radio colleagues?"

"I don't know. I'll be at the radio station in the morning. They told me that I will have lunch with all the members of the show, but I suppose I will have the night free. After all, they have to get up early for the next day's program, which starts at six, and I don't think they're going to bed too late."

"I know it's not an exciting plan, but if you feel like it, you could accompany me to the reception at the Embassy. The cocktails that the mixologist prepares are fantastic and then we could sweep Madrid. In a gala dress, we are going to be a hit!"

Rebecca had her mindset on the Embassy event.

"But aren't those ceremonies official, with personalities and under strict personal invitation?"

"Rebecca, my father is the cultural attaché and the organizer of the event! I can get an invitation for you without any problem."

"Who are they paying tribute to?"

"Nothing to do with the emotions you're going to experience on the radio tomorrow morning. He's an elderly academic with little life left."

"Yeah, you already told me that, but what is his name?"

"Bartolomé Bennassar. He's a close friend of my father, actually of the whole family. He's very ill. Possibly it's going to be his last public act; that's why I'm traveling to Madrid. It's kind of an official farewell."

"Bennassar! I know him! I mean, not personally, but his work. He's a very famous historian. In fact, he has written books that are a reference in some historical matters, such as the Spanish Inquisition," Rebecca said. Now she was the excited one. "I have studied him, and the truth is that I admire his work very much."

"What a coincidence!" Carol said excitedly.

"Well, that's it, we already have plans for tomorrow night. We will leave sweeping Madrid for another occasion. It will be a day of many emotions, and I don't think my body is ready for partying at night." Rebecca said.

"There's a little problem that I didn't think of," Carol said.

"Which one? Any security issues?"

"No, that's solvable. You have to understand that this is a reception and official tribute at the French Embassy in Spain. Some ministers will attend, both French and Spanish. They have given it a lot of hype. You have to go dressed in formal, specifically a ball gown, long and dark in color. Strict protocol rules."

Rebecca smiled.

"Don't worry, since I didn't know what the radio plan was, I brought half a closet from home, so I wouldn't mess up," she answered. "I think I have the appropriate outfit. I brought the Lorenzo Caprile that I wore on the day of the university graduation party. It costed me a real fortune. This way, buying it will pay off."

"Then everything is solved, he's also a well-known Spanish designer, it's perfect. I will send you a message with the personalized invitation on your cellphone. Anyway, I'll take care of you appearing on the official list that the gendarmes will have."

"I suppose there will be enough security, both Spanish and French, don't get scared by the deployment. As I just told you, keep in mind that many personalities and public officials from both countries will attend. Imagine its importance that a French television network is going to broadcast it live."

"I'm excited about meeting someone I have studied and who I thought was already dead."

"It's not right for me to say it because he's a lovely old man, but he's almost got both feet in the grave. I don't want to lower your expectations, but I don't even know if you'll be able to say hi to him," Carol replied. "He travels with a private doctor and nurse. Imagine his condition."

Carol didn't know how wrong she was, and Rebecca was unaware of the surprises that awaited her.

69   MARCH 23rd, 1524

Luis Vives had been teaching at Corpus Christi College, at Oxford University, for the last year, trying to revive the humanistic studies in England, whose level wasn't very good, to put it in a polite way. The cardinal and Lord Chancellor of the realm, Thomas Wosley, had kept his word. He had a stable job with a very decent salary and had time to write. Also, as he had promised, he had sent his sisters in Spain enough money to keep the ownership of the family home and all its furniture, which had been sequestrated by the Holy Office since his father was arrested. The formalities of the process were taking too long. They had been with them for four years, something excessive but not unusual with the Spanish Inquisition, which, at times, was desperately slow."

He received correspondence regularly from his sisters, who kept him informed of the process and everything seemed to indicate that the sentence was going to be convicted. Unfortunately for him, he didn't have much hope that it would lead to his release, even with a penalty of penance. Despite having done everything possible, Luis felt remorse for not being in Spain with his family. He had also received a letter from his friend Johan Corbera, worrying about his condition, but he was surprised that he didn't know anything about Don Bertrán, and it had been more than a year since they had said goodbye in Leuven. They had agreed to be discreet, but it seemed excessive not to send him a single letter in so long. They had had a deep conversation before parting ways."

Luis had integrated himself perfectly into court life since he had been warmly welcomed by the English monarch Henry VIII and his wife, the Spanish Catherine of Aragon, who used to invite him to numerous social events. Luis met great personalities and fostered his friendship with Thomas More and his family, who had adopted him almost as another member, treating him with deep affection.

He had also integrated into the teaching life with total harmony. Not in vain, he replaced Professor Lupset in the chair of Latin and Greek, languages that he mastered perfectly, having disciples of great value such as Edward Wotton or Richard Pate. He also had been able to write freely. In those first months, he had sent letters to the European monarchs in defense of peace and harmony among Christian princes, always faithful to that pacifist and Europeanist vocation that permeated his entire life and all of his work. He was a citizen of the world and he showed it every time he wrote. He didn't believe in borders or flags. Luis believed that they had caused too many deaths, more than the plague itself, throughout history. Without them, they would have lived better.

His existence seemed to go by with absolute normality, but there were some things that he hadn't gotten used to, despite all the efforts he had made, which weren't few.

Regarding the climate 'caelum grave pluvium, tempestatibus foedum et abdito sole, caeli laetitia triste'. That is storms, a little sun, and sadness. From his terrible accommodation to the meals, 'est ratio victus aliena stomacho meo atque adeo contraria,' the food wasn't suitable for the stomach. He missed the variety of food in Bruges. As for the diseases of the region, 'sunt morbi multi, sed aliquot fere citra remedium exitiabiles,' many without a cure and their bad digestions, 'concotio lenta, et sera, etiam maligna; itaque, quod numquam antea, e stomacho aliquoties, et ventris tormina, morbus jam tum in Flandria haud novus, hic mihi familiaris et quotidianus factus est.' In short, he missed Flanders, despite the wealthy life he led in England, without excessive luxuries, but with all his needs amply covered.

He was now sitting in front of his desk. He had just agreed to marry Margarita Valldaura, the maid he met when he was still a child during his first stay in Bruges, at the home of his friend Bernardo Valldaura, as soon as he finished his studies at the *Sorbonne* in Paris in 1512. He didn't find her displeasing at all, though he didn't feel any special emotion either. *I suppose these are stages that the Christian man has to go through in his life,* he said, trying to convince himself of that union.

In just two months, he would be married and had to send an invitation note to his friends. The betrothal would be held on May 26th in the city of Bruges, the home of his fiancé Margarita, coinciding with the Corpus Christi festival. Writing those notes gave him immense laziness.

Dear Johan... he began to write in that gloomy room at Oxford University.

He didn't know the surprises that awaited him.

70   NOWADAYS. THURSDAY, SEPTEMBER 13ᵗʰ

Rebecca had set her alarm clock for 5:30 in the morning. The show *Buenos días* began its broadcast at six, but she wasn't supposed to be on the radio station first thing in the morning since it was scheduled to go on air at eight. She wanted to wake up with enough time. She was very nervous and didn't want to be watching the clock all the time, never better said. She preferred to arrive early and see a program of this magnitude in action. For her, it was a new experience, and she wanted to squeeze it to enjoy it to the fullest.

She took a taxi and headed towards the radio station. When she got out of the car, she was already shocked by what she saw. That building was imposing. She entered the reception. *What a difference from La Crónica*, she thought immediately.

She walked over to one of the people behind the counter.

"Good morning, I'm Rebecca Mercader. I think they're waiting for me," Rebecca said, somewhat self-conscious.

"Rebecca! Of course! You've arrived in time," the receptionist said, grinning from ear to ear. "Sit in one of those armchairs in front. They'll come looking for you right now. And by the way, congratulations!"

"Thank you," Rebecca managed to say, who hadn't yet crossed the lobby of the station, and she no longer knew if she was more nervous or more embarrassed.

In just five minutes, a young woman approached her, greeted her, and indicated to accompany her. She got to some kind of room full of computers. Immediately, Javi Escarche went to greet her. He introduced her to the entire technical team behind the show. *So many people?* Rebecca thought, *they are like the whole newspaper staff.* She couldn't avoid constant comparisons, even if it didn't look anything like the editorial department of *La Crónica.* Mar Maluenda came out instantly to greet her as well.

"We already have our morning star!" She said, smiling.

"Right, make me even more nervous," Rebecca replied, smiling.

"Relax, today will be a small casual interview. We will simply introduce you, we will comment on your nomination for the Ondas Award, and we will announce your regular collaboration starting next week. We will hardly speak for about three or four minutes live."

"Will I have to come to Madrid every week?" Rebecca asked.

"It won't be necessary, of course! We have a studio in Valencia. Making you come today is for you to meet the whole team and then go out to eat together to celebrate your nomination. The network was already awarded the Ondas in 2012 for the best music radio, but it's the first time that someone from our team has been nominated individually in a category that has nothing to do with music. It's very important for everyone."

"You need to know that I have never spoken live on the radio," Rebecca said, somewhat embarrassed.

"Don't think about it. We will have a casual conversation between the three of us: Javi, you, and me. Act like if the microphones didn't exist, don't even look at them."

They entered the studio. *Here I go*, Rebecca thought.

In the end, everything was way better than Rebecca had anticipated. As Mar had informed her, it was a nice conversation that had its funny touch when they asked what a young and beautiful girl like her was planning to do tonight in Madrid. The response generated a lot of jokes since they didn't expect 'to attend a gala reception at the French Embassy, in homage to an old historian.' They thought something more like "sweep Madrid and drink the Cibeles fountain', typical of her friend Carol.

"You really know how to have fun," Javi said, unable to stop laughing at Rebecca's plan, even a few tears came to him. While everyone was laughing, Rebecca was somewhat embarrassed. *They surely think I'm a prude*, she told herself. *Am I?* She ended up wondering.

When the show ended, at eleven in the morning, they went down to have some beers at a nearby bar, and then she went to eat with her new colleagues. The truth is that she had a really good time. That had nothing to do with *La Crónica*. It was another world. She kept comparing them, although she should have stopped.

The lunch took longer than necessary. At six, when she left the restaurant, she looked at her cellphone. Carol had sent her the personalized invitation for the gala event tonight and a location. *The security guards already have your information*, she told her. She barely had an hour and a half to get ready and go to dinner.

I hope I don't get too bored, Rebecca thought. Although she wanted to meet historian Bartolomé Bennassar in person, she feared that the event would be too formal for her.

She was wrong, as she had always been lately.

71 APRIL 4ᵗʰ, 1524

"How do you intend to show us the impossible, little runt?" Amador asked. "Only two people live in the Royal Palace, the inquisitors Palacios and Churruca, and I believe that you are neither of the two."

"It's very simple. Although I have it expressly forbidden, I can invite you to my house, to the palace," he answered in a very calm voice.

Batiste and Amador stared at each other.

"Really, Jero, I don't want to be hard on you, but you seem to have gone crazy," Batiste said. "You can't enter there."

"I can," Jero insisted.

"Well, invite us to dinner," Amador said.

"Dinner is impossible. I'm not allowed to."

"You're starting to make excuses."

"Not to dinner, but I can invite you to visit it."

"Today? Do you dare?" Amador proposed the challenge.

"If I dare? When it gets dark, at eight o'clock, I'll see you at the front door," Jero said.

"Deal," Batiste and Amador replied in unison.

"Remember that I can't bring anyone to the palace, so I'll have to ask a small favor to the bailiff guarding the gate. I don't think it will bring me any trouble, but try to be discreet," Jero said as he left.

Batiste and Amador were left alone.

"You'll see how when we get to the door, he gives us some excuse for not being able to enter," Amador said, who didn't believe at all that his small friend could live in the Royal Palace.

Batiste had doubts.

"I don't know what to think, Amador. He told me that when I met him. At first, I didn't believe it, I thought he was fantasizing, but he isn't a liar. I have been spending time with him for almost two years, and I have never caught any obvious falsehood from him. As I told you at the beginning, right now, I don't know what to think," Batiste said. "Maybe, he even surprises us, and it's true."

"The good thing is that we'll find out in just a few hours," Amador replied.

72 NOWADAYS. THURSDAY, SEPTEMBER 13th

She showered, put on the Lorenzo Caprile that she had brought with her just in case, looked at herself in the mirror, and put on makeup, although not excessively. She didn't like to put too much makeup on; it gave her the impression that if she did it, she would stop looking like herself. She had to admit, much to her regret, that she, dressed and styled like that, had a resemblance to Taylor Swift. *I will never admit it in public, not even under torture*, she told herself as she smiled. Actually, she was even prettier. And younger.

She looked at her cellphone again. The location that her friend Carol had sent her didn't correspond to the French Embassy, which was located in the Arenzana Palace, but to the official residence of the French ambassador, on Serrano Street. She assumed the reception would be at that address.

She left the hotel and took a taxi. When she arrived at the door of the French residence, a friendly gendarme asked for her identification and checked her name on a list. With a big smile, he indicated that she could enter. There were also Spanish National Police officers standing at the door with long weapons. It was true what her friend Carol had told her. The security was impressive.

As soon she entered the gardens, she saw plenty of people dressed in ball gowns with glasses in hand and waiters serving canapes. She was surprised by the number of people there were. She couldn't imagine that such a crowd could gather to bid a historian farewell, even if it was Bartolomé Bennassar.

She also saw the assembly of the television cameras and the satellite transmission equipment. The truth is that the whole set was impressive.

She didn't see her friend Carol or her parents, so she decided to call her on the phone. She didn't know anyone present and felt somewhat out of place. She even had the feeling that people were looking at her, wondering what was such a young lady doing there. Her friend immediately answered her call and saw her making gestures to her from the entrance stairway to one of the buildings in the complex, the so-called *Villa Andalouse*. She walked over to her.

"Rebecca! You look awesome with that Caprile! You are going to get out with a boyfriend for sure," Carol said as she looked at her friend up and down.

"But the youngest one is sixty years old!" Rebecca protested, laughing. "It looks like a retirement meeting."

"Don't exaggerate!"

"But we're even younger than the waiters! We are all dressed up; if not, they will surely mistake us for them. By the way, your dress is absolutely spectacular, Carol, I have never seen you so beautiful as today. Did you say to go out in Madrid dressed like this? I wouldn't dare!"

"Come on, stop talking nonsense. Come with me and say hello to my parents," Carol said, "who are looking forward to seeing you after so long."

She followed her into a small room. She gave her friend's parents a hug. They hadn't seen each other for a long time. During their stay at the school, they had developed a great friendship. Rebecca and Carolina had spent many weekends together. Her parents had a great relationship.

"We are so glad to see you," Carmen said, Carol's mother. "You look spectacular. Over the years, you have converted into a complete swan. You look like a runway model, and more so with that great outfit that you are wearing. More than one guest in his sixties is going to have a heart attack when they see you."

"You look quite beautiful. It's an honor that an Ondas Award nominee deigns to visit us. We listened to your interview this morning," Jacques said, the father, with that usual derision that Rebecca still remembered from school. He was a joker, something her daughter Carol had inherited.

They were with a third person.

"Rebecca, this is Yves Saint-Malo, the French ambassador in Spain," Jacques said. "Yves, this is Rebecca Mercader, the radio star that we told you about this morning."

Rebecca was shocked. She didn't know the ambassador and had taken him as another guest at the reception.

"I see Jacques fell short with your description," the ambassador said in a very courteous tone as he gave Rebecca a couple of kisses. "I have also listened to your interview. *Très Magnifique*."

"It's a pleasure to meet you, Mr. Ambassador," Rebecca said, flushing with embarrassment.

"Yves, please. As a family, you don't need so many formalities," the ambassador said.

"And Bartolomé Bennassar?" Rebecca asked, trying to change the subject. "I haven't seen him in the gardens."

"You won't see him for now. Bartolomé is in a very poor health state, as my daughter has already told you. The trip to Madrid has exhausted him, so he's in his room resting. He will make a brief appearance; he will say a few words to us and will leave. It's probably his last act in public, and he himself has decided that it should be here, in Spain. It's an honor for us," Jacques explained.

"Of course," Rebecca said. "He's one of the great living Hispanists. For a recent history graduate, being able to see Mr. Bennassar in person is a luxury, even from a distance."

"That's why the Ministers of Culture and Internal Affairs of Spain and France have come to this last tribute, apart from a multitude of personalities from both countries," Carol said. "And they are broadcasting it on live television for a French cultural channel."

Well, I don't know anyone, or nobody knows who I am, Rebecca thought.

She once again was wrong, and they were already on their way...

73   APRIL 4th, 1524

It was a quarter to eight, and Batiste was heading towards the Royal Palace. He didn't know what to think of Jero. He had known him for a little over a year and he had him perplexed. At first, he would have sworn that he couldn't live in the Royal Palace, but now he wasn't so sure.

He met Amador about two hundred meters from the palace gate.

"Let's see what excuse the shrimp gives us," Amador said.

"We will see now," Batiste replied, who had all the doubts in the world.

They reached the front door. There was a huge bailiff standing at the door that looked like he had a bad temper.

"So, what can we do now?" Amador asked.

"Well, ask for Jerónimo."

"Do it yourself. I don't dare."

"Coward," Batiste said as he approached with some fear.

"Good evening, sir. We have a meeting with our schoolmate named Jerónimo," Batiste said with a trembling voice.

The bailiff stared them up and down. *Now is when he kicks us in the ass*, Amador thought. *Or something worse.*

"Wait a moment here, don't even think about moving," the bailiff replied, without changing his stern expression, as he entered the palace.

"Let's get out of here! Now is the moment; he doesn't see us," Amador said. "Can't you see? He has come in for reinforcements, to take us as prisoners."

"Let's wait; calm down a bit. We have done nothing wrong to get us arrested. And do you think a bailiff of that size would need backup to hold two brats like us?"

"That's also true," Amador replied, trying to reassure himself.

"If they don't know Jerónimo, they'll tell us, we'll go and that's it," Batiste replied. "We will go through nothing but embarrassment."

The door opened and the bailiff came out. Batiste and Amador held their breath.

"Go ahead."

"Go ahead, really? Can we enter the palace?" a surprised Amador asked.

"Didn't I just tell you that?" The bailiff answered with the same bad serious expression as before. "Or are you dumb?"

Batiste and Amador obeyed the bailiff and went through the door, not without some fear. They still couldn't believe it. The powerful exterior lighting made the interior seem dim to them.

"Hello, friends," they heard a voice say.

"Jero! How did you get in here?" Amador asked, still unable to believe that he was inside the palace.

"You are so annoying! I have already told you many times that I live here, in the Royal Palace."

"It's incredible," Batiste managed to say, who was more than impressed.

"Don't stay at the door. Come with me and I'll accompany you to my room."

They climbed some very luxurious stairs and reached the first floor. Both Amador and Batiste were left aghast. The entrance, seen from the railing where they were standing right now, was simply spectacular. Their eyes kept moving from detail to detail. They continued down a long corridor until they reached a living room with a burning fireplace.

Jero pointed precisely to the fireplace.

"Here I usually spend the afternoons, I sit in that armchair and I start reading. It's very comfortable and warm. In this area of the palace, except for the service, nobody usually comes. It's the wing that the Inquisition uses, and it's almost always empty."

Batiste and Amador still hadn't come out of their astonishment. It seemed that they hadn't reacted yet. They were silent, watching everything with idiotic faces.

Jero opened another door and they entered a hallway.

"How many doors does this palace have?" Amador asked, amazed.

"I don't know. I've never gone over all of it. I live in the area occupied by the Court of the Inquisition, but it's popularly known as the palace of the three hundred keys. They say it has three hundred rooms."

"I wouldn't be surprised by what I'm seeing," Amador said, who was still amazed and surprised.

They walked down the hall until Jero stopped at a door. He took a key from his pocket and opened it.

He stepped away from the door and gestured to his friends.

"You can come in. This is my room."

They went from surprise to surprise. They still hadn't closed their mouths since they had entered the palace. They were looking from the door into Jero's room, not even daring to enter. What they saw had them paralyzed, unable to react.

"This room is as big as my whole house," Batiste said.

"And much more luxurious than my own room," Amador said, "and my family is rich."

Batiste stared around, and when he finished, he fixed his gaze on Jero.

"Who the hell are you?"

74 NOWADAYS. THURSDAY, SEPTEMBER 13ᵗʰ

"Rebecca!"

She had camouflaged herself in the crowd of elderly people who were attending the gala reception in honor of Professor Bennassar, sipping a cocktail that her friend Carol had recommended. She didn't expect to meet anyone among so many elderly people. Suddenly, a familiar voice called out to her. Rebecca turned around. Her surprise was huge. She couldn't believe who was in front of her.

"Joanna!" Rebecca yelled, rushing toward her former professor and the former partner of her aunt Tote, giving her a big hug. "What are you doing here?"

"My university sent me to interview Professor Bennassar, and here I am."

"What a luxury! Did you do it already?"

"Yes, I interviewed him an hour ago. The man is in poor health. During the entire interview, there was a nurse next to him, with an oxygen cylinder ready; imagine his condition."

"They had told me that, but let's leave the professor alone. How are you?" Rebecca asked, who at that moment was much more interested in the former partner of her aunt than in Mr. Bennassar.

"Well, getting used to the new life. It hasn't been easy at all, but it is a path that must be traveled. And what are you doing here? I never imagined that I could find you at the residence of the French ambassador in Madrid. The word stunned falls short."

"It's a long story. I'm not going to bore you with the details," Rebecca replied.

Suddenly Carol appeared.

"Do you know each other?" She said, approaching them both.

"Kind of," Rebecca said, smiling. "Joanna was my professor when she taught at the University of Valencia. She's also friends with my aunt Tote."

"You see how you do know someone at the party!" Carol said as she looked at Rebecca. "I'll let you talk about your things, and then, I'll be right back," she said as she disappeared among the guests.

Joanna and Rebecca stared. They had so much to tell each other that they weren't able to articulate any word.

"How long are you staying in Spain?" Rebecca asked.

"I'm leaving tomorrow morning. I just came to interview the professor. How is your aunt?"

"I suppose that just like you, trying to heal the wounds. She isn't finding it easy at all. As an anecdote, last Sunday, she dared to cook your grandmother's cannelloni recipe."

"That's a good sign," Joanna said, smiling with a certain melancholy.

"Call her over the phone. She'll be glad to hear from you," Rebecca said.

"As soon as I return to the United States, I will. Don't worry. I told her I would do it in September."

Rebecca didn't want to miss the opportunity that this unexpected meeting had given her to bring up the issue that concerned her.

"Listen, Joanna, in your farewell in July you left me intrigued. You told me you had something important to tell me but that it could wait until September. Look where we are in September and reunited by surprise in Madrid."

Joanna smiled.

"It's true. It seems that today I have no escape. I'm going to do it. You will remember all the little scene that we put on in your house that night when I proclaimed myself as the Eleventh Door to save your ass."

"Of course, I remember it. How can I forget! You protected me like my Twelfth Door. Everything went wonderfully. Your performance was fantastic,"

"You're wrong."

"What do you mean?"

"I tell you that there is a loose end in the story, and I'm concerned about the importance it may have."

"I don't comprehend you. Everything went as we had planned. The club members left convinced of your performance. Everyone believed you."

"Not everyone."

"I still don't understand you. What do you mean?"

Joanna became very serious.

"Listen to me, Rebecca, I didn't inform Tania Rives of any of the advances we were making. Obviously, it wasn't Abraham Lunel either. You still don't understand me?"

Now, Joanna managed to catch Rebecca's attention. She had been stunned by what she had just heard. Right now, her mind was confused.

"It wasn't you?" She managed to ask, incredulous. "But you said it..."

"I said it as part of the little scene, but it wasn't me," Joanna interrupted. "That can only mean one thing, that you have a mole in your Speaker's Club who knows I wasn't the eleventh door."

Rebecca didn't react.

"I suppose that mole would be surprised by my performance. Didn't you notice anything unusual in any of those present?" Joanna asked.

Rebecca was speechless. She had long suspected about a person, but they had no relation with Tania Rives. There was also someone else who behaved somewhat strangely on some occasions. That could change things, and significantly.

Suddenly they heard a voice coming from the loudspeakers, interrupting Rebecca's thoughts. They turned to the lectern that was installed at the entrance of the *Villa Andalouse*.

"Honorable Ministers of Culture and Internal Affairs of the governments of France and Spain, Honorable Ambassadors and other guests, welcome to the Residence of France. Today I'm proud to be able to welcome a very special person to this house, an illustrious compatriot who, on many occasions, seems more Spanish than French," Yves Saint-Malo, the host's ambassador for the evening, announced. "Never better said, it's a real pride for me to give the floor to Bartolomé Bennassar."

Everyone present broke into loud applause. At first, Rebecca didn't see anyone behind the lectern, but she soon realized that the guest was traveling in a wheelchair."

They listened carefully to Professor Bennassar's speech. It was impressive to know that, in all probability, it would be the last of his life. It was short and emotional and ended with great applause, which lasted for at least two minutes. People seemed genuinely excited.

"Do you know him personally?" Joanna asked.

"Unfortunately, I don't. I would like to. I have read several of his books and they are exciting. I remember you recommended me one in our time at the Faculty of Geography and History."

"He's a very interesting personality. Too bad he's on the verge of death."

"Believe me, I envy you for having the opportunity to interview him, I would have liked to do it..."

Suddenly, two people dressed in black stood on each side of Rebecca. They looked like members of the embassy security service. Their faces reflected complete seriousness.

"Are you Miss Mercader?" they asked.

"Yes, that's me," she answered, somewhat intimidated when she saw herself between two people who were big as a cupboard.

"Please, join us."

"Is something wrong? I'm a friend of Jacques Antón, cultural attaché at the embassy. I have an official invitation," Rebecca said as she made a move to take her cell phone out of her tiny bag to show it to them.

"Is there a problem, gentlemen?" Joanna also asked them, intimidated by the presence of those two colossi.

271

"Don't worry, there's nothing wrong," they replied in a very calm tone. They turned to Rebecca. "We know exactly who you are; you don't need to show us any identification. The only thing that happens is that Professor Bennassar wants to speak to you privately in his chambers. He has asked us to locate you among the assistants."

Rebecca's face reflected great surprise.

"To me? Are you sure?" Rebecca asked incredulously. "Aren't you looking for the wrong person?"

"We're completely sure. Professor Bennassar knows you and has specifically asked for you," one of the security service members said. "He just wants to have a private interview with you discreetly, in his room. We assure you that nothing is happening, *Mademoiselle* Mercader. You are a VIP guest, according to the ambassador himself."

VIP guest? Rebecca thought, not knowing exactly what that meant.

Joanna couldn't help but smile.

"You won't know him, but it seems that Baltasar Bennassar does know you."

75 APRIL 4ᵗʰ, 1524

"That's what I would like to know," Jero replied. "I have no idea who I am and what I'm doing here. I don't even know who my family is."

"To live in this palace, your father must be someone very important," Batiste continued.

"His name is Don Alonso, and he knows your father. I already told you the first day you invited me to eat at your house, more than a year ago. I heard him name him in Seville," Jero exclaimed.

"I remember," he replied, "but I don't know who it could be. I didn't ask my father how many people he knows whose names are Alonso and are from Seville."

"Well, you should; you will clear up my doubt. And there's still one other thing I didn't tell you that day," Jero said. His tone was mysterious.

"Another thing you didn't tell me? And what are you waiting for?" Batiste said, addressing his friend Jero.

"I remember that when I was at your house, you received news of a certain Luis Vives and your father was very angry because he had stayed in England instead of returning to Spain, as he had planned."

"Yeah, he got a letter, and that's what it said. It's true that he got very angry."

"Well, I know a lot about the father of this Luis Vives, named Luis Vives Valeriola."

Batiste was surprised.

"It's true that's his name. And why do you know a lot about him?"

"Follow me, both of you," he said, waving his hand.

Jero walked to one end of the huge room. He bent over a heating rack, carefully undoing the screws that secured it to the wall and pulling it out. There was a hole of considerable size. He turned to Batiste.

"Bend down and look."

Batiste listened to him and looked through that hole. At first, he didn't see much, but when his eyes adjusted, he observed a large room. At that time, there were three people sitting at a table. He sat up in surprise.

"What is that?"

"It's the courtroom where the city's Holy Office Court is held. It's just below this room. You just saw the two inquisitors and the tax collector deliberating on a matter."

Amador also bent down to look.

"It's incredible. In theory, the Holy Office sessions are secret, but you can spy on them through that grid without anyone seeing you or suspecting anything," Batiste said excitedly.

"That's right. If you remain completely silent, in addition to seeing them, you can hear how they question witnesses, even when they deliberate among themselves. I have even heard how they wrote sentences and auto-da-fé. As you will understand, I'm alone and I get very bored, so I entertain myself with these things."

Batiste was stunned when he understood what his friend meant by all that.

"Did you hear the name of Luis Vives Valeriola through this grate?"

"I see you got it fast. I wanted to tell your father and you that day, but it didn't seem appropriate. You were so angry about that letter you just received that it didn't seem like the right time."

"But it's been more than a year of that! Haven't you found an opportunity to do it?"

"Actually, that moment has not yet come."

"What do you mean?" Batiste asked, surprised.

"From that moment, I continued spying on the meetings. I have learned that in exactly two weeks, they will make a decision on that matter. We could listen to it live and find out before they write the auto-da-fé and the sentence of this Luis Vives Valeriola if you are still interested in him."

"If I'm interested?" Batiste asked, surprised, still not quite believing everything that was happening.

76 NOWADAYS. THURSDAY, SEPTEMBER 13th

"Go on, you can come in," a voice from inside was heard after the two members of the security service escorted her to the door of Bartolomé Bennassar's room.

Rebecca got inside and saw the professor sitting in his wheelchair with a book on his lap.

"Hello, Mr. Bennassar. Two people just brought me here telling me you wanted to talk to me," Rebecca said, totally self-conscious about the situation.

The professor turned and stared at Rebecca.

"You are unmistakable," he said. "There's no doubt."

"Do we know each other?" Rebecca asked, in the presence of the strange welcome from the professor.

"Of course."

"Excuse my memory, but I don't remember it."

"It's reasonable; it would be a surprise if you remembered. You were barely a year old the last time we met."

Rebecca's face reflected great surprise.

"One year?" she asked, not understanding anything.

"You know what? You're identical to your mother. I recognized your face from the crowd immediately. With these glasses, I can see marvelously," he said, pointing to them. "I think it's the only sense that I still have, and thanks to technology."

"Do you know who I am, and did you know my mother?"

"Much more than that, Rebecca. Your mother and I became really good friends. I even spent two months at your house on one of my many trips to Spain."

Rebecca was astonished to hear the professor's revelations.

"Excuse me, I had no idea," she replied, unable to hide her surprise.

"That was about twenty years ago or more. It's funny, my memory has been disastrous for a long time, but I remember certain details from the past with extraordinary clarity. I suppose it is impossible to forget a whole woman like Catalina Rivera. *Quelle femme!*"

Rebecca felt a pang in her stomach when she heard her mother's name. She hadn't heard it in many, many years.

"And why did you know each other?"

"In the beginning, she came to me because she was interested in certain issues related to the Spanish Inquisition, which you will know is one of my specialties. Then we extended our friendship. It was a real pleasure to have conversations with someone of her intellectual level."

"The Inquisition? But my mother wasn't a historian or anything like that!" Rebecca said, surprised.

"I have already told you that my memory is a calamity, but I do remember that she had extensive knowledge of the Tribunal of the Holy Office of Valencia, and she still wanted to know more, especially about the process against the family of the great humanist Luis Vives."

"How curious! And what specific things did she want to know?"

"You are asking too much of my memory. I think I remember she wanted detailed information on two people, but I no longer remember who they were. It's been a long time," the professor said, whose voice seemed more tired than at the beginning of the conversation.

"What a pity!"

"My memory may be chaotic, but that's what pen and paper were invented for. I've always had the habit of writing everything down. In my residence in Toulouse in France, I have a file. I can consult it. I'm sure I took notes of all that. If I find something, I can send it to you by mail."

"I have a scheduled trip to France in a month, on the occasion of the master's degree that I'm going to start studying. If it's better for you, I could come in person to your residence and pick them up, thus avoiding the hassle of having to use the mail."

"One month? Too far for me. I don't know if I'll be alive by then. Doctors estimate that I have very little time left in this world."

"So little? Wow, I'm very sorry to hear that."

"Don't be sorry. I have done everything I wanted in this life and I can die in peace. The icing on the cake has been to coincide on my last trip to Spain with the daughter of the great Catalina. It was an unexpected gift from the Gods. In my eighty-nine years of life, she has been the only person I have met of the same intellectual level as me, although it sounds pretentious to say. I suppose a dying person can be allowed these liberties. Also, I see that her daughter is a clone of hers in all respects. You are truly amazing, even if you aren't aware of it right now. Within you, without a doubt, is the seed of your mother."

"Thank you, Professor, but I can't help feeling this whole business is strange to me."

"You were just a one-year-old little girl; however, even then, you looked like your mother. Do you know that with only seven months, you have already started walking? With a year, if we left you alone, you would almost run away."

Rebecca was on a cloud. She tried to focus on the subject that interested her.

"And why was my mother interested in the Spanish inquisition? She never told me anything."

"I guess it's normal. How old were you when she passed away?"

"Eight and a half years exactly."

"Think that the Spanish Inquisition wasn't a subject to discuss with a girl of that age either," the professor said.

Rebecca was thoughtful. At the age of eight, she had already discussed much deeper issues with her mother, that wasn't an excuse, but of course, she couldn't tell the professor about that. *Why wouldn't she tell me about all this*? She asked herself, not understanding. It was a very specific topic, and she didn't understand why she had never informed her about it. It was the strangest thing.

The professor continued speaking, unaware of Rebecca's perplexity with this topic.

"It was a real shame that all three suffered that unfortunate accident."

"All three?" Rebecca asked immediately, surprised. "Only my mother Catalina and my father Julián were in the car. Nobody else. It seems to me that you are confused."

Professor Bennassar changed his attitude. Now he looked visibly exhausted. His nurse appeared with an oxygen cylinder.

"Excuse my memory again," the professor said. "It was a real pleasure meeting you and being able to talk, even if it was only for a few minutes. Now you will forgive me. My nurse must supply me with oxygen. I need it every so often to continue in this world. My life is ending, but yours is beginning," the professor said by way of farewell. "Make the most of it. It's like if Catalina Rivera came back to life. A true gift for humanity."

Rebecca barely heard Bartolomé Bennassar's last words. She had her mind occupied.

All three? She was thoughtful as she left the room.

77 APRIL 15th, 1524

"He's getting married! I could have never imagined it!" Johan exclaimed as he opened a newly arrived letter. "He just invited me to his wedding."

"Who?" Batiste asked, surprised.

"Luis Vives. He's getting married in Bruges on May 26th to Margarita Valldaura. He met her in 1512 when he stayed with her parents after finishing his studies in Paris."

Batiste didn't understand the reaction of his father.

"Why couldn't you imagine his wedding?"

"He never seemed like that kind of man to me. I guess I was wrong. Now I have to start preparations, it's a long and exhausting journey, and I'm no longer young. It's going to take time."

"When will you leave?"

"Immediately. As soon as I'm ready."

"But the wedding is over a month away."

"It's not easy to get to Bruges these days. I will travel to the north of Spain by land, and there I will take a boat to Flanders. I don't trust going through France. The war has made everything complicated."

"Do you want me to accompany you?"

"No way, you also have a school. Endangering a member of the Corbera family is enough. You will stay home alone. You are already thirteen years old. You are almost an adult, and you can manage yourself alone."

"Don't worry about that."

"I do worry, but I have no choice but to make this trip. I can't miss his wedding."

"Is his wedding that important? I know you have a good relationship, but..."

"...But I don't give a damn about his wedding," Johan interrupted. "Well, I didn't really mean it exactly that, I'm happy for Luis, but it's not the main reason for my trip to Bruges."

"Oh! No? And then what are you going for?"

"To speak to him in person. There are very important issues that we have to deal with and that we can't entrust to postal correspondence. It isn't safe at all."

"And what are these important topics?" Batiste asked, with that curiosity that characterized him.

Johan stared at his son. *Has the time arrived?* He thought.

He was going on a dangerous journey. Batiste, despite being still a young man, was extremely intelligent, far more intelligent than him, he had to admit. Sometimes he thought that he might suspect something, although it wasn't possible. He had never spoken in his presence of anything related to the Great Council or *The Twelve Doors*, but he had the right to know his real roots and, above all, his great responsibility. The problem was choosing the right moment to initiate him. Maybe it was before his departure.

What if I don't come back? Johan thought. He had to think about it. On one hand, it was unwise to undertake such a journey without taking precautions regarding Number Eleven. On the other hand, Batiste was still young, and he wanted him to enjoy life with his friends. He didn't want to burden him with worries and responsibilities at such a young age.

"As I told you once, everything will come in due time," Johan replied.

Suddenly, he had an idea that combined both stances, although its execution carried some unwanted collateral damage. Still, he made up his mind; it seemed the sensible thing to do. *Let's get to work,* he told himself. *Batiste will understand it, at least, I suppose.*

Meanwhile, his son was looking at his father with a smile on his face. *It seems that soon I will find out what The Twelve Doors mean,* he thought with amusement. His father's face was an open book to him.

78 NOWADAYS. THURSDAY, SEPTEMBER 13th

"I've been looking for you. I had a good scare when I couldn't find you until I asked the security service, and they told me where you were," Carol said, who was standing in the doorway of Bartolomé Bennassar's room.

Rebecca almost tripped over her as she was on her way out.

"Yes, the professor called me into his room a moment ago," Rebecca replied. "He wanted to speak to me in private."

"Bartolomé? But didn't you say you didn't know him?"

"That's what I thought, but it turns out I do."

Carolina looked like she didn't understand anything.

"Did you forget that you knew the professor? How is that possible? Are you kidding me?"

"I was only a year old when we met, so I think it's normal that I don't remember."

"Heavens! You are going to tell me that story in the presence of my parents, who were also looking for you. We were all worried when we couldn't find you anywhere in the building."

Most of the guests had already left the Residence of France. Only a small group remained in the garden. Rebecca was searching with her sight, in case Joanna was among them. The sudden irruption of those two members of the security team had prevented her from saying goodbye to her, but she didn't see her. They had halted the conversation at the most exciting moment.

Carolina and Rebecca entered a room. At one end, seated in armchairs, were the parents of her friend. They invited her to sit in one of the armchairs.

"We were all concerned about you, and meanwhile, you were having a private meeting with our star host," Jacques said, a smirk on his face. "This deserves an explanation."

Rebecca stared at them. She was somewhat sad.

"You know what? I haven't talked to anyone about my parents in many years. Their sudden death in a car accident when they were so young seems to have made them a taboo subject, at least with me. Nobody tells me anything."

The expressions of Carolina's parents changed completely.

"Why do you say that, darling?" Carmen, Carol's mother, asked.

"Because Professor Bennassar seems to have been a good friend of my mother. I just found out that he even spent two months living in my house," Rebecca said.

"Oh! Really? We didn't know anything. Bartolomé used to stay in one of our residences whenever he came to Spain."

"Well, at least one time, it wasn't like that. He just told me right now," Rebecca said, with a certain air of melancholy.

"How curious! He never told us anything about your mother, and we talked very often," Carmen continued.

Rebecca continued with a nostalgic air

"How was she? You knew her a lot. I remember you went to dinner together before you separated, when you lived in Valencia."

"That's right," Jacques replied. "Your father and mother were two unusual people with dazzling minds, but the one who stood out was always her. She had a spark of brilliance that made the ordinary fun. Every time we met her, which was frequently, we had a great time."

"Do I look that much like her? The professor says that he recognized me in the crowd because I have the same face as her."

"Not that much when you were little, but now that you've grown up, you are physically identical, and from what Carol tells me, you also have a privileged mind. Without any doubt, you are just like your mother," Carmen replied. "If the professor knew your mother, no wonder he recognized you among the party guests."

"And why no one has talked to me about them?" Rebecca asked. She was sad.

Carolina's parents looked at each other as if they were thinking about what to answer. In the end, Carmen, the mother, was the one that went all out.

"You have to understand it. Her death was a very hard blow for everyone. You were a little girl and you went to live with your aunt. It was a radical change in your life. Understandably, we avoid mentioning that unpleasant subject. In reality, we didn't know what else to say about the situation. We all had a terrible time. Jacques and I were devastated."

"How many people were in the car when the accident happened?" Rebecca asked out of the blue.

Jacques winced, almost knocking his body out of the chair, and they were big chairs.

"Your father and your mother. Why do you ask that?" She answered. It was evident that he wasn't expecting the question and she had surprised him.

"Because Professor Bennassar told me about three people," Rebecca replied.

Jacques and Carmen were visibly upset.

"You must have realized that the professor is terminally ill. He has a terrible memory; he hardly remembers anything," Jacques replied. "It's clear that he's wrong. I don't know how he could say that nonsense."

Is it that clear? Rebecca thought, *a nonsense?* Each time she had more doubts.

79 APRIL 18ᵗʰ, 1524

Today was the day that Jero had specified as the day of the hearing of Luis Vives Valeriola, father of the humanist Luis Vives, in the Court of the Holy Office in the Royal Palace, the surprising place of residence of his friend. Batiste was very interested in listening to the deliberations so that he could tell them to his father.

He left his home at the usual time to go to school. Batiste, Amador, and Jero planned a meeting to talk about their date tonight during the break at classes.

"I've already warned the bailiff Damien that you will arrive around seven-thirty so that he can give you free entrance. Court deliberations always begin at eight, so we will have plenty of time. I've also told Jimena to prepare something for us to eat," Jero said.

"it's a good thing you wanted to be discreet," Batiste said.

"The service already found out that you came two weeks ago, so today they are already notified. Neither Pedro nor Andrés, who are the inquisitors, noticed anything, which is the important thing. That way, at least we won't go hungry. The court's deliberations are sometimes long and intense," Jero continued.

"We will be there," Batiste and Amador said in unison.

At noon each one went to their house. Upon reaching his, Batiste found it strangely silent.

"Hi, father, I'm back from school," he yelled as he put the books in their usual place.

Silence, there was no answer. He immediately went up to his father's room and realized that he had packed his bags because the closets were open and half empty. He went down to the kitchen to see if he was preparing food. There was no one.

How strange! He thought. At this hour, he's always at home.

He suddenly observed, on top of the kitchen mantel, a handwritten note and a sealed envelope. He approached it immediately. He read the note aloud.

I had to leave urgently for Bruges. You have a pantry full of food. You are not going to need anything. Don't worry about me; the trip is organized, and I won't go alone. If I don't return, be careful. Only if I don't do it, open the envelope next to this note and read its contents, but, I repeat, only if something happened to me during the trip and I didn't return home. See you in two months. Love you, your father, Johan."

A tear fell on Batiste's cheek. His father had embarked on a dangerous journey and he hadn't even said goodbye in person, only with a cold note and a sealed envelope that, furthermore, he couldn't open.

Can't I open it? He thought. He didn't waste any time, he looked for an iron pot, put water to boil, and with the steam that it gave off, he tried to discover the contents of that mysterious envelope without any external mark to be noticed.

That's how he did it, the envelope opened easily, and he read its contents. It was a very long letter. He took his time and when he finished, his eyes were wide open. He couldn't believe what he had just read. He looked more closely at the letter. It was undoubtedly his father's handwriting and the ink was still fresh. It had been written recently. There was no doubt about it. He reread it from the beginning. He took his good half hour again. He was dumbfounded, astonished, and shocked by its content; all the adjectives fell short. The life of his family had been a lie for over a hundred years.

It is very important that when you finish reading this letter, you throw it into the fireplace. There can be no written proof of what I have just told you. Assume your responsibility. Since reading this letter, you have just become an adult. I will always love you, your father, Johan.

That's how the letter ended. Obviously, the letter was written thinking that he would read it if his father died, that's why he said goodbye in such an effusive way. Batiste didn't throw it into the fire. He refolded it very carefully as he had found it at the beginning. He closed the envelope and put it under his mattress as if he had never read it.

He now understood the interest of his father in Luis Vives. This completely changed the perspective of this afternoon's meeting. *What about this afternoon's meeting? This letter has changed my whole life!* Batiste though, looking scared at the tremendous responsibility.

In all likelihood, his father would return from the trip to Bruges, but he already knew the meaning of *The Twelve Doors* and who the Corbera family really was, as well as the role he was going to play in the whole plan. Although he wasn't formally part of it yet, because his father was still alive and he wasn't supposed to be able to read that letter until his death, *de facto,* he had just become the third Eleventh Door in the history of the Great Council.

He had a lump in his throat. He would never have imagined who the Corbera family really was or their origins.

80 NOWADAYS. FRIDAY, SEPTEMBER 14th

"Rebecca! We didn't expect to see you here today," Alba said.

Rebecca had just landed from her trip to Madrid. She had no obligation to go to *La Crónica* since editor Fornell had excused her from work until next week, but it was ten in the morning and she felt bad for missing so many days in a row, so she went to the editorial department with the suitcase, without even going to her house.

"Hi, Alba," Rebecca said, surprised that the editor's secretary greeted her. She usually didn't speak to her.

"We all heard you on the radio. We interrupted our work to hear your interview. You were very spontaneous," Alba said.

"How embarrassing!" Rebecca replied, blushing as soon as she imagined the situation.

As she approached her table, she greeted all her colleagues, who couldn't stop congratulating her.

"You're a star!" Her friend Tere told her as soon as she saw her, giving her a big hug.

"Tere is right. I recognize talent when I see it, in this case, when I hear it. Your future isn't here but on the radio." Fabio said, who was sitting next to her friend.

"Do you already want to get rid of me to leave both of you alone?"

Tere turned red as a tomato, and Fabio laughed.

"Hey! We're saying it for your sake," her friend protested.

The morning flew by for her while she talked to all of her coworkers about her anecdotes on her day at the radio station and answered all their questions. At one o'clock she took a taxi and went to her house. After all the hustle and bustle of the week, she was in the mood for some silence. She entered and went to the kitchen. Her aunt hadn't arrived yet from the police station. She decided to wait for her to eat. Besides, she wanted to see her after having spent two days away from home. She had things to tell her and some questions to ask.

Without intending it, Bartolomé Bennassar had opened Pandora's box. He had lifted the ban.

81 APRIL 18ᵗʰ, 1524

Batiste and Amador met in front of the Royal Palace at quarter past seven. They didn't want to be late for their meeting with Jero and the Court of the Holy Office, especially today.

"Are you nervous?" Amador asked, seeing the somewhat disturbed face of his friend.

"You know how it feels," Batiste answered, who had to concentrate on not being obvious about what he had just read a few hours ago in the letter from his father.

They approached the door. The bailiff, as soon as he saw them coming, waved them to stop without saying a single word. He entered the palace. In a few minutes, he came back, and he made another gesture, this time to accompany him. They entered. This time they weren't that impressed by the monumental staircase as the first time they saw it, they already knew it. They watched Jero go down from it.

"We have a problem," he told them as soon as he saw his friends.

"What happens?" Amador asked, concerned.

"Usually, the right-wing, which is the one used by the Holy Office, is inhabited only by the inquisitors, as you already know. When I got back from school this afternoon, I noticed that there are more people staying at the palace."

"Have they come for the deliberations of Luis Vives Valeriola?" Batiste asked, alarmed.

"It's a curious coincidence. They seem to be more important than we supposed. It may be the end of the process and they will decide what to do with him."

"But is it customary that more people are present when inquisitors discuss a sentence?" Batiste asked.

"No, it's unusual, but I have observed it on other occasions, in very specific cases. Apparently, this is one of them."

"And what should we do?" Amador asked.

"Let's sneak up to my room and we won't leave until the meeting we're spying on is over. We'll have to be very careful not to run into other people in the corridors," Jero said. "If we hear anything, for example, that people are coming, we hide in the first place we see. The palace is usually in darkness, so the easiest thing is that they don't notice our presence."

They climbed the stairs and walked down the hall. They went through the living room with the burning fireplace, opened the door, and entered the other corridor until they reached Jero's room. This time the road was longer than on the previous occasion. They neither heard anything nor met anyone.

"Well, we've already cleared the first obstacle. I'm going to remove the rack. It isn't eight o'clock yet, so they will not have started, but we should start preparing."

He removed the screws as he had done before and left the hole clear so they could watch and listen to what was happening just below his room.

All three peeked out. The room was lit, there was a large table, but it was empty. There seemed to be no one inside the room.

"They haven't started yet, but they tend to be very punctual, so it's only five minutes until the deliberations begin," Jero said.

Batiste had been staring through the hole.

"People are coming into the room now. It seems like there are five."

"Five?" Jero asked, surprised, while he also peeked through.

Indeed, Batiste was right. There were five people in the room.

Jero was obviously surprised.

"This is really strange. I had never seen so many people in a deliberation. The two inquisitors are usually there, sometimes the prosecutor joins them, and I've even seen four people, but never five," he said, puzzled.

"Let's hear what they say," Amador said. "It promises to be interesting."

From a distance, their faces couldn't be seen, nor their voices could be distinguished because the echoes from the room distorted them, but if they remained silent, they could understand what they were saying, even if they didn't know who was speaking.

"Good evening. How was the trip?"

"Tiresome, as always, but you know that tomorrow morning I'm leaving for Bruges. That will be a tedious trip."

Are they going to Bruges tomorrow? Batiste thought curiously. Just like my father. Is he also invited to the wedding of Luis Vives?

"Let's start as soon as possible. I want to go back to my room as soon as possible," the same person who was traveling to Bruges in the morning said.

Two voices explained the entire process of Luis Vives' father. They had the testimony of many witnesses, including that of direct relatives, who accused him of Judaizing. They made reference to a synagogue that they had discovered more than twenty years ago, whose rabbi was his brother, a certain Miguel Vives. At first, he didn't accuse him of anything but being subjected to torture, he confessed that Luis Vives Valeriola frequented the clandestine synagogue together with his wife Blanquina March.

"Why weren't they captured then?" a voice asked.

"Luis Vives Valeriola was arrested by the prosecutor Vergara and gave a statement the following day before the inquisitors Monasterio and Mercado. Both considered that they only had a vague accusatory statement from Miguel Vives against his brother Luis, also obtained under torture. There were obvious signs that Miguel Vives was kind of crazy and his behavior was very extravagant, as all his neighbors attested unanimously. They even stated that his mother locked him in a room while he yelled meaninglessly. No one else confessed to having seen them Judaize. The inquisitors ruled that they didn't have strong enough evidence to initiate heresy proceedings against him and released him almost immediately. To think that they had only a vague accusation of a nut, also subjected to torture," another voice said. "The Vives family left the city the next day."

The voice of the person who was going to Bruges didn't seem entirely convinced by the explanations.

"Were those the Inquisitors relieved by the king after the synagogue's discovery for their incompetence or collusion with the Jews?"

"Yes, the king dismissed them outright. He condemned their negligent behavior. It was a disgrace for the Holy Office that a clandestine synagogue had been active for many years, under the very noses of the inquisition. He appointed Juan de Loaysa and Justo de San Sebastián as the new inquisitors of the Court of Valencia."

"And what has changed now in the prosecution compared to twenty years ago?"

"Now we have recent, reliable witnesses who have provided solid evidence that Luis Vives Valeriola respects the Fast of Forgiveness and continues to perform the typical Shabbat rituals without working that day. In addition, he confessed that he did it in the company of Joan Valeriola, Daniel Valeriola, and Isabel Santángel. Except for Daniel Valeriola, who we haven't been able to question because he's dead, we have taken statements from all the others, and their statements are corresponding and contrasted, not like twenty years ago. We now have a strong case with strong evidence."

"Have you used torture?"

"Yes, of course, but we have followed the manual to the letter. Everything has been done according to the procedure. "

Jero spoke up and addressed his friends, who were following the conversation attentively through the gap in the vent.

"Although you can't see their faces or distinguish their voices, I suppose that those who are giving the information against the accused are the inquisitors Juan de Churruca and Andrés Palacios. I don't know who the others are."

They kept listening.

"Luis Vives Valeriola must be relieved; there is no other possible sentence," one of those presents said.

Contrary to what is believed, the courts of the Holy Office of the Inquisition couldn't sentence anyone to death since they had the category of ecclesiastical courts. What they did was "relieve" the convicted so that the secular arm, that is, the civil justice could declare the death sentence. If they had confessed their crimes before being burned, they were executed by means of the *garrote vil*, but if they were unrepentant, that is, they hadn't confessed their crimes, they were burned alive. The relief took place during the so-called auto-da-fé.

"Besides, as soon as possible," one of the voices that had given the whole explanation said. "We have been in this process for almost four years, and we must conclude it at once."

The person who had announced their trip to Bruges got up from the table, slapping it hard.

"You have been ineffective for almost four years, and now, that his son is getting married next month, do you want to burn his father just a few days before his wedding?" they said, screaming.

"Your Excellency, please understand that the evidence is conclusive," another person dared to say in a frightened voice, "and we have already told you that we have a very solid case. Your excellency has at your disposal all the documentation you consider."

"I do not deny that Luis Vives Valeriola should be relieved. I'm not arguing if the case is solid, but now? No way! I'm about to leave for Bruges tomorrow."

They were visibly angry. They continued speaking. More than that, it seemed that they were giving orders.

"The sentence will be made public and he will be executed within five months. I don't want his son's wedding to be used to magnify this already unpleasant affair. These processes can't take that long. I want you to organize a great auto-da-fé for the month of September, with at least fifty people. In it, Luis Vives Valeriola will be relieved."

They all went silent. It was clear that the person speaking had a lot of authority.

"Did you all understand? Are you clear about it?" The same voice repeated. "I don't want any doubt left about my instructions. They seem to me to be very precise."

"Of course, your Excellency, everything will be done according to your wishes," one of the voices, which must have been one of the inquisitors, said.

"The meeting has concluded," the person they were addressing with the title of their excellency said as they rose from the table, visibly angry.

Batiste, Amador, and Jero stared at each other.

"Who is this person they call their excellency?" Amador asked, intrigued.

"I don't know, but they're certainly a very important person," Jero said.

Batiste was confused.

"Who has the authority to behave like this before the court of the Holy Office?" He asked, still flabbergasted and, why not say it, a little afraid.

Jero, more than confused, was stunned.

"Do you have an idea of what we have witnessed today?"

"The truth is that it was all very strange," Amador said. "It's surprising to see two inquisitors being treated like this. Who would be their excellency?"

"Thinking about it, only two people have authority above the inquisitors of the city court," Jero replied thoughtfully.

"Who are they?"

"The first one, the King of Spain Charles I, and I doubt very much that he cares about such mundane matters. Besides, he isn't addressed as his excellency. The second one, the Grand Inquisitor of Spain, who I don't think would travel to Valencia for a minor issue like this. They could also be an envoy of any of them, but with a lot of authority. I have never seen the inquisitors being treated with such rudeness and contempt, who also seemed genuinely scared with the scolding they were receiving. We have witnessed something extraordinary, although we don't understand it," Jero said, who was also surprised.

"We do have understood it. You are getting lost in the details. The important thing is that in September, Luis Vives

Valeriola will be sentenced to die at the stake," Batiste said. "That has become very clear."

I should tell my father this news, and I can't, Batiste thought. It was important that he had known it before his trip to Bruges.

"I have suspended the snack I had ordered to Jimena; I'm sorry. There's too much movement around this area of the palace. I don't want to be discovered," Jero said apologetically.

"Don't worry about it. We're leaving now," Amador said. "Also, it's getting a little late."

"Let's go out carefully. Remember, if you hear someone approaching, hide in the first place you see. It's all pretty dark and I don't think they'll see us," Jero repeated.

They opened the bedroom door and went out into the hall. It was completely silent. They walked as stealthily as possible. They crossed the living room with the burning fireplace. At one point, they heard a noise coming from one of the armchairs in the room. Jero and Amador went out the door as fast as they could, but Batiste froze. Sitting there, lounging in one of the armchairs, was a person who had just opened their eyes and was staring at him.

"What are you doing at the Royal Palace?" they asked him rudely.

Batiste didn't react. He was kind of astonished.

"Are you not going to answer?" They insisted.

"Sorry, I didn't expect to see you here," he finally said, completely taken aback. Of course, he had immediately recognized his interlocutor and didn't come out of his astonishment.

"Well, here I am, as you can see."

"I can see that."

"Well, you haven't seen it."

"What?" Batiste asked, who didn't even understand what they were saying to each other.

"I mean that this conversation has never taken place, you haven't seen me in the Royal Palace and when we meet again, upon my return from Bruges, you will not speak a single word of it. When you meet again with your friends, at the exit of this room, if they have seen me sitting in this chair, you tell them that I didn't wake up. In this case, you won't tell them that you know me either. In short, forget everything that just happened. Is that clear to you?"

"Very clear."

His stupefied face still reached a higher degree when he suspected that the person who was sitting on the couch and with whom he was speaking was the same one they were addressing as Their Excellency at the Holy Office meeting that he had just spied on. Now he really was confused. He didn't know how to react.

This can't be happening, Batiste thought, dazed- His jaw dropped.

"Now, I'll wake up and it will all have been a dream."

It was not.

82 NOWADAYS. FRIDAY, SEPTEMBER 14th

Rebecca opened a red label Chimay, the toasted Belgian Trappist beer she loved so much, while she waited for her aunt Tote to arrive from work. She laid down on one of the lounge chairs. *What a pleasant tranquility!* She thought, trying to clear her mind. She wasn't able to do it. She couldn't get her dead parents out of her mind.

She heard the door of the house open and, immediately, she saw her aunt enter the living room.

"It didn't take long for you to get comfortable!" Tote said, looking at her niece lounging on the couch. Rebecca got up and they hugged.

"I'm exhausted and I wanted to relax," she replied.

"I heard you on the radio. In fact, half the police station did. The word was spread out and now you're a celebrity at my job too. Can you believe that the policeman who brought you into my office the last time you came, asked me if you have a boyfriend?"

"Hey, I remember he didn't look bad at all," Rebecca replied, laughing.

"He's not, no, but don't even think of hooking up with a subordinate of mine, with all the free guys out there," Tote said, laughing too.

They moved into the kitchen. Her aunt started cooking while Rebecca tried to help her, even though she was in denial.

"Come on, sit at the table with your beer. You are only bothering in the kitchen," Tote said.

"For the record, I've tried, don't call me lazy," Rebecca said as she took a sip of her Chimay.

"I don't. I'm calling you useless directly," Tote said, with a smile on her lips. "While I make the food, at least tell me how your day on the radio was."

Rebecca told her how nice they had all been to her, the tremendous differences that existed with *La Crónica,* and that from now on, she was going to have a small section on the radio once a week.

"On the *Buenos días* show? But don't they broadcast from Madrid?"

"Sure, but I won't need to move there. I will go on air from the studio in Valencia."

"Are you aware of the leap your career is going to take? Apparently, that program has a large audience nationwide, according to what I have been told at the police station. I didn't know it."

"I know, and don't think it doesn't scare me."

"Apart from visiting the radio studios, what else did you do in Madrid?"

"On the outbound journey, I ran into Carolina Antón on the train. Do you remember her?"

"Sure, what a coincidence! Was she going to see her father at the embassy?"

"Yes, he had organized a reception for a very famous French historian, a Hispanist of international renown."

"Don't tell me that she invited you to such a drag?"

"She did."

"And did you go?"

"Well, of course!"

"How are you going to find a boyfriend like that! Surely all the guests were very boring and over sixty years old."

"Those in their sixties were young people," Rebecca answered, who didn't know how to tell her aunt that she had met Joanna in Madrid, so her comment came in handy.

"What I was saying, a meeting of distinguished retired people."

"Well, they weren't all retired. There was a guest that, curiously, you also know," Rebecca said with a certain mystery.

"Let's see, who can attend such a boring ceremony that I know?" Tote asked curiously.

Rebecca broke the news.

"Joanna," she replied, in the most impersonal voice she could imitate.

Tote's eyes widened.

She informed her of their coincidental encounter and what she told her, that she hadn't been the person who had informed Tania Rives of the progress in our investigations when they were searching for the ancient tree of Jewish knowledge.

"She told me that she would call you when she arrived in the United States," Rebecca concluded, "in September, just as she had promised when she left."

"That's not the important part, right now. Have you thought about the repercussions of her revelation?" Tote asked worriedly.

"Actually, I haven't had time, but we clearly have a mole at the Speaker's Club."

"Didn't you say you knew about the existence of the Seventh Door, that it was part of your club?"

"Yes, I think so, but that person had no relationship with Tania Rives. It doesn't add up to me at all that they are the mole who could leak that information."

"That's good! So, there is a member of the Great Council and a mole inside the Speaker's Club at the same time? Almost nothing. Your group of friends has more holes than a Gruyère cheese. How are you going to trust them?"

Rebecca was silent.

"There's something else that worries you even more, isn't it?" Tote asked, seeing her niece with that expression on her face.

"Do you know Bartolomé Bennassar?" Rebecca asked.

83 MAY 5th, 1524

Johan Corbera, after many ups and downs, finally reached Bruges. It had been a tiresome journey, just as he had anticipated. He dedicated the first two days to rest. He preferred not to visit his friend Luis Vives immediately, taking advantage of the fact that he hadn't told him when he was going to arrive.

On the third day, he went to the Valldaura residence, located downtown. It was a small palace in which luxury corresponded to the comfortable life that the family led, headed by Bernardo Valldaura, a well-known Valencian merchant who enjoyed an excellent reputation in Bruges. They were all of Jewish origin. He had had three sons and a girl, Margarita, who was now nineteen years old and who in a few weeks was going to become the wife of his friend.

He asked for Luis Vives, and as soon as they saw each other, they melted into a hug. They hadn't seen each other in person for two and a half years, since the last time Johan visited him when he was still living in Leuven. He found him a bit shabby. It was clear that his stay in England hadn't done him too well. That's what he told him.

"If I look thinner to you now, you should have seen me a month ago when I came to Bruges from Oxford. Now, with the care of my future wife and her mother, I have gained on a few pounds," he replied.

"You've always liked good food and the best wines," Johan said. "I imagine you were suffering in England, where there is none of that."

"How is my father?"

"Your father has been ill and in prison for two years. He will not leave the Tower of the Hall. I'm afraid that, at the latest in September, he will be relieved and burned. Regarding that, we haven't been able to do anything. I'm not going to fool you: we have no hope."

"And my sisters? How are they?"

"Beatriz and Leonor are surviving as best as they can and appreciate the financial aid you sent them. Thanks to it, they were able to keep the family home and all its furniture from the Inquisition's claws."

"And Isabel-Ana? You haven't mentioned her."

Johan made a small pause. He noted the anguish of his friend.

"I'm sorry, Luis. I'm sorry to tell you that she passed away almost a year ago, specifically on May 31st, 1523, Trinity Sunday.

Luis got up from the chair, covering his face with his hands.

"Please, she was so young!" He wailed.

"She didn't even get married; she died maiden at the age of sixteen."

"It was the bloody Inquisition too?" He asked with immense sadness.

"In this case, it was God's will, although the Holy Office wouldn't have cared. She died of pestilence."

"Like my mother Blanquina, even in death, they have ended up looking alike," Luis said, who was on the verge of tears. "Although Isabel-Ana was just a one-year-old baby when she left Valencia, she had a special affection for her from a distance because everyone told her that she resembled, in body and soul, to her mother Blanquina, who she always worshiped."

With regard to his father, he had sent letters to all the influential personalities he knew, from the king to the pope of Rome himself. As he had imagined, it was of no use. He had received kind responses but empty of content and without any practical effect.

He decided to change the subject. The thought of his family broke him down. He told him about all the ups and downs of his supposed trip to Spain at the beginning of 1523 and how Cardinal Wosley had plotted for him to stay in England, taking advantage of an unexpected stopover in the port of Dover as a result of a gale.

"Unexpected for you because it seems that the sly cardinal had everything ready," Johan said. "I'm sure that even the storm was his doing."

"I know you don't like him very much, but Wosley kept all of his promises. He sent money to my sisters so that they could maintain the family home and I'm the Professor of Latin and Greek at Corpus Christi College, Oxford University. I'm bringing back the study of the humanities in England, and I frequently attend social events organized by King Henry VIII and Catherine of Aragon, besides from my close relationship with Thomas More and his family. You can say that I'm happy."

Johan stared at his friend closely.

"Excuse me, Luis, but you don't seem like it at all. I've been your friend for sixteen years since you were just a child. You have lost that spark that you have always had in your eyes. Now they look dull."

"It's true that I haven't adapted to the English weather. It has no comparison to the one from Valencia, not even with the gray of Flanders. Neither I nor my stomach has adapted to the food of the islands. They cause me intestinal problems continuously. Sometimes it's real torture, and I spend whole days in horrible pain."

"Luis, listen to me carefully. Now you're going to get married. You're going to form a new family, which are also of Valencian origin. You will have to make decisions about your future life."

"I can see that you aren't giving up on trying to get me back to Spain, right?"

"Do I have to remind you that you are the Number One in the Great Council, which is paralyzed because of you?"

"You're wrong about that," Luis answered with a hint of a vague smile.

"In that, the Great Council is paralyzed because of you?"

"No, the other thing."

"What other?"

"I'm not Number One anymore."

Johan Corbera's face was quite a poem.

"What are you talking about! And when were you going to tell me?" Johan asked, absolutely surprised by Luis' revelation.

"Now at my wedding. I knew you wouldn't miss it."

"Who have you initiated? You don't have any children."

"I'll tell you that later; there's no such rush. First, I have to inform you of something much more important, now that I'm clear that I will never set foot on Spanish land again."

"More important than the identity of the Number One of the Great Council?"

"To our misfortune, it's much more important," Luis answered, with a tone of voice that reflected sadness. "Do you remember how we said goodbye the last time we saw each other in Leuven?"

"Yes, you intrigued me with a revelation that it wasn't yet the time to reveal to me."

"Well, that moment has come. Now you must know it."

"I'm all ears," Johan said, who couldn't understand what could be so important. Luis continued talking.

"In 1508, you came looking for me at my house in Valencia because you couldn't find anyone from the Great Council, do you remember it? I was hardly a young man full of ideas that no one seemed to understand."

"How can I forget! It was the same day we met," Johan replied with some emotion.

"Do you also remember what I said to you?"

"Yes, that an incident had occurred a few years before in the Great Council, but you didn't want to tell me about it. You said that the time would come for me to know."

"Well, it has arrived. We already have two moments and two key events."

There was silence between them. You could feel the tension in the air. Luis continued with the explanation.

"What you are going to hear will make you understand some past events that you may not have understood well."

"Come on! Tell me once for all, stop beating around the bush."

"Here I go, don't be surprised by what you're going to hear. In March 1500, the Holy Office broke into the midst of a meeting of the Great Council. There was a general escape; even some members were arrested and later burned at the stake."

Johan was scared.

"You asked me not to be surprised? It is awful!"

"But that wasn't the worst."

"That the Inquisition discovered a meeting of the Great Council wasn't the worst?" Johan asked, amazed. "And what was it?"

"The most relevant of those events was the decision made by my mother Blanquina, who, as you know, was Number One at that time."

"And what was that decision?"

"The termination of the Great Council. That's why you couldn't find them. Do you know why? Because it hasn't existed for more than twenty-four years. There is no Great Council nowadays."

"What are you telling me! And who is guarding the tree that we so carefully hide?"

"Just you, no one else."

Johan Corbera was scandalized.

"But that can't be possible! The Great Council must be rebuilt immediately!"

Luis Vives was very serious.

"That's not the worst part. There's still more."

"More serious?" Johan asked, his face contorted. "But what you just told me is catastrophic! You just told me that the Great Council hasn't existed for twenty-four years."

"We will continue with the conversation before you leave Bruges. My wedding is still three weeks away. Enjoy the city and the hospitality of the Valldaura family. We will have time to continue talking."

84 NOWADAYS. FRIDAY, SEPTEMBER 14th

"What Bartolomé? It doesn't sound like anything familiar to me. Am I supposed to know that man?" Tote asked, surprised.

"He was a very good friend of my mother, that is, of your sister," Rebecca replied, "so I supposed you should know him."

"How do you know they were friends? I had never heard his name."

"Bartolomé Bennassar told me himself. He even lived in our house for two months when I was one year old."

"I have no idea who he is, he was never introduced to me, and we must not have met on any occasion."

Rebecca addressed the topic she wanted to talk about, the topic that she really cared about.

"Why don't we ever talk about my parents?" She asked.

Tote stared at her niece. They had always avoided that conversation, but it had been a long time since that unfortunate accident and Rebecca was getting older. It was only natural that the questions would spring from her mind. After all, she had the right to know.

"Soon, you will be twenty-two. I think the time has come for me to give you something that belonged to my sister, your mother," Tote said.

"To give me something?" Rebecca asked, surprised.

"When the accident occurred, everything happened very quickly. You lived happily with your parents, and suddenly, when you were barely eight years old, you had to move to live with an aunt who, in turn, shared the apartment with another woman, her partner," Tote began.

"Auntie, you already know that this topic..." Rebecca began.

"I know you never cared about it and since you were a little girl, you saw it as it was normal. I already realized that I wasn't an idiot," Tote interrupted her. "I wasn't saying it for that reason. I wanted to express that your universe changed radically from one day to the next one. This must have been very hard for an eight-year-old girl, even if it was you."

"I was perfectly aware of what was happening around me, believe it or not."

"I believe it and I also comprehended it. You're your mother's daughter, physically and intellectually. Although it's a word that I have never liked, you were a gifted person and it showed perfectly. In those days, your eight years were the fifteen of any other person. You were and are extremely intelligent, but even so, there were too many changes in a very short time," Tote tried to explain. "and radical ones."

Rebecca stared at her aunt, trying to understand what she wanted to convey to her.

"Deep down, I know what you mean. I fully understood what was happening, I was aware of my new situation from the first moment, but it's true that I had a small period of inner confusion, not because I didn't know what was happening around me, but because I thought that I didn't deserve what had happened," Rebecca said. "Why me? That was the question I asked myself and it tormented me."

"I could tell; that's why I decided the day would come when we would have this conversation, it would come out naturally."

"Well, that day has come. What happened?"

Tote tried to measure her words.

"To not make it too long, the car your parents were traveling in was hit by a drunk driver. Your father, who was behind the wheel, died on the spot. My sister, your mother, died in the hospital a few hours later. She didn't regain consciousness. I couldn't even say goodbye to her," Tote said, with tears in her eyes. Although a long time had passed, the memories were still painful.

Rebecca asked the question that worried her.

"Was anyone else in the car?"

Tote looked puzzled.

"What strange question are you asking me? Of course not!" She answered flatly.

Rebecca was struck by the intensity of her aunt's answer. A simple 'no' would have been enough. *Why do the people I ask this question overreact and act inappropriately?* She thought. It wasn't normal.

Rebecca broke out of her thoughts and continued the conversation.

"You were telling me the time had come for you to give me something that belonged to my mother."

"Yes, over the years, I've kept it very affectionately, but in reality, it belongs to you," Tote said as she got up and disappeared down the hall of the house. In a moment, she was back. She put some kind of book on the table.

"What is this?" Rebecca asked, hardly daring to look at it.

"It's the family photo album. It's like your mother left it. I haven't touched it all these years," Tote said. "I considered that it was better to wait a while for you to have it."

Rebecca didn't react. She stared at it, not knowing if she should open it or not. In the end, she did. She went page by page without dwelling too much on the details. She would do it later. There were pictures of her since she was a baby to eight years old, with her parents and with other people. She recognized Carolina's parents in several of them. Even in another, she was in the arms of Bartolomé Bennassar.

She turned to her aunt.

"This man is Professor Bennassar, the person I was talking about a little while ago," Rebecca said as she pointed at him.

"I had seen the image, but I didn't know him. I didn't know who he was."

"There are damaged photos; the album isn't very well preserved."

"I know, but that's how your mother had it. She took it with her everywhere; that's why it's pretty tattered," Tote replied.

Rebecca's eyes were watery.

"There are beautiful photos. We looked like a happy family," Rebecca said, who you could tell was very affected.

"You were. That's why I considered not giving it to you until you were old enough to come to terms with it."

"You could have done it before, aunt. I'm going to be twenty-two years old," Rebecca said reproachfully. "I stopped being a little girl a long time ago."

"That's the truth, but I never saw the right moment. I'm sorry," Tote apologized. "I guess I had my sentimental motives too."

"No, don't worry. I know your intention has always been to protect me. You don't need to apologize. I'm the one who should apologize," Rebecca said.

"Why do you say that?"

"Are you really asking me? Because for my fault, you have broken up with two partners, Sandra and Joanna. I can't help feeling that the people around me will never be happy. It's like a curse."

"What nonsense you just said!" Tote replied. "Don't even think about that."

"Aunt, did you know my mother was the Eleventh Door?" Rebecca asked in a seemingly innocent way.

"No. Until you told me, I didn't know anything about the Great Council or the tree," Tote replied.

Why doesn't she tell me the truth? Rebecca wondered, surprised by the lie that she didn't understand.

I suppose everything will come in its own time, she thought.

She was right.

85   MAY 26ᵗʰ, 1524

Johan Corbera spent three weeks exploring Bruges and enjoying the hospitality of the Valldaura family, just as his friend Luis had indicated. The city was beautiful, and one could eat very well. Despite the fact that he couldn't get out of his mind the revelations Luis had made, he had enjoyed his stay. He now understood a few things, among them that the Great Council seemed to have disappeared. Not that it seemed, it actually had happened. According to his friend, it didn't exist. It had been dissolved by his mother Blanquina, although it was difficult for Johan to understand why. They are supposed to protect the ancient Jewish tree of knowledge, and if they didn't exist, they couldn't do it.

But today wasn't the appropriate day to think about these questions. Today Luis Vives was getting married to Margarita Valldaura. It was quite a social event in Bruges, and personalities from all over Europe had come. The wedding was going to be celebrated in style, despite Luis, whose shyness had led him not to invite famous friends like Erasmus of Rotterdam himself.

"Mr. Corbera, you have a note."

Johan was startled and snapped out of his thoughts. A servant carried a letter to him.

"Who is the sender?"

"Don Luis Vives, sir."

Is Luis sending me a note on the same day of his wedding? Johan thought. He had spent three weeks in Bruges doing hardly anything, and now, a few hours before his marriage, he was sending him a letter. He opened it curiously.

See you in an hour at the Church of San Salvador.

Of course, the note was brief. Had something happened? It crossed his mind that his friend had regretted the wedding and was devising an escape plan. *It's absurd*, he told himself, on second thought. *He wouldn't have made me meet him in such a crowded place.*

It was still too early, but Johan decided to go to the church for a little walk through the city and its canals. He never got tired of seeing it. Bruges was beautiful, without a doubt the most beautiful city in Flanders, if Ghent excuses me.

He entered the Church of San Salvador. It was one of the oldest in Bruges, after the Cathedral of San Donaciano, the largest in the city, and the spectacular Church of Nuestra Señora, with its brick tower, which was one of the highest in the world.

He went into the church and sat down. There were still fifteen minutes before his appointment with Luis. Not even ten had passed when he saw his friend walk through the door. He made a little gesture and went to meet him. They greeted each other, and Luis sat down next to Johan.

"Have you gone mad? You are getting married in four hours! I've spent three weeks in Bruges doing practically nothing, and we haven't even seen each other. You've ignored me, and now all of a sudden, you're making me meet you just hours before your wedding. You're nuts!"

"I wanted to wait for the last minute."

"Of course, you have! A little more, and whatever you have to tell me, you would do it at the altar."

"Did you enjoy your stay in Bruges?" Luis asked.

"Of course! It's a unique city, but don't beat around the bush. We don't have much time, at least you don't. Soon everyone will start asking for you."

"It's true, and I have important things to tell you."

"More important than that the Great Council doesn't exist? I'm still shocked by the news."

"Much more."

"Well, start talking."

"Do you remember when we hid the ancient Jewish tree of knowledge in Valencia sixteen years ago?"

"Of course, I remember. How can I forget! We had just met."

"Do you remember that we created a secret message, and we divided it into two parts, and each of us kept one of them? Do you remember that we also divided it into ten parts for me to give to each member of the Great Council?" Luis asked.

"Of course, I remember. It's the procedure established according to the norms created by the founders of the Great Council."

"And what did I tell you when you arrived in Bruges?"

Johan went pale when he understood what his friend wanted to tell him.

"You didn't deliver a tenth of the message to every member of the Great Council because it didn't exist since 1500!" Johan exclaimed. "Your mother, former Number One, had dissolved it twenty-four years ago!"

"Don't yell; people around us are looking at us. The last thing we want is that they recognize me," Luis said.

"But that's a catastrophe," Johan said, covering his face with his hands.

"You already said that when I informed you that the Great Council didn't exist."

"Yes, but I hadn't realized its consequences. According to this, now only two people know the location of the Jewish tree, you and me. Nobody else."

"Although it's half true, you're wrong again. Don't you remember I told you I'm not Number One anymore? Actually, my part of the message is known to the new Number One of the Great Council. Instead, your half of the message is only known by you."

Johan smiled for the first time since they started the conversation.

"Now, the one who's wrong is you," he said.

"I don't understand you."

"I'm not young anymore. This trip I undertook to Flanders for your wedding is dangerous in times of war and I don't know if I will return to Spain. I left a written envelope for my son, Batiste, with all the explanations and his functions as a new Number Eleven, with the only condition that he only must open it if I didn't return, that is, if I died during the trip."

"Then, he hasn't opened it yet."

"You don't know Batiste. As soon as he saw the envelope, the first thing he would have done is open it. Consequently, I'm also not Number Eleven right now. My son must already be it."

Luis started laughing. The people in the church turned to look at them.

"Do you see the irony? We are concerned about the Great Council and the tree, and you are not Number Eleven and I'm not Number One. We are no longer doors; we aren't the *Keter* and the *Daat*. We don't even belong to the plan."

Johan smiled too, but he was still worried about everything he had learned.

"And who is the new Number One of the Great Council, if you can tell?" Johan asked curiously.

"I told him to get in touch with you, hasn't he?"

"No, at least if he has, I haven't heard about it."

"That's weird! It's been a long time," Luis answered, surprised.

"How long is a long time?"

"More than a year."

"And in more than a year, the new Number One hasn't found it appropriate to contact me?" Johan asked. "It's beyond strange."

"Yes, it's surprising."

"And who have you chosen for such an honor or responsibility, depending on how we look at it?"

Luis told him the name.

As soon as he heard it, Johan jumped from his seat in the church. His face reflected deep terror.

"My God, Luis! What have you done?" he managed to say, kind of shocked.

86 NOWADAYS. SATURDAY, SEPTEMBER 15th

Rebecca woke up at eight, despite being Saturday and being able to get up later. She looked out the window; it was a magnificent day. She decided to go running around the Malvarrosa and La Patacona beach areas, in the Alboraya area, a heavenly place. Every time she ran through that zone, she couldn't help but evoke the painter Joaquín Sorolla and his oil paintings, with that light and those typical colors of the Mediterranean. Rebecca thought that she wouldn't know how to live without those sensations.

She remembered her friend Carlota. They hadn't spoken since the death of her mother. She didn't know anything about her. She considered sending her a message to come and exercise with her, but after the beating she gave her last Saturday, she thought she wouldn't even answer her. Besides, she didn't know how she was feeling emotionally. She decided to stop by her house and pay her a visit; after all, she lived next to the Malvarrosa beach, and it was on her way. She also remembered that when they said goodbye, the last time she saw her, she told her that when the whole issue of her mother's death was over, she wanted to talk to her. She remembered that she had used the expression 'curious.'

It's decided. I'm going to stop by her house, Rebecca thought.

She arrived and rang the bell. Her sister Rocío opened the door for her. They embraced for an instant. She told her to sit on the patio, that she was going to let Carlota know, who had

315

remained locked in her room all week. Rebecca worried about her friend. She silently felt guilty for not having sent a single message to ask how she was. The confusion of the week had absorbed her. She saw her friend coming down the stairs. She had a hideous face.

"Carlota, how are you?" She asked as she hugged her friend.

"As you see, not too good, to say the least."

"I'm sorry I didn't send you a message. I've been...." Rebecca began to apologize.

"...very busy, I know," Carlota interrupted. "We all heard you on the radio. You were on point, fantastic."

"You know that I'm honest with you. Looking at you now, I'm a bit worried."

"Don't worry about me. I actually think I have almost overcome my mother's death."

"Excuse me, I don't mean to be rude, but it doesn't seem like it at all," Rebecca replied, looking her up and down. "You are always full of life and now you seem like a ghost of yourself."

"Thanks for the encouragement," Carlota said, "and for your honesty, but my current appearance has nothing to do with my mother's death exactly."

"Not exactly?" Rebecca asked, surprised, without understanding what her friend meant.

"No," Carlota answered flatly.

"I was going to offer you to come with me for a run, but would you rather if we talk?"

"The truth is that yes, I would appreciate it. It's not because I don't want to exercise. You know I'm very passionate about it," Carlota said, with a grimace on her face that seemed to simulate a half-smile.

"I know, you have nothing to thank me for," Rebecca said, somewhat relieved to see that her friend hadn't completely lost her sense of humor. Actually, Carlota hated exercising.

"Let's go up to my room."

To her room? Rebecca thought. It seemed strange to her. They had never spoken there. They had always sat in the farmyard or the patio of the house, a very pleasant area in the open air, where they were now.

"Don't be surprised because I asked you to come up to my room," Carlota said, looking at her friend. "In a moment, you will understand why."

"I didn't remember that I can't hide anything from you. You can read my mind," Rebecca replied, trying to cheer up her friend.

"Not your mind. I read your expressions," Carlota answered, smiling.

Rebecca had never entered her room. It was simple, though very spacious. The decor looked like from the 19th century, including the bed.

"You look at it as if it was a museum," Carlota said.

"It is. It's the original furniture from when this house was built, right?"

"Yes. The whole house is furnished like this, except for the appliances, which are obviously modern. We have had a lot of offers for them, even some absurdly high for kitchenware, but my mother always refused to sell anything," Carlota explained. "And it's not because she didn't need the money. It would have been good for us."

"Well, she was right. There are hardly any traditional houses like yours left and in such a very good state of conservation."

"Come on, let's get to the point. We haven't gone up to my room to talk about the decoration of my house. The reason for being here, the two of us, is that I don't want my siblings to listen to this conversation."

"I can imagine, which I don't know if it's because of the Kinder surprise egg from the party at my house or because of what you told me the last time we met."

Carlota smiled.

"Haven't you yet guessed what was out of place at your home party last Saturday?" Carlota asked, pretending to be surprised. "It was strange and amazing at the same time."

"I have no idea, I promise you," Rebecca said.

"Now, that doesn't matter, I'll tell you about it another time. It isn't the reason we are here and now."

"And why then?"

"My mother, shortly before she died, asked to speak with me."

"And what's so strange about that? I suppose she would want to say goodbye to her children, knowing that she was dying."

"You aren't listening to me. She asked to speak to me alone."

"Alone? And your siblings?" Rebecca asked, surprised.

"That's what I told her, but she insisted on talking to me without the two of them being present," Carlota said.

"That's really weird."

"She told me a series of absolutely amazing things. I still have to process some of them that I didn't quite understand. The oncologist had just visited her, and knowing her imminent death, he had administered a considerable amount of sedatives, so her conversation wasn't entirely coherent. In the end, she seemed like a crazy old woman."

"Hey, be respectful. She was your mother!" Rebecca said.

"That's the point; she wasn't."

Rebecca stared at her friend.

"What do you mean?" Rebecca asked, without understanding her.

"That my mother wasn't my mother, nor my father my father, nor my siblings my siblings."

"What do you mean?" Rebecca asked, not understanding anything.

"That I'm adopted, that is precisely what my mother wanted to tell me before she died, without my so-called siblings knowing."

87 MAY 26ᵗʰ, 1524

"Why do you look terrified?" Luis Vives asked.

"Do you know who you have named Number One in the Great Council?" Johan Corbera returned the question.

"Well, of course! He's a good man. I don't see where the problem is," Luis said, who didn't understand his friend's negative reaction. "I've known him for a long time."

Johan didn't know how to approach the subject. It was a delicate matter.

"Doesn't it surprise you that for over a year, he hasn't contacted me?" He asked. "Even more so, has he been in contact with you since you appointed him?"

"No, but him not contacting me is normal. The strange thing is that he didn't do it with you. Are you sure about it?"

"Luis, please, of course, I'm sure. Besides, it would be impossible for him to do so," Johan said with a horrified expression.

"From your expression, anyone would say that I named a ghost."

"That is precisely what you have done."

"What are you saying? I don't comprehend you. Explain yourself at once."

"Don Bertrán died more than a year ago in Nantes in an ambush by the French army. Despite the fact that in 1522 he organized your boat trip to Spain for security reasons, he tried to return by land, ignoring the dangers of war with France."

Luis was undaunted.

"He told me that he had urgent questions to attend in Spain and that he had to return as soon as possible, so he couldn't wait for the scheduled departure date of the ship," he managed to stammer. He seemed impressed by the news.

"Only a member of his entourage was able to escape the ambush, who was able to reach Spain and tell the story. The French King, Francis I, refused to give him a Christian burial and publicly burned his body."

"It's terrible," Luis said, a look of horror on his face. "I invited him to my wedding; he's supposed to come."

"How do you want him to come if he's dead? Weren't you surprised that he didn't answer your invitation or confirm his attendance? Did he do it? It would be a true miracle."

Luis was silent. He seemed genuinely shocked.

"Do you realize? Not only does the Great Council not exist, but we also don't have a Number One, and we need it for its reconstruction."

"Number One and Eleven," Luis mumbled.

"Exactly. You must name someone else as soon as possible," Johan asked.

"I can't," Luis answered emphatically. "It's impossible."

"Why?"

"Because since I designated another Number One, I stopped being it. I have no longer been a member of the Great Council for over a year. I can't name anyone because I don't have any authority to do so."

"So, what do we do? Has the Great Council disappeared forever? Who will care for the millennial tree of knowledge in the centuries to come? Are we going to sit and do nothing in the face of this disaster?"

Luis continued with that expression of absolute amazement on his face. Johan thought that he was becoming aware of the tremendous consequences of Don Bertrán's death. The death of the Number One dismantled any possibility of rebuilding the Great Council.

In reality, Luis Vives' astonishment was due to another matter that Johan was unaware of.

The Great Council definitely doesn't exist, Johan thought in horror.

88 NOWADAYS. SATURDAY, SEPTEMBER 15th

Rebecca didn't react immediately after hearing the amazing news that her friend Carlota had just given her. She wasn't expecting it.

"Are you sure you're adopted?" She said the first thing that occurred to her. She didn't know what to say at this delicate moment.

"Of course not, but why would my mother lie to me on her deathbed? I have to assume that it's true, that she adopted me as a baby, just as she told me."

"So, your siblings don't know anything?"

"Not a word. She wanted it that way."

"And who are your biological parents?"

"I don't know. I don't even know if she tried to tell me. She gave me a rather large book half torn, according to her, she told me that my father wanted me to have it. Inside the book, there was a photograph of a baby. I suppose it will be me with only a few months old, although she didn't tell me anything about the photo. At times she seemed delirious, I suppose that it was the result of the strong painkillers that she had been given, but at other times she appeared to be lucid. You know how much she liked good wine because almost at the end of the conversation, she dared to ask me for a drink. Imagine what state of mind she was in!"

"Were those memories she gave you of your biological father?"

"That's one of the things I told you that I didn't quite understand. I barely met my supposed mother's husband, so I'm inclined to think that these are memories of my biological father, but I have yet to analyze and reflect on them. I'm still a bit confused."

Suddenly, they heard someone knock on the door of the room. Carlota's sister entered.

"Álvaro Enguix is in the courtyard. He's asking for you, Carlota."

"Thanks, Rocío. I'll be right down to get him," she said.

Her sister left the room.

"Not a word of all this to Álvaro or anyone else. It's a secret between us," Carlota warned.

"Of course," Rebecca replied.

Carlota went in search of her summer fling, as she herself had described it. For a simple love affair, he took a lot of trouble going to her friend's house at these delicate moments. It was quite a gesture.

A moment later, Carlota and Álvaro entered. Rebecca got up and gave him a couple of kisses. The three of them sat down.

"How are you, Carlota? I didn't know if it was appropriate for me to come to your house to see you. Sorry if I have interrupted or disturbed you in these delicate moments," Álvaro said, in a very polite tone, as always.

"You never bother me, and you haven't interrupted us either," Carlota lied, also out of politeness.

"Excuse me for telling you this, but I see you in a bad state," Álvaro continued. "You haven't answered the question. Are you okay? Can I do anything for you? You know you can count on me for anything you want."

"I can't get over my mother's death, no matter how hard I try. It was a very hard blow; I suppose it's going to take some time," Carlota said with a truly astonishing sad face.

What an actress Hollywood has missed! Rebecca thought as she watched Carlota's fantastic performance. If it weren't for the previous conversation they'd had, she would have believed it too.

323

Álvaro Enguix didn't have a very good appearance either.

"I understand you. I also went through the same thing as you a little over two years ago. Although now you see everything black, I assure you that you will end up overcoming it. You are an extraordinary woman," he said.

How cute is this boy! Rebecca thought. I like him even more over time.

"Did your mother pass away too?" Carlota asked. Her eyes were watery.

"No, my mother is still alive."

"So, who died?"

"My father."

Rebecca and Carlota jumped up from the chair and, at the same time, almost without realizing it, knocked them to the ground. Álvaro was surprised by the simultaneous reaction, which almost seemed coordinated.

"But didn't your father retire three years ago, which was when you took over the jewelry store?" Carlota asked. 'You told us about it at the Speaker's Club meeting."

"That's right."

"But you just told us that he died," Carlota insisted.

"Because shortly after he retired, he died of a heart attack," Álvaro said, who was looking at his two friends without understanding their strange reaction.

"So, your father has been dead for more than two years?" Carlota kept asking. Her eyes were wide open.

"Yes, I just told you. What's the matter with you? You look scared. It seems that I have named you a ghost."

"You have," Carlota said, while she stared at Rebecca with an expression that reflected she wanted to say something, *I told you, I wasn't wrong. Let's see what Detective Richie has to say now.* This is what her friend understood.

The Great Council definitely exists, Rebecca thought in horror.

End of part III
Everything Is So Dark

Continues in part IV
All You Believe Is a Lie

You are in the middle of a great mystery,
and now, all you believe is a lie?

VIP CLUB

If you've read any of my novels, I think you know me a bit. **There will always be surprises and big ones**.

If you want to be informed and don't miss any of them, **I recommend you to join my club, called, of course, Speaker's Club**.

It's free forever and it only has advantages: giveaway novels and ebook readers, special discounts, exclusive access to my new books, reading their first chapters before they are published, etc.

You can do it through my website. I don't share your email with anyone:

www.vicenteraga.com/en/club

SOCIAL MEDIA

Follow me to keep up to date

BookBub
www.bookbub.com/authors/vicente-raga

Goodreads
www.goodreads.com/vicenteraga

Facebook
www.facebook.com/vicente.raga.author

Instagram
www.instagram.com/vicente.raga.author

Twitter
www.twitter.com/vicent_raga

Author website
www.vicenteraga.com

IF YOU LIKED THE NOVEL, PLEASE, WRITE A REVIEW.

For you, it's just a moment, but it's more important for independent authors than you may think.

With them, you support culture.

If you didn't like my book or you want to send me a message, please, feel free to contact me:

www.vicenteraga.com/en/contact

Novel series "The Twelve Doors"

All available on *Amazon*

The Twelve Doors

Nothing Is What It Seems (Part II)

Everything Is So Dark (Part III)

All You Believe Is a Lie (Part IV)

The Uncertain Smile (Part V)

Rebecca Must Die (Part VI)

Expect the Unexpected (Part VII)

The Final Mystery (Part VIII)

Duology
«Look Around You»

Look Around You (Part I)

The Queen of the Sea (Part II) – Final Chapter

NEW TRILOGY IN ONE BOOK BY VICENTE RAGA «JAQUE A NAPOLEÓN»

"CHECKMATE TO NAPOLEÓN"

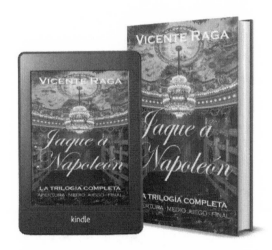

Jaque a Napoleón, la trilogía: apertura, medio juego y final (Spanish Edition)